VERMILION

Also Available in Large Print
by Phyllis A. Whitney:

Domino
The Golden Unicorn
Hunter's Green
Poinciana
The Stone Bull

VERMILION

Phyllis A. Whitney

G.K. HALL & CO.
Boston, Massachusetts
1982

103015

Library of Congress Cataloging in Publication Data

Whitney, Phyllis A., 1903-
  Vermilion.

"Published in large print"--T.p. verso.
  1. Large type books. I. Title.
[PS3545.H8363V4   1982]   813'.54   81-23524
ISBN 0-8161-3312-3   AACR2

B 017-1968

Published in Large Print by arrangement with
Doubleday & Company, Inc.

Set in 16 pt English Times

*For Lucinda Baker, whose
generous gift of her time,
company, and advice enabled
me to write about Sedona.*

With special thanks to Marion Ramsbotham, June Kovacovich, and Beckie Laughman, for their kindness in driving me around; to Al and Pat Purchase, for letting me borrow their terrace and view, and bits of their house; to Kim LaBarbera, for helping to keep me straight on police detail; to Larry Brooks of Search and Rescue, who taught me about the red rock country; and to Kelsey Thompson, who showed me how beautiful Tlaquepaque can be by moonlight.

VERMILION

1

The first step that would take me to Arizona began at the time of Jed Phillips' murder.

Jed was my father, and for most of my life I'd both loved and resented him. I had seen all too clearly what he was doing to my mother, and some time ago, in spite of the wrench it cost me, I'd made the choice to stand by her when she needed me. Now that she was so terribly ill in the hospital, she needed me more than ever.

The telephone call that told me of my father's death didn't come from my sister Sybil—my half sister—but from her husband, Rick Adams. I sat at my desk that morning in my Manhattan office, feeling only disbelief as I listened to Rick's remembered voice calling from Arizona.

Jed had died in a hotel in Las Vegas, Rick said. He had been entertaining lavishly, as usual, while probably flat broke. Both Rick had Sybil had been invited to the party he had thrown at a luxury hotel in his favorite gambling town—undoubtedly in order to raise money for some new scheme. How well I knew that he'd always been a gambler on a grand scale. Casinos and race tracks were small time to him, however, for Jed's schemes were a lot larger and more imaginative. Also a great deal more expensive and disastrous than any ordinary gambling.

"Lindsay, are you all right?" Rick was asking in my ear.

"I'm all right," I said, and heard the break in my voice. "I'm listening."

I knew I must listen. I must try to understand, even though I was merely holding off grief that waited to engulf me.

"Early this morning," Rick went on, "someone got into Jed's room and struck him down with his own ivory-headed cane. He wasn't found until a maid came in later. Money and his keys were missing. So perhaps it was robbery."

As I listened, my memory of that frightful cane seemed more real than what Rick was telling me. I remembered how I'd hated the dragon's head with which it was decorated. One of Jed's macabre little jokes—and now the weapon for his death.

"What about your mother?" Rick asked. His voice was still strong, deep timbred and recognizable, even though I hadn't heard it in years. "Sybil said you'd written that she was ill."

"She's in the hospital. The doctor told me yesterday that she may not have much longer

2

to live. I would have called Sybil later today. I can't tell Mother this—I can't."

"Then wait a while. It's been hard on us all—pretty shattering. Sybil's gone home to be with Marilla, before anyone else tells her what's happened. She's only nine, and she was devoted to her Grandpa Jed. As we all were."

Not all, I thought dully. "Have you any idea who killed him?"

"There isn't a lead so far. Sybil thought your mother would want him brought home."

Home? His real home, his heart's home, was in the West, to which he'd always returned. He and my mother had never been officially separated, but through no wish of hers they'd moved farther and farther apart over the years. Yet this news would cause her unbearable pain.

"I'll stay on here, Lindsay, and look after everything, if you wish," Rick offered. "You'll have time to work out the details at your end, since the police aren't ready to—to release him yet. Are you really all right, Lindsay?"

I wasn't. But I had to hold on. It was better to be numb for a little while and let reality seep through to me slowly.

"I'll manage," I said.

"He cared about you a great deal. He always talked about you with such pride and affection."

I didn't doubt that this was true. Yet my feeling about all this was one of anger as well as sorrow. When it came to Jed Phillips these

3

two emotions had always gone hand in hand.

Rick continued, "If you'd like, Lindsay, I'll bring Jed's body to New York."

I said, "Please, Rick. And thank you . . . *thank you.*"

Feeble words. After he hung up, I sat at my desk dry-eyed and unable to cry, even though I felt sick and shaken. I could remember so well how both Sybil and I had adored Jed when we were children. Nevertheless, my sister had never forgiven him for fathering me outside of his marriage and bringing me home as a baby only a few weeks old. If there had been deep pain in this for the woman I called my mother, she had never let us know. But my half sister, who was eight at the time, had never forgiven *me* either.

I knew nothing about the real mother who had let me go, and as I grew up I'd had too much pride to ask Jed any questions. I told myself I didn't care. All my defiant loyalty was for my stepmother. And still was. My father had always been able to look after himself.

Only apparently he hadn't. He'd chosen to live dramatically, and now he had died in the same theatrical way. There had been a gallant sort of recklessness about him that one could almost admire, however ruefully. Even the limp that had plagued him in his last years had been earned in characteristic fashion. Two years ago he'd been driving in the rain down the precipitous hills of San Francisco when his car

4

plunged off a 'steep incline, rolling over and over. The woman with him—wasn't there always a woman?—had died in the crash, but Jed came out with a few broken bones that mended, and a limp that enabled him to look even more romantic than before. That was when he'd bought himself the cane with the ivory dragon's head. I shivered, thinking of it, and something strange and sad seemed to touch the outskirts of my mind like a hint of foreboding.

Memory swept back to a time ten years ago when Sybil had been twenty-five, a stunningly successful New York model, with a distinction of her own in presenting fashions for the business woman. I'd been seventeen and still in school. Jed came swooping into our lives on one of those waves of electric enthusiasm that always enveloped him when he returned without warning from the West.

On that occasion he had brought a protégé with him—Rick Adams. Rick was twenty-six and I had seen in him some of that same adventurous, enthusiastic quality that surrounded my father. In my young and romantic vision he had seemed a *Western* man. Not a cowboy with ten-gallon hat and high-heeled boots, but a man who had a look of the outdoors about him, and who didn't fit in with concrete and steel.

What I'd liked most was his joyful quality. I knew hardly anyone except my father who laughed out loud. Rick was full of laughter, and he could make other people laugh. Me, especially. He had gone out of his way to be my friend. It had seemed more than a casual kindness—as though he really liked me and wished me well. He would share jokes with me that made us both laugh, and which never carried hurtful barbs or put-downs. Jokes that I'm sure Sybil never understood. They might have made her grumpy if she hadn't been putting on such a beautiful act.

Of course when Rick looked at *her* there was a bedazzlement in him, a longing and admiration that he couldn't possibly turn on a child like me. With me he was kind and thoughtful, and very dear, so naturally I fell for him with all the passionate adoration of one who was too young and new when it came to love.

I suppose his laughter grew from his being so exuberantly alive. He was filled with triumphant joy because he had found this beautiful, intelligent, altogether glorious woman who was Sybil Phillips—and because she loved him back.

As I watched, there was a wryness in me born of long experience. I could have told Rick that my sister had never loved anyone. What she loved was her own power over others. What she enjoyed most was making others do as *she* wished. What she admired most was her own performance. And in that admiration there had always been a strong grain of cruelty toward anyone who crossed her. I'd seen her torment our mother on occasion. I'd seen her heartless treatment of some pretty decent men, and of course my own very existence crossed her, so that I was often her target and too young to defend myself. Oh, I could have quoted him chapter and verse.

Of course I didn't. He would never have believed me, and I wanted so much to have him at least like me. I could still remember my sense of loss after the wedding party, when Rick had searched me out to say good-bye. I'd been hiding from everyone, deep in the gloomy despair of youth. He'd kissed me on the cheek and hugged me, and I'd wept a little in his arms. He understood my foolishness and he'd never laughed at me.

He said, "Being young is very tough. But it's not permanent. You'll recover," and we had laughed together for one last time before he went away. Went off to Arizona, taking with him his enchanting and willing Sybil—who had worn out her fields of influence in New York and wanted new worlds to conquer.

In the years that followed they'd had only one child—their daughter, Marilla. I had seen her just once when she was three and they had come East. Mother wouldn't go to Arizona to visit—because Jed was there and she wouldn't pursue him—so of course I wouldn't go either. I didn't want to see Rick again anyway. Sybil came East only a few times during those years, and then, I suspected, only because it looked better if she visited her mother once in a while.

I managed to be away whenever she came.

Rick's prophecy had come true, and I had grown up. I had my own absorbing work in the fashion world, and I was my own person, with no need to worry about an older sister who despised me. Or a father whom I'd loved so desperately, and who left me filled with angry resentment because I'd always wanted more from him than he could give. There had been men in my life, but no one I'd ever become serious about. Watching my mother suffer over Jed had made me wary of any full commitment. Besides, New York was not an easy place for the successful woman who might want a personal life as well. While men might give lip service to the new "equality," some of them still found the old ways more comfortable. It had always been hard for a strong woman to find a strong man.

Not that I was all that strong—if they really knew. What I had achieved made me look that way, and vulnerability was not something one wore like a badge.

Now, with the phone call from Arizona, the past had burst into the open. My father had died brutally, and Rick was coming here. I couldn't escape from searing grief, nor could I escape seeing Rick again. The grief I would manage to face, and of course it didn't mean anything anymore—that old, very young love of mine. Yet I suppose we never quite lose the selves we once were, and I was a little afraid of

8

the girl who still hid inside the woman. Though surely in ten years we would all have changed, and I could count on that to get me through.

I wasn't prepared, however, for the startling change in Rick. A week later he brought my father's body to New York, and he drove me to Connecticut, where Jed Phillips was buried in a country cemetery not far from the town where he'd been born. My mother wasn't told. The doctors said it was pointless to add to her pain. In spite of everything, I knew she would have suffered. Somehow, my father was a man one never stopped loving, no matter how strong the bitterness.

I stood with Rick Adams beside the raw new grave, and still I couldn't cry, though there was a stone in my chest.

"When it was possible, he helped a great many people," Rick said. "He had a joyful spirit. He may have committed all the sins of the flesh—I don't know—but I never knew him to commit a sin of the spirit."

The words were a benediction, even though I couldn't wholly accept them. I had nothing to add.

Rick took me to dinner in New York that night before he went back to Arizona, and as we faced each other across a table I became increasingly aware that the young man whom I'd loved so desperately was gone. In his place was a stranger who had no laughter in him.

Not that he wasn't even more attractive, with his sun-browned look, deep-set dark eyes, and springy brown hair that had a tendency to tumble. His face had always squared at the jawbones, but the expression of his generous mouth had hardened with deepening crescent lines, and there seemed a skepticism in his eyes that hadn't been there before. Perhaps he was a stronger, more forceful man than the one I'd known, but with a troubled restlessness in him that surfaced now and then. I knew the answer. Sybil had been at her destructive work again.

Though he didn't speak of my sister, he told me a little of his work in Arizona. There had been a time before he married when he'd worked for the government on a Hopi reservation in a place called Keams Canyon. He had always been interested in Indian crafts, and he could see the danger of their dying out, giving way to cheaply manufactured tourist junk. In the pueblos women still wore exquisite turquoise jewelry, and the Hopi were still weaving and making beautiful pottery.

Rick had begun modestly with a small shop in Phoenix that had been a gratifying success. But he was no shopkeeper, and he discovered quickly that his skills lay in finding and developing Indian artists and craftsmen, and that he could leave the selling of goods to others. What he did was on a cooperative basis with the Indians, and all profited.

His first shop had grown into several—and

the prospering had been quite spectacular because what he had to offer was work for which wealthy buyers were willing to pay well. The shop in Sedona was the finest of all, and was managed by his partner, a woman named Clara Robins, who kept an eye on the other shops as well.

As Rick talked with growing enthusiasm, I could glimpse again the younger man I had known, and I listened eagerly, warmly. But he wanted to talk about me, too, and of the success I had achieved for myself. Apparently Jed had briefed him well. Though he was puzzled that I should be a designer in the fashion world—which seemed strange to him— perhaps because of what he regarded as its artificiality.

"Are you happy in what you're doing?" he asked bluntly.

I ate another mouthful of lemon sole and thought about his question. For some reason, it seemed necessary to defend and justify what I was doing.

"Apparently I have a talent for designing women's clothes," I told him. "Though I suppose I'm something of a maverick. I go my own way. I don't think beauty need preclude comfort. Good clothes ought to be good for any time. The great designers have always known that. Clothes should never forget the woman who'll wear them, and fortunately, women are wiser these days, smarter, more natural. They don't want to look like everyone else or be slaves to changing fashions.''

Perhaps he thought I protested too much, and he watched me with a half smile that questioned, even doubted. I couldn't explain one of the forces that had always driven me toward success. I had known very early that I would never be content to remain as insignificant and invisible as Sybil thought me. If she had given me nothing else, she had taught me how to fight. In refusing to be her victim as I grew up, I'd learned how to stand on my own feet and develop the self-reliance that I'd needed. Now I could take satisfaction in knowing that I'd done well against enormous odds, that I was respected and recognized in my own field. No one had ever suspected the hollowness in me. But before I could leap into further defense of my work, Rick went down another road.

"It's time you came West for a visit, Lindsay. It's time Marilla got to know you. She needs more family in her life."

There was something in his voice . . .

"You're worried about your daughter?" I asked.

"I worry a lot. She's a pretty special person."

And what sort of mother had Sybil made? But he didn't need to say any more. Perhaps he didn't even realize that he'd let down his new, instinctive guard and allowed me to see a tormented man. A strange confusion of love and compassion, as well as anger with Sybil, rose in me, and I reached out to him across the table. He took my hand gently and without surprise.

"Thank you for growing up like this," he said. "I know there was a time when you thought you never would."

Once more we laughed together—and were no longer strangers.

"Will you come to Arizona?" he said. "After all, you were born in the West."

The old, unacknowledged fear sprang up in me, and I let his hand go. Undoubtedly Rick Adams knew more about me than I did about myself, and I must shut this door quickly and firmly. Long ago I'd resolved that I didn't want to know about the past. All my loyalties were for the woman I considered to be my mother—not for someone unknown and faceless who had given me up long ago, valuing me so little.

"No," I said, too sharply, "I can't come to Arizona."

"You'll come," he said with a quiet assurance. "Eventually you'll come."

But I wouldn't. Not ever. Because, although I'd conquered other fears, I was still afraid of what lay hidden out there in the West. Questions about my real mother, the woman who hadn't wanted me, were too painful to face. It was possible that I had other relatives on her side who didn't know about me, or didn't care to know. There might be an ugliness that I didn't want to unearth.

Now there was even more reason not to go. I was afraid of Rick Adams, too. If I saw him again how could I trust myself not to fall hopelessly in love with my sister's husband? I was half in love with him right now.

"I like it here in the East," I said, and hated it that my voice broke a little.

His eyes were kind in the old way, and I wouldn't meet them. He let the matter go and spoke about other things.

The next day he went home, and once he was gone and safely out of reach, I ached for his presence, and thought of him too often.

In a month he shipped back my father's possessions, preceded by a letter to tell me they were coming.

"I've kept out his cane," he wrote. "I thought you might not want to see it again. Nothing has come to light with the police, and there are apparently no clues for them to go on. I will let you know if anything develops. Take care of yourself, Lindsay."

He had been Jed's friend, and he was mine. If there was anything to be done, he would do it, I thought. So now it was better to work as hard as I could in order to put the unhappy and painful out of my mind. Old wounds from my girlhood must never be allowed to reopen. Wounds connected with both my father and Rick.

My mother died two months after Jed, without ever knowing that he was gone. Since he had never written to us regularly, the deception was easy enough to carry out. Now for the first time, I was nobody's daughter, and the knowledge brought me a doubled sense of loss and emptiness. Mother had never expected very much of life, and she had received so little. I told myself that I expected a great deal, but I still didn't know exactly what that was.

Luckily, my partner, Nan Griffith, and I were busy with a new resort collection, and I worked all hours with my models and at my drawing board. Nan had been with me since I'd become established, and I depended on her for a great deal. She was a good designer herself, and she also took care of a lot of the legwork with which I'd grown bored, visiting buyers, manufacturers, helping with shows. Our hard-won customers were the fine stores, and they were always waiting: Bergdorf's, Neiman-Marcus, Saks, Bloomingdale's, and Marshall Field's.

When I'd started out, my mother had been able to finance me for a while. But I had won my laurels the hard way, and now the Lindsay Phillips label meant something. It meant something in the world of fashion, but more and more I was wondering how much it meant to me. My creativity was dulling around the edges, and I drove myself into longer hours. As though by wearing myself out physically I could recapture what was slipping away. I wasn't the first to find success and then wonder what it all meant anyway. Nor was I the first to suffer this sense of loss and emptiness. Jed, my mother, Rick—all lost to me. No words could help me. Pain must be lived with until it diminished.

More than a year passed before the astonishing letter arrived to turn my life upside down. Ordinarily, I would have discarded an unsigned letter and never given it another thought. But the black, block-lettered words immediately captured my attention and could not be ignored. The letter began without salutation, just as it ended without signature.

You are Jed Phillips' daughter and you should be interested in the facts behind his death. You should know about the role your sister played in what happened.

Come to Sedona. Once I have confidence in you, I will tell you everything. I must remain anonymous for now, but when you are ready for the truth, you will know who I am.

I think your own conscience will not let you refuse to come.

Of course I would refuse! How could I know this was the truth anyhow? I wouldn't dream of going to Arizona and mixing myself up in something so unsavory. Besides, I must never go near Rick again.

I went home with a pounding headache and slept hardly at all that night. I fought the thing for three days, refusing to so much as reread the letter. Then I took it out and read it over and over again without stopping. Compulsively.

All the *good* memories of my father swept back. Echoes of laughter, of sound and scent and touch. A memory of the time he'd taken me on the Staten Island Ferry to show me the drama of Manhattan's towers from the water. The time we'd gone to climb the Statue of Liberty, and he'd read aloud for me the moving words that had greeted America's immigrants. We'd rowed in Central Park and visited China-town and the Brooklyn Botanical Gardens. Our companionship had been more satisfying than anything else in my life, though these special moments took place over the years, and not all at once.

When he went away each time, as he always did, there was Sybil's jealousy to cope with. He should have taken us both on those excursions, but it was me he chose, and afterward Sybil punished me—because he loved me best. I was too young then to recognize my half sister's hurt and resentment, or to blame my father for their cause. Perhaps in those years his own treatment began to mold us both for the future—Sybil no less than me.

He had been the one who first saw talent in the little dresses I designed for my dolls. He'd

17

made me glow with a sense of pride in my own achievement, and recognizing this, Sybil had cut up several of the dresses with her sharp scissors and only laughed at my tears. Of course, my father was never there to settle anything, and when he went away emptiness was left behind. It had always been like that, though with the years I'd grown resentful, too, and protective of my mother. Her hurt was the hardest to bear.

Now, all this time later, the loss was deeper than ever—because of a cruel and unwarranted act that had struck down Jed Phillips. Strange that I should want so much to believe that it was unwarranted, when I knew very well that he had hurt a great many people and that it might not have been robbery at all. He never hurt anyone deliberately, or cruelly, but just walked away to follow his own will-o'-the-wisp into a world that had to stay exciting and exhilarating, or he couldn't live with it. But no matter what he'd been, or how much I'd come to resent his absence in some ways, he had given me more than anyone else ever had, and I would always be richer for having known him.

Because of this, wasn't it my obligation to follow through, even if the note might be no more than the work of some crank? Involved with my reluctance to go to Arizona was my old, childish fear about my own heritage, and my feeling as well that it could only hurt me if I saw Rick Adams again. Nevertheless, in the face of what had been done to my father, mustn't I deny these arguments? There were risks I would have to take if I were to live with myself. The writer of the note had seen this very well.

That night I sat in the living room of my apartment, with a single lamp burning; sat with my eyes closed, weighted down by questions I couldn't answer, concentrating intensely. And suddenly the old feeling came—of not being alone. *She* was there in the room with me, secretly laughing, listening, watching—always ready to speak out. How real she could seem in the shadows of my mind—perhaps even in the shadows of the room—I was never quite sure. Though not for years had she emerged so clearly or so alive. Now that she had come, I was almost relieved—even grateful. Perhaps I wouldn't have to make up my own mind after all.

Strangely enough, it was Jed who had made me a present of Vermilion. I could remember vividly that time when he had come home for a little while when I must have been no more than five. I was already imaginative and creative, and that day I was sitting in my room with my paint box and colored papers, laid out on a card table before me.

When he came in to see me, however, I was crying, with my brush dropped in its glass of water, my painting of a lady in a fancy dress neglected, while tears stained my cheeks. He'd caught me up in his arms and sat down in the room's one grown-up-size chair to hold me on his lap. I could remember the very smell of him—somehow like pine forests and the outdoors, and I liked the comforting feel of a tanned and prickly cheek against my own.

A few sympathetic questions brought out the fact that I was lonely. I had no one to play with, and Sybil didn't like me. I wished I had a *real* sister, instead of just half a one. Someone I could play with and talk to, and who would talk to me.

Jed said, "But of course you can have a real sister. Let's make her up right now. How do you want her to look?"

This was a lovely game. We decided that she must look like me and be just my age. Only, of course, Jed must be able to tell us apart—so perhaps her hair should be a different color from mine. Not black, but some brighter color that I more admired.

I looked at the open paint box on the table and pointed to a wonderful brilliant red. That would be the color of my new sister's hair, and it wouldn't be straight and smooth like mine, but flyaway and shiny and always dancing.

"What will you name her?" Jed asked.

Even though it was a big word, I'd learned to recognize and pronounce it, and I pointed to where it was lettered under the very color in my paint box.

"Vermilion," I said.

My father said, "That's a wonderful name. Sometimes when the sun is right, there are rocks in Sedona that can look almost that color. Someday I'll show you."

So she was born, my make-believe playmate, and very much alive in my mind. She was always there the moment I wanted her. When I was sad and confused she would comfort me, and she was always ready to play any games I suggested. She seemed perfectly comfortable in the outside world when I wanted her to be. At the dining table she would sit beside me and eat whatever I ate. It was Vermilion who tried on clothes that came straight out of my imagination. She was my first model, really. I began to collect bits of lace and ribbon, scraps of patterned cloth, and we gloated over these together. She would deck herself in outlandish costumes, though it was only Lindsay I saw when I looked in my mirror.

If I wanted her there, her shining head would lie on the pillow beside my own at night, and I was never lonely anymore. Mother didn't mind and she would play the game, though with less enthusiasm than Jed. Sybil, of course, had a fit.

By that time Sybil had learned the word "bastard," and she applied it to me freely, never hesitating to point out that her mother was not really my mother. I didn't understand exactly what the word meant. I only knew it was something terrible and demeaning, and that it hurt my mother too. But by the time I could better understand that being a bastard was not my fault, the wound had gone very deep.

There was a difference between my Vermilion and other make-believe companions I'd read about. To begin with, she'd been deliberately invented. She didn't fade as the years went by. In a way, she seemed to grow up with me, though perhaps less outside of me than she was at first. Even when I went to school and no longer needed her to play with me, she would come whenever I felt discouraged or uncertain. She was my confidante, and never vulnerable and afraid like me. When I grew older, I laughed a little over this, knowing that instead of Vermilion being a part of me, I had only to pretend that I was Vermilion—and I could do anything. I could even stand up to Sybil!

Of course, I knew well enough that such make-believe was only an extension of my own needs, but Vermilion became my secret weapon. Sybil learned that when Vermilion was there she had better leave me alone. Vermilion was a very good fighter, and through me she could sometimes give as good as she got—even startling and frightening *me* on occasion. I seldom intended the things Vermilion prompted me to do.

Perhaps part of the reason I was successful while I was still very young was because of this odd ability of mine to become someone stronger and wiser and more ruthless than I felt I really was. Now and then, when some impulsive act of mine shocked me, I found myself blaming Vermilion, excusing myself. But at least I had the good sense to realize that this might be a dangerous course and must not be allowed to get out of hand.

Mostly I'd succeeded in suppressing such extravagance, and eventually Vermilion took her place in the shadows and seldom emerged anymore, seeming to accept her banishment. As "Lindsay Phillips" began to be recognized as a name in the fashion world, there was no more "materializing." I was, I told myself, an entirely well-balanced woman, and no longer needed the pretense of someone stronger to help and defend me. All such childishness was behind me, I certainly hoped.

Yet now, faced by a problem that so disturbed and perplexed me, I could sense her presence, insistent and gently pushing. I was almost amused to discover that the old feeling was still there in me, and just for fun I let her in. I said half-mockingly, *All right, what would you do?*

At once it was as though she was in the room with me—fully my own age of twenty-eight—a shining, dancing figure that seemed to whirl about me. What was in the mind's eye could become all too vividly real, as I very well knew. She seemed to toss bright, flyaway hair that could never be restrained, and she spoke one resounding word in my mind: *GO!*

That was when I made my second mistake. Still amused, I asked her why. And she told me.

Sybil is out there. Sybil got the man you always wanted. There are old scores to pay off. Go and settle them.

I slammed the door on her hard. I shut her out almost violently, and was relieved to see her fade away with not even a trace of laughter left behind. There are motivations one can't accept and live with in self-respect. So I would not go to Sedona unless I could be sure of myself—sure that I went only because of what I owed my father.

At the end of three days I was able to make my decision coolly. I wrote to Sybil and Rick and told them I needed a change and a rest. I would save the reason behind my coming to tell them later when I produced the note.

Unexpectedly, it was Sybil who wrote back. Yes, of course I must come. Rick would meet me in Phoenix. I had only to let them know my plane time and date of arrival. They would of course look forward to my visit. In spite of those "of courses," the letter was cool—but not rejecting. Perhaps she'd changed, as I had changed. Perhaps everything would be better between us now since, after all, we'd both grown up. I would give her the benefit of any doubt.

I told Nan, my partner, that I would leave everything in her hands for a little while, and she said wryly that I wasn't worth having around in my present mood: "Good riddance—and get some rest!"

The arrangements were made, I caught my plane, and all the way to Arizona the thing that beat in my mind was the knowledge that I would see Rick again, stay in the same house with him, get to know him better. But there could never be any more than that. I must ignore the rush of anticipation that was so ready to sweep me up. I must whip that feeling down until it lay quiet. I knew I was strong enough now to do this. Rick and I were friends, no more than that—never any more than that.

At least I would see him as a friend again. And I would not listen to Vermilion laughing.

2

I stood on the high strip of deck that ran outside the guesthouse and stared at rock formations towering across a dry wash. This was Sedona—at least its edge—and the sense of isolation was really an illusion, since I knew there were houses out there. It was a strange and unfamiliar world that exhilarated as much as it threatened.

The first meeting with my sister still lay ahead, and I hoped I was braced for it. Not only because of the unanswered questions raised in the letter from Arizona, but also because it would be so easy to slip back to that insignificant position into which she'd always thrust me. For as long as I could remember the deliberate put-down had been one of Sybil's major weapons. This time I wouldn't let her use it. This time, if she tried, she'd meet her match. And I'd do it without Vermilion.

My meeting with Rick at the airport had not been an easy one. There seemed a remoteness about him when I came off the plane and found him waiting. His greeting was preoccupied, and he appeared disturbingly different from the man I'd seen in New York a little over a year ago. Once more, we were strangers.

On the drive north toward Sedona, I'd tried to question him openly in order to clear the air. "Is anything wrong? Have I come at a bad time?"

He glanced at me and then returned his attention to the road, so that I had only a swift impression of some terrible desolation before he turned away. It was a look that shocked me.

"It needn't concern you," he said, and made an effort to be more friendly. Not a very convincing effort.

"We're going by way of Prescott and Jerome and Cottonwood," he explained. "It's the longer route, but you might as well see something of Arizona."

Words came out abruptly that I hadn't meant to speak. "Was I born in Arizona?"

Again he gave me a quick, studying look. "Didn't Jed tell you *anything?*"

"I never asked," I admitted. "I didn't want to know. I'm not sure how much I want to know even now."

"You were born in northern Arizona," he said curtly, and let silence fall between us.

I asked nothing more, and he offered nothing. It was best that way, although it hurt me that Rick chose to put such distance between us. As far as my own birthright was concerned, if what was so long past and secret must now become part of my present life, then let it come gradually. Let me have time to orient myself and digest new facts that I could learn to live with. It was disconcerting to realize that half my blood heritage came from this land through which we were passing—though I had to admit to a strange attraction. I gave the scene my full attention and tried not to think about Rick.

The colors of the southwest were very different from the world I was used to. The all-pervading turquoise of the sky spread above desert tans and beiges. Adobe colors in which the sun could be absorbed, and in which gray was almost totally absent. What a lot of gray I'd been looking at lately! There were subtle greens as well—the greens of sage and juniper and other unfamiliar desert growth. Like an artist, I had learned to appreciate texture, and this new world offered so many new and exciting textures.

Behind Phoenix, the bare volcanic peaks lacked the wooded friendliness of Eastern mountains, yet I liked their strong earth colors. North of the city the saguaro cactus sprang up in desert soil, reaching candelabra arms toward a vast sky. Rick identified palo verde trees, thick and bushy, with green trunks, and the soft-looking cholla, that was really filled with prickly spines. I saw green tumbleweed growing in great clumps that would later dry out, break off, and go blowing across the landscape as it did in Western movies.

Texture! Color! All new and fresh. In this country I might come to life again. Because half my roots were here? Because men and women to whom I was related had stood in this earth and seen what I was seeing now? Had they been pioneers, I wondered.

But that was sentimental whimsy. I belonged to the East. Not just to the places I knew, but to a stepmother who had raised and loved me. Of course I would enjoy and respond to all that was fresh and different here, but there must be no digging for facts that might only hurt me. I wasn't ready to accept one of my father's many passing fancies as my real mother. I had come because I wanted to know how Jed had died. I wanted to know whatever connection might lie between Sybil and my father's death. But all else in the past could stay buried forever as far as I was concerned.

As we began to climb, my ears popped with the rising elevation, and the vegetation turned into varieties of pine. The miles flowed by, mostly in silence. Once Rick inquired politely about my work, and I told him that everything was in the hands of my partner and would be fine. Then, quite suddenly he stopped being polite.

"Why *did* you come?" he asked. "Why did you *really* come?"

The letter was folded in my handbag and I had debated with myself as to whether I should show it to Rick immediately, or wait a while. Each time I had decided that it was better to wait until the reason that brought me here became clear. The letter concerned Sybil in a possibly ugly way, and there was no point in showing it to Rick, if in the long run it proved to be no more than a hoax, or perhaps an act of spite. My sister had always had a gift for making enemies.

I decided to evade the real reason. "Everything's been going stale for me in New York. I'm tired, and perhaps a change will really help."

"But not Europe this time?"

I shrugged. "Europe, for me, is necessarily one fashion show after another. It wouldn't be much of a change right now."

"All right. I'll accept that. Marilla is excited about your coming."

"And I'm eager to see her."

After that we were silent again, and I knew my specious explanation had not convinced him. *Oh, Rick,* I said silently, *be my friend. I need a friend.*

Prescott was a high, sprawling town, with houses whose roofs were built with steep peaks to shed the heavy snows. Beyond, we drove past strange rock formations, and as we went on, the mountains grew higher, more formidable. We climbed through stands of white pine, through cedar and piñon and juniper, and I drank in the high, clear air as though it would nourish me, turn me into someone new.

Above Jerome, we came at last to an escarpment that looked out over the edge of the world, and Rick stopped the car and pulled over. "There!" he said. "Your first view."

I gazed across a wide stretch of the Verde Valley to the dramatic sight that marked the far horizon. A jagged line of red rocks cut into the sky. Strange mountains of bare sandstone that had been thrust up to stand alone in contrast to the more subdued coloring of the lower country. A strong response surged through me, as though that far line of burning rocks promised something; as though they involved me in their very being—perhaps threatening, perhaps delighting. For the moment, I had no idea which. I knew only that something in me lifted and responded.

"That's where we're going," Rick said. "The red rock country."

We went over Mingus Mountain and down through the ghost town of Jerome, which was a name out of history. I could remember my father telling me about it with excitement in his voice—the place of the great copper mines. The town had been built on the side of a mountain, with narrow streets running one almost on top of the other. Today the main street was lined with little shops intended to attract tourists, and two cars could barely pass. Traffic was heavy both ways, and Rick said it was

31

always like that.

In recent years the houses had been taken over by artists and others who loved the locality. Many had been rebuilt at some expense, and repainted, so that pastels and splashes of white mingled with the gray. Near the mine structures, huge mounds of dull-gray tailings fell down the mountainside, scarring it forever.

The highway ran through the town, and as we followed it down steep switchback turns till we reached the valley, I had no sense of fatality about this place. No faintest suspicion that I would return under strange and frightening circumstances.

"It's about thirty miles from here to Sedona," Rick said. "To Oak Creek Canyon and the red rocks. You either love the rocks, or they scare the wits out of you and you move on. Your father loved them."

Clearly, Rick did too, for he had stayed. But would I? That burning red was a new color for me, and so strong that I wasn't sure I could deal with it, however exciting it seemed. I must wait to find out.

I was still waiting, still uncertain, as I stood on the narrow deck of the guesthouse, where Rick had brought me when we arrived. I hadn't seen Sybil at all. She was out for the afternoon on a speaking engagement, he'd said. Something to do with ecology. The picture of Sybil on a platform espousing a cause bemused me, but I still dreaded our first meeting. I would know at once whether she had really changed, and what our relationship would be.

Marilla was not around either when we arrived, so there had been no family welcome. Rick saw me to my rooms, set down my bags, and indicated a bell I could ring for anything I wanted. It was necessary for him to get out to the shop before it closed. He would see me at dinner. I'd found no way to break through this new guard he had raised against me.

At least I couldn't have been made more comfortable, as far as my surroundings went. The little guesthouse had a generous living room furnished in soothing greens and buffs, a bedroom with twin beds, an easy chair, good lamps, and a row of books between carved bookends.

Since I could never live without reading, I ran through the titles. An effort had been made to provide guests with books about the Southwest. There was a popular history that began with the Conquistadores, a volume of beautiful color photographs of Indians of the area, one called *Book of the Hopi,* and several suspense novels by Southwestern writers. Perhaps I would dip into them all, but now I wanted to see the rest of the house.

The bedroom closet was built-in and spacious. Even the bathroom was perfectly appointed, with tiles of pale green, and a huge tub. A dining and kitchen arrangement showed me a refrigerator stocked with eggs, cheese, bacon, and a carton of milk. Flowers and fruit on a table welcomed me, yet I felt uneasy and anything but welcome. I was here on a pretext, and whatever face I looked into from now on I would question because of the letter in my handbag. More than that, Rick's behavior disturbed me. And there was still Sybil to be faced.

I'd unpacked, bathed, changed to a dress of meadow-green suede with a touch of gold— my own design—and had come out here to the deck, where I could stare at the stupendous view and await developments.

The quiet and the sense of isolation seemed somehow oppressive. This guesthouse, set at a distance from the main structure, was like a high island, occupying a mound of rock that went steeply down on all sides. It was connected with the main house area by a private bridge across a gully. If I wanted privacy, this was it, and I wasn't altogether sure I liked it.

On my left, the main house spread across a larger outcropping of rock, with a half moon of tiled terrace, where one could sit and look out at all those everlasting red mountains of rock. The low house was built of reddish-brown redwood, with wide overhangs on all sides and a great deal of glass. There were a few trees, oak and pine, but no grass. Instead, small cactus plantings bedded in chips of red rock substituted for patches of lawn. There could be floods in Arizona, but most of the time this was dry country and water would be at a premium.

"Hi!" A light, inquiring voice addressed me from the direction of the bridge and I turned to see a little girl dressed in jeans and plaid shirt, thumbs tucked into her silver-studded belt, as she stood watching me. This was the daughter Rick had been concerned about at our last meeting in New York. I warmed to her at once.

"Hello, Marilla," I said. "I'm your mother's sister. Will you come and join me? It's time we got acquainted."

"I know who you are," she assured me, and stayed where she was. If, as Rick had said, she was pleased about my coming, she wasn't showing it. "And you're not my mother's sister. You're her *half* sister," she corrected.

So Sybil had once more emphasized the distinction—this time to her daughter. As she'd done so often to me when we were growing up. I waited expectantly, and after a moment the child came the rest of the way across the bridge and approached my deck. Her hair was as fair as Sybil's, and she wore it in short curls like a cap about her head—curls that were ruffled now by a wind that swept up the canyon. When she reached the end of the deck, she stopped to study me with enormous brown eyes in a small, piquant face.

I sat down in a deck chair and waved her toward its companion. Under such solemn scrutiny, it was hard to find the right thing to say. Marilla could be as disconcerting as her father.

Instead of taking the chair, she climbed astride the open rail, hooking her feet together underneath. The rocky cliff plunged off steeply beyond, and I put out my hand to steady her. She ignored it, her silent interest in me continuing.

"It's all so beautiful," I said, nodding toward the red pinnacles. "But—a little scary too."

She turned her head to look over one shoulder, as though checking my words. "There're lots of rocks more scary than those. Wait till you see the Fire People. They're the ones who're really spooky."

"Fire People?"

"Didn't Grandpa Jed tell you about them?"

"I'm afraid not."

She nodded in odd satisfaction, as though pleased to have shared something with my father that I had not. I could understand how she felt. When Jed's attention was on you, no one else existed for him. He'd had a talent for giving himself completely—for however short a time. But this was a faculty that could arouse jealousy in those he seemed to forget all too quickly. I had seen such jealousy surface violently in Sybil, and I'd felt it in myself, too. Now it was evident even in this child. You scored in the game when Jed Phillips made you feel special.

Marilla was running on. "It was Grandpa Jed who showed me the Fire People. I was only little when he drove me out in the back country one time in a jeep. That's when he first took me inside the secret place where they live."

"He could make everything seem exciting," I said, remembering all too well.

Sunset caught a glint of tears in her eyes, but she brushed them away. "Did you know that Clara Hale is upset about your coming here? She used to be Clara Robins before she got married."

The sudden segue from my father to Rick's partner in his shops seemed strange, and I didn't understand it until the next day. At the moment her words were merely puzzling.

"Why should she be upset?" I asked. "What have I to do with her?"

"I expect you'll find out." Then, perhaps because she had said too much, she made another quick switch of subjects. "My mother's a real good speaker. She can stand up in front of hundreds of people and make them think just what she wants. Today she's in Flagstaff at the ecology meeting, and I'll bet she's really wowed them. Brian drove her up there in her car. I expect they'll be home soon."

Marilla was going too fast for me. This new facet of my sister continued to surprise me.

"Who is Brian?" I asked.

"Brian Montgomery. He knows more about animals and plants and rocks than anybody. Right now he works for his mother a couple of afternoons taking tourists around in a jeep. So he can earn money and still have time to write his book. Brian is nonviolent—that's what he says. He's seen the Fire People too."

"What are the Fire People?"

"*Maybe* I'll show you sometime. You aren't much like your father, are you? I mean, you look kind of like Grandpa Jed, but you don't seem like him."

I hoped that was true. "You aren't like your father either."

"Mom says I have a temper like his. Mom never gets excited mad the way we do."

I understood very well, and felt uncomfortable, remembering. As a child she'd been dangerously excitable, but as she grew up Sybil had acquired an icy control over her emotions that could seem more devastating than hot anger. I had seen her behave cruelly at times, while she remained coldly calm—and those around her fell apart. I remembered one occasion when she had thrown her pair of pointed scissors at me, and had done it without the slightest passion, though with full intent to injure. Either my friend Vermilion, or some inner instinct, had caused me to move just in time for her aim to miss my throat.

Marilla was regarding me curiously. "Did you bring *her* with you?" she asked.

For a moment I didn't know what she was talking about and merely stared.

"You know—the make-believe one. Grandpa told me how you made her up together, and what fun you had with her. What was her name—Vermilion? Did you bring her with you?"

"I don't think so," I said, and quickly shut all the doors in my mind.

"Grandpa Jed said he'd help me make up a sister too, but I didn't want one, and Mom wouldn't like it."

That was certainly true, I thought wryly.

"Anyway," Marilla said, "I like unicorns better."

"A very sensible choice," I agreed, but I wished Jed hadn't told his granddaughter about Vermilion. Somehow, it seemed a betrayal. Yet I had to be amused at myself, too. He could still make everyone jealous.

Marilla tipped her head, listening, and I heard the distant sound of a car coming up the hill from town. When it came nearer and stopped close by, Marilla hopped down from the rail.

"That's Mom's car. Brian's brought her home. Let's go meet them."

I had no wish to hurry toward a meeting with my sister, but it must be faced, and Marilla was already tugging me along. She was an appealing child, though at the same time disquieting. Some tantalizing quality in her eluded me. We crossed the redwood bridge together, and at the end she stopped.

"I have a present for you," she whispered, her eyes very bright. "One you'll like. Maybe I'll bring it to you tonight. So wait up for me."

Then she was running ahead toward the house, pushing open a glass door, beckoning. When I'd first arrived, Rick had brought me to the guesthouse by way of the outer walk, so this was the first time I'd been inside the main house. I followed Marilla into an enormous living room that stretched the width of the terrace and ran back in a narrower extension toward the street. A beamed cathedral ceiling arched overhead, and great glass panels looked out upon the rocks. It was a room filled with fascinating treasures, but I had no time to study it just then. I heard voices from the front door. My sister was coming toward me, and I stiffened anxiously.

She had indeed changed, matured—no longer the thin, beautiful young model but a handsome, self-assured woman. Her blond hair was elegantly coiled on top of her head, and she wore a lightweight suit in a gold as pale as ripening wheat. A good deal of fine turquoise jewelry was in evidence—a mark of the Southwest, as I'd already noticed at the airport. The front of her suit was spattered now with a darker yellow stain that spilled from breast to lower pocket.

The younger man who followed her into the room was as tall as Sybil, broad-shouldered and muscular, with sunbleached hair, a curly golden beard, and a manner that seemed protective of her and affectionately concerned.

Marilla rushed toward her mother but stopped cautiously just short of touching her. "Mom! What happened to your suit? What did you spill on it?"

Sybil brushed past her daughter without answering, and I recognized that she was being consumed by one of her cold and dangerous angers. The chill seemed directed toward me, yet her control was superb as she embraced me quickly, dutifully.

"Lindsay, you do look marvelous!"

The words were right, even the tone of her voice, but I knew from all those long years in the same house with my sister that something had made her furious. I managed to return her greeting pleasantly and stepped back from the embrace.

"Don't worry about the stain, Marilla," she went on. "It's dry by this time. Can you imagine—someone threw an egg at me. Never in my life has that happened before."

Marilla squealed with excitement. "Mom! Why would anyone throw an egg on you? What did you do?"

"It was nothing. I went right on, and the audience was with me all the more. But don't carry on, Marilla. Lindsay, I'd like you to meet Brian Montgomery, who's been a wonderful help to me in this entire ecology project."

The young man took my hand and held it

for a moment, his look rather searching. So this was the "nonviolent" one, I thought, and at once my mind began its questioning—as I was to question everyone silently from now on. Had *he* written that letter to me—the summons that had brought me here?

"I'm happy to meet Sybil's sister," he said. "I know how much she's looked forward to your visit." Was there something a little dry about the words, as though he didn't entirely believe them?

"I'm sorry I couldn't be here to meet you." Sybil continued. "I'd expected to be home a lot sooner, but there was quite a commotion after the egg throwing. Though once they quieted down, they listened to me. Whoever it was got away without being noticed, and I'm relieved, really. We don't need that sort of publicity."

"Just the same, that note left under your windshield wiper was serious," Brian said. "I couldn't help wondering if it was connected. I still think you should've given it to the police."

"Nonsense!" The word dripped scorn, and Brian winced. "Everyone who speaks out on a controversial subject becomes a target now and then. There are always fanatics in opposition to any good cause. Brian," her tone softened, "I'm planning a little dinner while Lindsay is here. Just a few people who'll want to meet my sister. You'll come, of course, and bring your mother? Clara and Parker Hale will be here, and I'll see if I can get Parker to cook us one of his terrific dinners. He was trained by a Swiss chef, you know."

She was talking more than I remembered, and I wondered if she was uneasy too. Or perhaps she was just filling time, until we could be alone and she could show me her real face.

Now she turned to me in explanation. "Clara and Parker were married only a few months ago. He used to be a professional chef and a very fine one. So sometimes he does special dinners locally."

Brian seemed disturbed by her words. "But Sybil, if Clara—"

She interrupted at once, as confident as ever. "Oh, I know about all that. Don't worry. I'll handle it. We can count on you, Brian?"

"Of course. And you'd never keep Ma away. She's dying to meet Jed's younger daughter."

"I know you want to get home," Sybil said a little too smoothly. "Thank you for driving me to Flagstaff. It helped save my energy for the talk. I hope I haven't made you late."

She was dismissing him, and he knew it.

"Ma will wait dinner," he said. "It's fine that your talk went so well. You really cut into the opposition today. Let me know when you get the Phoenix thing lined up."

He was on his way to the door, when Marilla improvised suddenly. "Brian, I told Lindsay you'd take her out in one of the jeeps sometime. Into the back country, I mean. Then I can go too, can't I?"

He looked a little surprised but nodded cheerfully enough. "Oh, sure. I'll be glad to. Any time."

He went off to where he'd parked his car, and Marilla accompanied him to the door. For the first time, Sybil and I were alone.

For a moment she stood looking after him, nodding as though in satisfaction. "I'm glad he's over that girl."

If she expected me to ask, "What girl?" I was silent. It meant nothing to me.

"Well, Lindsay?" she went on, and the veneer of cordiality she'd worn fell away with the challenge of her words.

"Thanks for letting me come," I said mildly.

"It was Rick's idea—not mine. He's been making plans. *We* don't have to pretend with each other, do we?"

"I don't know about any plans."

"Oh, he has them for you, but I don't think you should get carried away. Not to the point of staying here for long, Lindsay."

"I haven't any intention of staying long."

"That's wise of you. Come and sit down for a minute, since we have this chance alone. Why *did* you come? It wasn't just because you wanted a rest, was it?"

She *had* changed, I thought in dismay. And for the worse. What had been rather spiteful and unformed efforts to dominate me in the past had now crystallized and grown a great deal stronger. She had always been able to put me down with a look and a few words, and she was trying to do the same thing again, though for some more threatening purpose. But I was no longer a child to be bullied. In the old days I'd needed to summon Vermilion in order to stand up to her, but I didn't need any imaginary support now, and I answered her quietly.

"I came because of Jed, Sybil. I want to know what really happened to him."

Her laughter had the sound of ice in it, and she was not really amused. "How stupid we were, Lindsay. All that hero worship for a father who never gave a damn about either one of us. Though of course you haven't had the advantage I've had in the last few years of watching him closely and recognizing just what he was like. He wasn't worth your coming here, if he really is your reason. What on earth could you possibly do?"

By an effort, I kept my voice low and even. "I don't know yet. That's what I'm here to find out."

She switched her direction without warning. "Has Rick told you about your mother? Your *real* mother?"

This time her attack startled me, but I still managed an outward calm. "If there's something to tell, I suppose he will, eventually."

The old word she had loved to use echoed in my mind as it had not done for years— "bastard"—and it took an effort of will to keep from dropping my eyes. Somehow I was able to stare her down, and I think she recognized that her old domination of me was over.

"You may not like what you learn," she told me, and let the matter go.

A young Mexican woman came into the room just then, and Sybil spoke to her. "Consuela, will you get Miss Phillips whatever she'd like to drink, please." And to me, "Do go out on the terrace and make yourself comfortable, Lindsay. The air cools off at sunset. I'll change and be with you soon."

Sybil waited while I spoke to Consuela, and then went away. I watched her go with a tiny feeling of satisfaction. I'd stood up to my sister, and for once she hadn't been able to beat me down. Nevertheless, the threat of some intent I didn't understand stayed with me, and I knew I wouldn't dare allow a chink of weakness to become visible. This time, any attack she made on me wouldn't be for her own passing satisfaction but because of something that went a great deal deeper. What had happened between us just now was no light crossing of words. This time Sybil had some far more serious intent, though I had no idea as yet what it was.

Let me in, Vermilion whispered. *You need me now.*

I didn't need her. I was my own woman and I would fight my own battles from now on.

When Consuela brought my cinzano, I didn't carry it out to the terrace but took the stemmed

46

glass and walked slowly around the room. There was so much to see. So much that might tell me, not only about Arizona, but perhaps about Sybil and Rick as well. I needed to *know*.

As I moved about, studying the room, a frieze of heads caught my eye. They were of carved wood brightly painted, and all alike—perhaps twenty of them mounted along a high shelf that stretched across the opening to the entry hall. The repetition of staring black eyes and slightly sneering red mouths was hypnotic, and I could hardly take my eyes from them.

Marilla came running in from the front door, and she turned around to see what held my attention.

"Oh, those. They're Hopi. Dad bought them from an old man in the Pueblo village of Oraibi up north. Dad says they aren't typical. The old man just does that same funny head over and over. And then he paints tham all alike. Grandpa Jed used to talk to those heads when he was here. He knew some Hopi words, and he said they talked back to him, but I never heard them."

The familiar stab of pain come so easily at mention of my father. But reminders of him would come often out here. I had better learn how to meet them, and close my ears to Sybil's derogatory words. There was nothing she could say about Jed that I hadn't told myself, yet none of this changed what I felt I owed him.

As I sipped my drink, I examined a collection

of handsome Indian pottery, all earthen tones, with decorations of blue and henna. A combination that would be interesting in a dress. On the wall above hung the framed painting of an Indian woman. The figure was full length, and she wore a blue dress with a lighter overskirt on which flowers had been appliquéd. Her legs were encased in long white leggings with moccasin feet. In one hand, she held up a basket heaped with what seemed to be blue grain while, from the other, five ears of blue corn were suspended.

But it was her face that had most interested the artist—as it interested me. She had great dark eyes, with a slashing of black brows above. Her cheeks and chin were softly contoured, the lips full and parted breathlessly, as though she listened to something just out of sight. A beating of ceremonial drums, perhaps? Her black hair was brushed down the sides from a central part, but there were no traditional braids from the old days—as I'd seen in pictures of Indians. She wore it in a short, straight bob that seemed modern in concept.

Again, Marilla was just behind me. "That picture is called *The Blue Corn Maiden*. Grandpa Jed loaned it to my father. He was always doing that. People gave him things, but he moved around so much that he never had any place to keep them, so he sort of parked them with friends. And sometimes he brought us presents. I have two kachina dolls that are from him, and some other things too. Once he gave Brian a real Hopi drum.''

"Are there Indians in Sedona?" I asked.

"Not now. But the Yavapai tribe believes that a valley in the vicinity of Soldier's Wash, right here in Sedona, is the place where the world began. Of course there're Hopi on Black Mesa, where the reservation is, but that's a long way off. Dad says the Hopi are like a small island with a sea of Navajo all around.''

I knew very little about the Indians of the Southwest, and I moved on to study a woven wall hanging with a crested blue-gray bird darting across it. Everywhere I looked I saw marvelous color combinations, great design symbols, new textures. But at the moment I was more interested in the people I was meeting here than in inspiration for design.

"Tell me about Brian," I said.

"What do you want to know?"

"You said he was writing a book."

"I guess he is. But what he likes best is to be outdoors and not inside houses. Even when he's working, he sets his typewriter out on the patio when it's not too cold or windy. Mostly he climbs around in the dry washes and all along Oak Creek looking for whatever he can find.''

"What sort of things does he find?"

"Oh—plants and rocks and bugs. His mother, Mrs. Orva Montgomery, used to be an art teacher in our school. She's retired and now that she's a widow she runs the jeep tours that her husband used to run. She still gives private art lessons, too. Mom used to let me go to her—but I don't know if I will anymore." Marilla hesitated and her voice dropped. "I don't know if I really want to paint."

"Why not? I like to paint too, though mostly I do peculiar ladies with long necks and skinny bodies to show off the dresses I design."

Before she could respond, a car door slammed, and Rick came into the house.

Marilla hurled herself toward her father and this time she didn't stop short, as she'd done with Sybil. He caught her up and swung her around, planted a kiss on her cheek and set her down.

The excitement of telling her news set her chattering. "Somebody threw an egg at Mom while she was making her speech! It got all over the front of her suit. And Brian said there was a note left on the windshield of her car. But I don't know what it said."

"Then maybe I'd better wait until your mother tells me about it," Rick said. "Scoot now. You know she won't like it if you're not out of jeans by dinnertime—and neither will I." He patted her bottom, and she ran off, laughing.

"What's all this about egg throwing?" he asked me.

"I don't know any more than Marilla told you. Sybil didn't seem to think it was important. Rick, I do like your house. It fits into the landscape.''

He looked tired, and perhaps even more somber than he'd seemed on the drive from Phoenix, though he made an effort and smiled at me.

"I worked with the architect on it all the way. I wanted something low and spacious, with windows looking out at the rocks.''

In his voice I heard his fondness for this place, this house. For Sybil it would be a prize possession, but for Rick it was more.

He went on. ''Tomorrow, if you feel like it, I'd like to show you our Sedona shop. Clara wants to meet you.''

I remembered his daughter's disquieting words. ''Marilla seems to think that Mrs. Hale is upset about my coming here.''

"Oh, that.'' Rick brushed the matter aside. "What Clara is miffed about has nothing to do with you. She'll get over it.''

"Sybil doesn't want me here either,'' I said. "We were never close as sisters, as you know perfectly well. I wouldn't have come here if I'd known how strongly she feels.''

He rubbed his forehead with one finger, and it was a gesture of weariness. "You had to come to Sedona because you're Jed's daughter. You had to come eventually, didn't you?''

"Tomorrow I'll tell you why. Then you can decide whether or not I ought to stay for a while.''

"All right, I'll wait. Now if you'll excuse

me, I'll shower and change for dinner. Have you everything you want?"

I nodded and he reached out to touch my shoulder lightly. It was a gesture of reassurance, but I was not reassured. It was as though he knew something I didn't—something that still lay ahead of me—and he didn't want me to be frightened. But his touch carried understanding as well, so perhaps he hadn't changed altogether. He knew that coming here had not been easy for me, whatever it was that had brought me. I wanted to thank him, but I couldn't put anything so nebulous into words. Nor did I want him to raise his guard against me again, as he might if I said the wrong thing.

I watched him disappear toward the bedroom area and sipped my drink thoughtfully. It wasn't my foolish first-love feeling for him as a young girl that mattered now, but the stronger, far more troubling emotions that stirred in me as a woman. I wondered if I would be strong enough to keep them from surfacing. Because Rick must never guess. Nor Sybil. And I must question myself, too. Had I been attracted so deeply again simply because he was Sybil's husband? Must I always envy what she possessed?

The great beamed room with its collected treasures began to seem oppressive, and I took Sybil's suggestion and carried my drink onto the half moon of terra-cotta tiles that formed the terrace. The sun had set, and against the sky huge rock shapes blackened in the fading light, resembling spiny-backed monsters crouching too close for comfort. At each end of the terrace a mushroom lamp had come on, so that I was encased in a small area of light that held off the encroaching darkness. There were no lights up there among the rocks, though on either hand lighted windows showed in a scattering of houses, none of them very close. The night seemed utterly quiet and lonely.

I sat in a folding chair and placed my thin-stemmed glass on the small table beside me. Sybil's words with their barbed challenge had roused questions about the mother I'd never known. A mother who had been unwilling to face whatever difficulties a baby might have brought into her life. It wasn't often that I brooded about this any more. The fact that she had existed was something I'd seldom faced in the course of my life. Yet this mother, whoever she was, belonged to an Arizona I was seeing for the first time. Her family had probably lived here, perhaps still lived here. That was something I was less than ever ready to face after the veiled warning in Sybil's words.

An early evening breeze refreshed me after the warm day, and I raised my face to its touch. Far off in the hills an animal cried out—a sound curiously between a bark and a note that was almost human. A coyote, I supposed. Jed had written about night sounds out in the back country. A mountain wilderness crowded close around small Sedona. It was a wealthy little town, yet wealth meant nothing out there where emptiness ruled. In New York the voice of the city was always awake. It hummed stridently all night long, and you could hear it even in high-rise apartment buildings. There could be loneliness there too, of a different sort. Here the night was too quiet.

A nearby sound, reassuringly normal, reached me from the house—door chimes. I heard Consuela hurrying to answer. A moment later she appeared on the terrace with an envelope in her hand.

"For you, miss," she said. "A boy just brought it to the door."

I thanked her and she went away. The letters that spelled my name had been blocked in with a black felt-tipped pen, and I knew at once where this message came from. I'd seen the same block letters on the sheet of notebook paper that had brought me here.

Opening the envelope, I took out a similar sheet. The words were only a few:

I knew you would come. Be careful of you sister. She has something to hide. Be patient.

I had brought my handbag with me and it contained the note I had received in New York. Now I took it out and compared the two. The writers were identical. I must show these to

54

Rick, and yet reluctance still held me. How could I make accusations against my sister, when I didn't know whether these notes were a hoax? If they weren't, what damage might they cause in my sister's life, or in Rick's? Or to Marilla? Someone was watching—someone who knew I'd arrived. I must be wary, yet I *must* find out who had watched me, summoned me, who concealed motives I couldn't yet understand.

I put both notes in my bag just as Rick came through the living room to the terrace. He had changed to gray slacks and a light jacket, his dark hair damp from the shower. It seemed to me that he was more rested, more cheerful than a little while ago. As always, I liked to look at him. Just to look seemed enough for now.

"I feel a lot better," he said. "There have been problems, and there still are. But I don't want to worry you with them. And I don't want you to worry about Clara Hale. She can't hold your relationship to Jed against you, once she gets to know you. I do want you to meet her tomorrow."

"So that's it—my relationship to Jed? What did she have against my father?"

"It isn't something she likes to talk about."

Rick knew, I thought, and he didn't mean to discuss it with me.

Sybil appeared at one of the glass doors with two martinis in her hands, and Rick went to take one of the glasses. He didn't kiss her in greeting, and his manner seemed reserved as he drew a chair near my table for her, and she sat down, all but ignoring him.

She had changed to a flowing gown in a print of pale green with red poppies—a couturier creation, obviously—that enhanced a figure that was no longer too thin. I would have said that she looked perfectly cool and serene, and beautifully in control of her world. But when she placed an envelope on the table before her, she knocked over her glass, cracking the delicate Baccarat crystal.

Consuela was summoned, the broken glass removed, the spill mopped up, and a second glass brought—while through it all Sybil controlled an obvious tendency to tremble. Not in weakness, I suddenly realized, but because she was shaken by some inner rage. I wondered what would happen if she ever let go and blew up. That, however, was never her way. She had always preferred the quiet stiletto to the roaring gun.

"According to Marilla, someone threw an egg at you during the meeting this afternoon," Rick said when everything was calm again.

"That wasn't important," she told him. "This is what I want you to see." She removed a sheet from the envelope and held it out to him. "Brian found this tucked under my windshield wiper when we were ready to drive home this afternoon."

As Rick took the sheet, I noted that it was

cheap paper, though not torn from a school notebook. Rick read the single sentence aloud: " 'Get out of Sedona if you know what's good for you.' "

"I'll show this to the police," he said. "Did you report the egg throwing?"

Sybil's eyes were on me, and I realized that I'd been staring at Rick, hanging on his words. I must be more careful. Sybil was no fool, and the last thing I wanted was to have her armed with new ammunition.

After a moment she answered Rick almost carelessly. "There was no point in reporting it. Whoever it was got away while all the attention was on me. I suppose this sort of thing can be expected when people are being stirred up."

I suspected that Rick didn't believe in this dismissal of the incident. Nor did I. Sybil undoubtedly had something to conceal—as the second note to me had hinted.

"I'll turn this in tomorrow at the sheriff's office," Rick said. "I'm just glad you weren't hurt."

Sybil shrugged and finished her fresh drink. I still sensed an anger that she held under steely control.

"What is this controversial topic?" I asked her.

At least she could warm to the subject, and she came out of her preoccupation. "Until recently, we've had no pollution in Sedona. There are septic systems for houses already built, and our water comes from mountain wells and reservoirs. It's as pure as our air has always been. There's been no problem until recently."

"Oak Creek flows into the Verde River near Cottonwood and its purity is important down there too," Rick added.

Sybil went on. "New subdivisions are springing up. Some promoters want to build condominiums and restaurants up the canyon and we're becoming alarmed as the contamination level rises. That's the battle I'm helping to fight."

"You can do it, too," Rick said warmly. "You know I'll help, if I can."

Her look flicked briefly to his face, and then away, and I sensed that his warmth was for what she would regard as the wrong reason.

"I hope you were into all this when Dad was here," I told her. "He'd have been pleased."

She stared off at the black peaks, and when she turned her head and looked at me I knew she would no more accept me now as a sister than she had done in the past. Inexplicably, her hostility toward me had deepened.

"I understand some of the reasons why you've come, Lindsay," she said, "but it's a mistake for you to be here."

With Rick present, she was being more careful than she had been with me alone, though she was still challenging me. However, when she went on, her words took an unexpected turn.

"Obviously, Jed had enemies—and he's dead. Has it ever occurred to you, Lindsay, that the same people who hated him may not be fond of his daughters?"

"What are you talking about?" Rick demanded.

"Perhaps that thrown egg and the windshield note had nothing to do with our conservationist project. Perhaps there will be worse before this ends."

"You'd better explain." Rick was curt.

She only shrugged again. "Perhaps I will—and very soon. But not right now." Again she turned a quick glance in my direction, as though hinting of something unpleasant to come. I had no realization then of how quickly prophetic her earlier words were to be.

It was as though some unseen hand suddenly pushed me. Instantly I scraped my chair backward on the terrace. I had no time to think—I simply reacted—and as I did so I caught a glimpse of movement off the terrace to my right. I was the only one facing that way, and I had an instant's impression of a face, a raised hand, as a rock came hurtling across the terrace. It flashed through the air where my head had been, and smashed upon the tiles.

Rick was on his feet at once, snatching up a flashlight from a nearby rack as he ran. He vaulted over the railing, to crash down through brush, while I sat shaking in reaction.

A few times before in my life I'd experienced

warnings just like the push I'd felt, and I was always disturbed afterward, not only because of danger that had barely missed me, but because I had *known* ahead of time.

Again, Sybil was watching me. "You look terrified, Lindsay. I wonder which one of us that was intended for?" Though she spoke calmly enough, I sensed underlying tension as malice toward me surfaced. "A rock is rather more serious than an egg. Do *you* have any enemies, Lindsay?"

It was possible that I did have, and meeting her look I knew her for my enemy. She had always been that, and now her antagonism toward me had deepened to a frightening degree.

I didn't answer her.

"He won't find anyone," Sybil went on, setting down her empty glass as though nothing had happened, and now her hand didn't shake. "Not at night. Whoever threw that rock was sure of not being caught."

She was right. After five minutes of fruitless searching, Rick returned angrily and came directly to me.

"Are you all right, Lindsay? That was very close." His concern reached out to me, and I was all too aware of Sybil watching.

"I'm fine," I said, and kept myself sternly in hand.

He went on, his anger mounting. "I'm not going to wait until tomorrow. I'll call the sheriff's office now."

As he spoke, Marilla ran out upon the terrace, eager to join us. In contrast to what had just happened, she seemed a vision of bright innocence in neat blue chambray, with a jonquil embroidered on the pocket. Her fair hair had been brushed into a semblance of order before it sprang into unruly curls again, and there was an elfin appeal about her. Nevertheless, her eyes held an awareness that belied her nine years.

Before anyone could speak, she challenged us. "Something's happened, hasn't it?"

Rick started to reassure her, but Sybil broke in sharply. "Yes! And for the second time today I seem to have been in the line of fire. The aim just wasn't as good this time. That rock came closer to Lindsay. Unless, of course, Lindsay was really the target."

"Stop that!" Rick said, and put an arm about his daughter's shoulders. "Someone threw a stone," he told her quietly. "Some kid, probably. I'm going to phone the sheriff, but it's nothing to be scared of. Go inside now with your mother and Lindsay, and sit down to dinner. I'll be with you soon."

The heat of anger was in him as he strode off, and I knew how he felt. It was one thing to fight a known enemy, to stand up and defend oneself, but something else when that enemy was faceless and offered nothing tangible to fight against.

As we moved toward the dining room, my foot crunched on rock. I could still feel the violence of disturbed air close to my face. The stone would have injured one of us, though it was unlikely that it could have been fatal. A warning had been given. To whom? Was there any question, in spite of Sybil's words? I had a feeling that the aim had been very good indeed, and that the chunk of sandstone had landed exactly toward the target intended—*me*. Had the intent been to miss? This time.

3

It was nearly ten o'clock and I was ready for bed. The remainder of the evening had been upsetting. A deputy had come from the sheriff's office, and we'd told him what little we could. I had seen a face, a hand, but only for an instant. I had no remembered impression of either.

It was all an exercise in futility, but at least the sheriff had been alerted, both about what had happened in Flagstaff, and on the terrace of Rick's house. When he left, the deputy took with him the note left on Sybil's windshield, as well as the rock. I had still said nothing about the two notes I'd received. They were quite different and I was convinced that they had come from another source. I wanted to put them into Rick's hands first. He had a right to be prepared before they were shown to anyone else.

Marilla had stayed with us, in spite of a half-hearted attempt by Rick to send her away, and the child almost seethed with excitement as she listened to everything.

We had finished dinner late, and it had been an uncomfortable meal.

"Nothing so dramatic as this usually happens around here," Sybil assured me as we finished our dessert. "Sedona is a remarkably peaceful community."

Marilla said, "Just the same, Mom, things *do* happen here. People get lost up in the rocks, or they have accidents there and fall. That can be exciting. Then Brian has to go searching for them, and sometimes he brings them down safely. If they don't get killed first."

"Why Brian?" I asked.

"Because he belongs to Search and Rescue," Marilla said. "I'll bet he's about the best they've got on the whole crew."

Sybil explained. "Tourists who don't know any better sometimes go rock climbing, and that's not always safe on crumbling sandstone. Even experienced rock climbers can have accidents. And it's easier to get lost in the back country than outsiders think. So Search and Rescue, which is made up of volunteers, performs a real service. Brian *is* an expert."

Rick had been silent and preoccupied through most of the meal. What had occurred on the terrace seemed to trouble him deeply, and I wondered again if there was any connection between my father's death and what was happening now. Did someone besides the letter writer know why I was here?

Later that night, as I sat up in bed trying to read *The Book of the Hopi,* my thoughts were melancholy and not on the pages. Two men were insistent in my mind, with a hurtful longing that connected them both.

If only I could have seen my father again. While the loss of my mother was a constant sadness, it was a quiet grief, without anguish. She had wanted the release of death and I could wish nothing else for her. But Jed had never desired anything more than the life he'd lived so richly, and which had been cut off with cruel suddenness. Perhaps I had really lost him long ago. Perhaps my own anger had shut me away from him. Yet I'd always known he was there, had I wanted to reach out for reconciliation. Now he was truly gone, and I was left with an emptiness I'd never expected, and a growing need to know what had really happened.

But Rick was in my thoughts as well, as I had known he would be. The coolness between him and Sybil was evident, as was his love and concern for Marilla. I must be careful, very careful to upset no delicate balances with my presence. Nothing was going to be easy.

The voice I knew so well spoke softly in my mind. *Things won't be easy if you're not more careful. If I hadn't pushed you tonight, you'd have taken that rock right in the face.*

My moving was pure instinct, I told her. *I don't want you here.*

Surprisingly, she faded away, and I felt a

small sense of triumph. Aberrations I could do without!

Mountain silence pressed all around this small guesthouse, and now the silence seemed to threaten me. I couldn't concentrate on the beliefs of the Hopi, and I was about to put my book aside and attempt to fall asleep when a light tapping sounded on the outside door. In my present state of mind the sound was unnerving. Nevertheless, I drew on my robe and went into the little hallway that led to the louvered front door.

"Who's there?" I called.

"It's me—Marilla. Open the door, Lindsay."

I sighed and turned that latch, not at all sure that I could cope with Marilla just then. She stood on the flagstones outside, dressed in pajamas and one of her father's sweaters, which hung below her knees. She held both hands behind her back and smiled at me angelically.

"Invite me in, Lindsay. It's cold out here."

"Of course," I said. "Please come in."

"You go first," she directed, clearly unwilling to show me what she held behind her back.

I led the way into the living room and switched on a lamp. "It's pretty late—shouldn't you be in bed?"

"Yes, I should. But I like to get up at night when nobody else is around. That's when the Fire People dance in the moonlight, and everything gets spooky and thrilling."

No wonder she had been fond of her grandfather. This sounded like the sort of speech he might have made. I could remember his leprechaun stories when I was little.

"All right," I said. "Why are you here?"

"I have something for you. I told you I'd bring it. It's something I knew you'd want."

She drew her right hand from behind her back and thrust it toward me with a suddenness that made me jump. Her fingers were clasped tightly around the black stick of my father's cane, and the ivory dragon's head glared at me, teeth bared. Stumbling backward so that it wouldn't touch me, I felt the couch behind my knees and dropped weakly onto its cushions.

Marilla said, "They'd hidden it away in a closet, but I knew it was there. Sometimes I take it out and walk around with it at night—the way Grandpa Jed used to do after he started to limp. He never could sleep much at night. He said that mornings were for sleeping. I thought you'd like to have it because it belonged to him."

Her eyes were dancing, and the fair cap of curls shone in lamplight, but I couldn't be sure whether she had wanted to please or to torment me.

"Do you know how your grandfather died?" I asked.

"Of course! I was there. I wasn't even eight years old then, so they wouldn't let me talk to the police or anything."

"You were at the hotel in Las Vegas?"

"Yes! I just told you." She perched herself, knees pulled up, on the wide arm of the sofa, regarding me intently. "Grandpa Jed invited all of us for a couple of days. Me especially. He thought I'd like to see Las Vegas once anyway, since I never had, and have dinner at one of those big hotels. Clara was there too, but not Parker, because she didn't know him then. So were Brian and Orva. Orva Montgomery—Brian's mother. And of course my father and mother. It was a Sedona party."

I ran my fingers through hair brushed behind my ears, tugging a little to pull myself back to reality. When I spoke, it was more to myself than to this strange and bewildering child.

"Why would he give an expensive party when he had no money at all?" Though I knew that was a foolish question, since this was exactly what Jed would have done. He'd have had some plan afoot to raise funds for a new scheme, and he'd always said that you had to spend money to get more. Probably his guests had been targets as possible investors.

I studied Marilla's bright face. "Then you know about the cane?"

She nodded vigorously. "Sure—it was the weapon the murderer used. You don't need to worry. It was cleaned up ages ago, when the police let my father have it. You can see how beautiful it looks."

Children were realists, so perhaps she wasn't

being malicious. The young can accept death with open grief and without mystic ramifications. *I* would not touch the cane for anything, and I could only regard it with repugnance.

"You're upset," Marilla said. "I didn't mean to upset you. I just thought —" Her voice trailed away. She looked downcast and disappointed, but I still couldn't be sure this wasn't an act she was putting on.

"Perhaps there's something we all need to understand when we make a gift," I said, speaking as gently as I could. "It's a good idea to be sure ahead of time that what we're giving is something the person would really like to have. Do you know what I'm talking about?"

She looked again at the dragon's head with its horrid teeth and the eyes that always seemed to watch me. "You mean you don't want this cane because of—of what was done with it?"

"That's right. Is that so hard to understand?"

"No, I guess not." She sounded doubtful. "I really did love Grandpa Jed a lot. Sometimes I still make believe he isn't gone. I pretend that he'll walk through the door any time and talk to me the way he used to."

"I know what you mean," I said, understanding very well.

"This cane was just something he liked. Dad explained to me about it. He said the cane wasn't to blame for what happened. It was only the—the *instrument* that somebody used. It was a *person* who killed him. Grandpa Jed liked his cane, and he was proud to carry it while he was alive. It was sort of a part of him after that accident, when he started to limp.''

"That's a good way to think of it," I said. "But just the same, your father didn't include the cane when he sent the rest of Jed's things to me. He knew I would never want to see it again."

She stared at me for a moment, while tears welled up in her eyes and rolled unheeded down her cheeks. "My mother says I never figure anything out right."

I felt immediately guilty. "Don't feel that way. I'm to blame too. I should have tried to understand why you brought it to me. There was nothing wrong about that, really. You thought I'd like to have it."

"I'll take it away." She jumped off the arm of the sofa and picked up the cane, not touching the dragon's head. "I didn't mean to scare you or make you feel sad, Lindsay. I guess I had a different picture in my head that I was looking at."

Most of us looked at different pictures in our heads, I thought. And we seldom understood the other fellow's picture. But this was a late hour for philosophy.

I got up, steeling myself to take the cane from her hand. "Leave it here, Marilla. It's time I got over my feeling about it. Thank you

70

for bringing it to me."

She brightened at once, her face still wet and shiny. "Then you aren't mad at me?"

"No. Not now that we understand each other a little better."

We went to the door together and she stepped outside upon red rock flagstones.

"I wish *I* could see her," she said. "I mean your Vermilion. Does she come so close you can really see and hear her?"

"Only in my head," I told her firmly. "And that was long ago. We all have to grow up, you know." But I was trying to reassure myself.

She looked disappointed. "I'll go now. Be sure to lock up, Lindsay. Don't let the night things get in!" Then she was off, running across the redwood bridge to the main house, looking back only to wave her hand.

I didn't close my door at once. I stood for a moment staring up at the great rocks riding like ships in black silhouette against the sky, their edges silvered by moonlight. Every time I looked at them they seemed to take on different characteristics, resembling something I hadn't seen in them before. Up there was where Marilla's "Fire People" belonged, and I wanted nothing to do with them. Yet this harsh red landscape with its dramatic beauty was something Rick loved, and I wished I could see it with his eyes. Or the eyes of those unknown ones of my own ancestry who had come before me, and who, perhaps, had looked at these very rocks with a lifting of the spirit. For the first time, a wondering arose in me—a marveling that I'd always suppressed before. Who *had* they been? Perhaps, after all, it wouldn't be too terrible to know. Yet at the very moment of weakening, I stepped back, still afraid of the truth—lest it damage me in some way I couldn't yet understand.

I obeyed Marilla and locked my door with its key—there was no bolt—and came inside. I couldn't quickly forget that moment when a rock had come crashing out of the darkness to whiz past me and smash on the tiles. If there was any connection between past and present, I didn't know what it was and it was useless to speculate.

When I went to bed, I left a light burning.

I awakened early and lay quietly, trying to orient myself. Last night I had been very tired and there had been too much that was strange and perplexing. The answers would come gradually, I told myself, and perhaps today I could begin to help them along. I needed to move about Sedona, meet Rick's and Sybil's friends—learn which one of them was a watcher. Though of course there was no guarantee that whoever it was need be a "friend." In any case, I must certainly consult with Rick now and tell him why I had come.

Decision helped a little, and when I'd dressed I fixed myself breakfast in the small kitchen.

Afterward, I stepped outside to breathe the marvelous mountain air. Under a deep blue and cloudless sky, the rocks were a flat carmine, with shadows erased by brilliant sunlight, so that they seemed less mysterious than in the evening. I leaned against the railing on the narrow deck.

In the gully of the wash below me, bushes trembled, and something moved down there. Even as alarm started up in me, a man stepped into view, in waist-high juniper growth. It was Brian Montgomery. This morning he wore khaki pants and a shirt with a gold and blue insignia of crossed hammer and pick on his sleeve. His beard looked even more golden by morning sun, and his thick hair more sun-bleached. He smiled up at me, his eyes dark in contrast to his hair, and very solemn. An earnest young man, and perhaps not quite as young as he looked. Last night I'd thought him to be in his early twenties but now I was less sure. Nevertheless, I didn't think he was my letter writer. Though I wasn't sure why I should believe those notes to be the work of a woman, that was what I thought.

"Good morning," Brian called, climbing up the cliff to join me on the deck. "Sybil phoned last night about what happened. She wanted me to come over early and see if I could pick up any traces down there. Maybe she sees me as an Indian tracker."

"Did you find anything?"

"Not really. Anybody could have climbed up

73

and down here last night. Rocks have slipped, where someone might have stood. But I expect Rick left some of the traces himself. Sybil says you saw something."

"Not clearly enough. Just a quick flash—like a face and a hand. Then the rock came flying and I didn't see anything else."

"That's all you remember?"

"I'm afraid it is," I admitted. "When I think of it now, it doesn't seem very real."

Yet the thrown rock *had* been real. But since there was nothing more I could offer, Brian returned to the subject of the meeting.

"Your sister really wowed that crowd in the auditorium. They loved the way she went on after that egg hit her." There was admiration in his voice, and I knew that Sybil had acquired a loyal follower in Brian Montgomery.

"She always had courage," I said, trying not to sound grudging.

He nodded agreement. "I'll go along now, and phone her later. Have fun." His smile was attractive, lifting briefly his slightly frowning earnestness. When he chose to exert himself, Brian had a certain charm. For a moment longer he stood staring at me and then loped off toward the street.

When he'd gone, I looked toward the house, where nothing moved. Rick had set no time for taking me to the shop this morning, though since I knew that was his plan, I'd put on a pair of gray slacks and a blue blouse with a black string tie at the throat, so I was ready to leave whenever he wanted me. By the way the heat of the sun was intensifying, I wouldn't need a jacket, but I'd better get my sunglasses.

After I'd taken them from my suitcase I went into the living room for a moment and stood looking at Jed's ivory-mounted cane with the same feeling of revulsion I'd experienced the night before. The dragon's shining eyes seemed to watch me with a knowing air, and I was sure the creature had always been aware of how much I disliked it. It would be easy to believe that the thing had used its own malevolent will in that attack on my father.

Reluctantly, I picked up the cane and thrust it into the back of a closet. For Marilla's sake, I would tell neither her father nor her mother what she had done. Let it remain our secret.

"May I come in?" That was Rick at the door I'd left open, and I went to greet him.

"How is Sybil?" I asked. "She seemed remarkably calm about everything last night, yet at the same time wound up inside."

He followed me into the living room and sat down. "She seems all right. She was up early for a trip to Jerome with Brian. For some reason she seems to have developed an obsession with Jerome lately, though I don't know why. Anyway, she won't be home until after lunch. The shop at Tlaquepaque doesn't open until nine, but Clara's coming in early, so we needn't wait to get started. Have you had breakfast?"

I nodded, focusing upon the strange name he had spoken, repeating it phonetically. "Tlockapockey?"

He spelled it for me. "It's a fantastic place. I wish I'd had the imagination to dream it up myself. A Southwesterner named Abe Miller created it, and he has based the architecture on a real town in Mexico—Tlaquepaque, a suburb of Guadalajara."

I had a feeling that Rick was marking time, and that he wanted to talk about something else. Yet it was an enticing picture he drew for me as he went on.

"It's a bit of old Mexico right here on the banks of Oak Creek. Five acres, complete with sycamores and pines and glorious flowers. The buildings are the best of Spanish Mexico, and stunningly beautiful. There are shops selling silver and leather, stained glass, sculpture, paintings, all the Indian crafts at their best— anything creative and beautiful. You could roam through it for days, and you may want to. It's still growing, and visitors come from everywhere to explore what it offers."

I watched Rick's face as I listened and he warmed to what he was saying. Not since I'd come here had I seen this glow in him, this enthusiasm.

I hated to quench it, but this was the moment to talk to him.

"I want to show you something," I said and took the two notes from my handbag, giving him the first one. "This is what brought me here."

He read the lettered words aloud slowly, and when he came to Sybil's name he gave the paper an angry flick. "I've no use for anonymous threats, Lindsay."

"I know. But I could hardly ignore it, could I? Not even for Sybil's sake. How do I know what's behind it? Have you any idea what it could mean as far as she's concerned?"

"None at all. That is—" He broke off as though he might not be as positive as he sounded, and I knew with a stab of concern how torn he was.

I wouldn't challenge him, but I held out the other note. "This is a second one, and it was brought here for me yesterday. Consuela took it from a boy at the door."

This time Rick read in silence, his expression grim.

"I can't let this go," I said miserably. "My father was murdered. Has anything ever turned up to tell you why?"

"There are plenty of *whys,* robbery aside. What we don't know is *who.* I loved him too, you know. And perhaps I knew him better than you did."

A great many people had known him better than I had. The thought was bitter, and I thrust it away. "Do you think we should show these notes to Sybil?"

He gave them back to me with a curt gesture.

"Not yet. You saw her yesterday when she knocked over her glass. She's not as calm as she pretends. Something's stretching her out. I can guess a few reasons for this but not all of them, and it worries me. She's capable of—" Again he broke off, as though he'd said too much, and went to stand before a window.

"Do you think what's troubling her could possibly tie in with Jed's death?"

"No, of course not. She was no more to blame than the rest of us who were there with him in Las Vegas. He was her father too, even though neither of you was close to him."

He turned to look at me as he spoke. I knew I'd been reproved, and I didn't like it. He wasn't being completely open with me, and he had no right to judge me when he knew so little about the past.

I stood up abruptly. "Shall we leave now?"

He led the way to the garage, a large one built at one side of the house and holding a Mercedes sedan, a red Triumph Spitfire, and a Ford pickup truck.

"I've some things to drop off at the shop," Rick said and went to open the door of the pickup for me.

I climbed in and felt immediately comfortable. As a small girl, when I'd gone camping in Connecticut with Jed, he'd driven this sort of vehicle, and one summer when I was older, he'd even taught me to drive it.

As we started down the hill, I could see the

houses and subdivisions of Sedona spread along the thread of the highway, with a wilderness of rocks and undeveloped forest crowding all around. It seemed a very *long* town, though not especially dense. Some of the rock shapes that hemmed it in were becoming familiar to me, though it seemed startling to see them rising so close at one end of the business section of town. Most had names, Rick said—Coffee Pot, Bell Rock, the Giant's Thumb, and many more—and I thought their beauty far more impressive than such prosaic names. It was a good thing *they* didn't know what they were called!

We drove through the village along the wide main street that was also the highway. Shops and restaurants and motels stretched along either side, typically Southwestern architecture— adobe or trading post—and usually no more than a single story high. Red rocks backed the town and closed it in, rising from spotty green juniper that encroached wherever it could gain roothold.

We turned at the "Y" and drove the short distance to the bottom of the canyon, where Tlaquepaque had been built near the creek. We entered the compound through an arched gateway to a parking area. Rick's spirits seemed to lift, as though he put all that concerned him deliberately from his mind for the present. Together, we lifted the few cartons from the truck and he led the way in.

Tall trees and the canyon walls had hidden

all this until we were almost there, so the first impact of Tlaquepaque was stunning. The buildings were larger and more dense than I'd expected—a small Spanish town set down on its own acres. The paving stones of a wide plaza shone pale in the sunlight, while arches and balconies offered the flavor of old Mexico. Tiled walkways rimmed the rectangle we had entered, and led into other courtyards. On every hand masonry gleamed with a creamy whiteness, tinged by deep rose in the shadows. In several of the courts fountains played, and twisted gray sycamores raised leafy branches to soften the darkness of stone. Everywhere there were plants and flowers and vines. Bougainvillea and chrysanthemums, geraniums and begonias brushed lavish color wherever I looked. Loving hands had planted and cared for all this, contributing a living beauty to the man-made angles of stone.

Commanding all else rose the square bell tower. It could be seen all over the compound—with an intensity of turquoise sky burning above.

Rick was watching me, waiting, and I wanted to tell him how much it meant to me that *he* had brought me here. But none of this feeling could be spoken.

"I haven't any words," I said. "I can't take it in all in one breath."

"We'll get rid of these cartons first," he said, and went through a stone arch, following another red-tiled passageway. The maze of courts and fountains and walks in a place that was still growing led one continually into new and marvelous vistas, warm with the colors of Mexico and the Southwest—and of the very sun itself.

Surrounding each plaza were shops that were out of the ordinary. In one window stood a bronze armadillo with a red head, and I set down my boxes to look closer, discovering beyond him a multitude of imaginative creatures that inhabited the shop.

"You can come back and see everything another time," Rick said. "I'd like you to meet Clara before the shop opens. Have I told you its name? We call it Silvercloud." There seemed something almost questioning in the way he spoke the word—as though he expected some response from me.

"It's a beautiful name," I said.

"You've never heard it before—from Jed?"

"No. Should I have?"

"He suggested it for the shop and Clara and I liked it. We'll go and meet her now."

I'd rather have roamed these courtyards and explored enticing arcades instead of meeting a woman who, for some reason, was already prejudiced against me. I wasn't sure why Rick seemed so insistent about this meeting, and I found myself wondering if Clara Hale could be the writer of my notes.

We crossed another paved courtyard, rounded

a pool that gleamed in greenish shadow, and stopped before a window that displayed the arts of the West. A grinning Indian mask looked out at me through the glass, and just inside the door was a stand that held an intricately tooled saddle—one of Rick's specialties, I'd learned. Over the window curved the name: SILVER-CLOUD.

"Here we are," Rick said.

The door was locked and when he opened it with a key I went ahead into a warmly lighted area of redwood paneling. Rick piled our cartons at one side of the shop, while I stood looking around.

Well-spaced shelves and tables and glass counters displayed pottery, sculpture, weaving, turquoise mosaics, sand paintings, jewelry—everything imaginable that had been created by fine craftsmen and artists. Even at first glance, it all seemed fresh and original in concept. I identified the smell of leather, a smoky hint of oriental sandalwood—oddly out of place—and another odor suspiciously like garlic. No one seemed to be about.

Rick caught the garlic odor and wrinkled his nose. "Clara won't like this. Probably it's why the incense is burning."

He nodded toward an earthen bowl of lighted punk sticks, from which aromatic smoke curled in wisps that were losing the battle with the stronger smells that drifted out from a burner somewhere in the rear. Rick smiled wryly, and

I tried to relax and not think about Clara as I looked around the shop.

My eye was caught at once by a dramatic wall hanging—a coiled straw plaque, bordered by a geometric design in terra-cotta red. In the center, done in the same red-earth tones, a formalized eagle spread its great wings. Fanned tail feathers were formed in the natural straw color of the background, and etched in red. For all my working life, travel had meant to me an infusion of fresh ideas to feed my imagination. I had trained myself to be open to impressions, to receive and store and imagine creatively. Now I felt the familiar tingling of excitement that meant this faculty was stirring again.

I forgot Rick and the rest of the shop and went to stand before the straw circle on the wall. "Blue," I said. "Denim, perhaps. A dress, not jeans, and it should be the blue of the sky over Tlaquepaque. Tiny birds of terra-cotta red, woven in a narrow strip that could be appliquéd."

I closed my eyes, visualizing as I went on aloud.

"The strip could start at the round neck and follow the shoulders and the outside of the arms down each side all the way to the narrow cuff. A continuous strip of color, with the bird pattern very small. Perhaps a narrow leather belt with an enameled buckle that would carry out the terra-cotta motif." I turned to find Rick watching me, and an enthusiasm I hadn't felt in a long while spilled over in me. "I can see the dress in every detail! I could even cut a pattern and—" I broke off, hearing my own words as I came to my senses. "That was foolish, wasn't it? To look at something beautiful and think of clothes."

Rick was smiling at me. "That's your job. And clothes can be an art form, can't they? Go on."

"It's not a practical idea. I'd drive the textile manufacturers crazy asking for little red birds in an Indian design. They don't warm to individual orders. That's the trouble. I have to compromise with what's available, what I can find—so, I'm always at war with myself. My best ideas are apt to be expensive—and impossible."

"Not necessarily impossible," Rick said. "Look at yourself! Until this minute, all I've seen has been the slick polish of New York. Then you looked at that thunderbird done in straw, and you came to life. You're excited, you're *real*. And you know something? You look just the way your father used to when an imaginative idea seized him. Excitement's good for you."

Even as he spoke, the elation I'd felt faded, and I sighed. In any case, I didn't want to look like my father—or be like him. Jed's dreams usually came to nothing. That was one reason why I always tried to be practical—however dull practicality had grown.

I shook my head at Rick. "It's no use. Oh, I'm sure when I get home I'll find myself using ideas I've picked up in Arizona. I'll look for new color combinations, textures. But I can't really do what I'd like to do. In the old days Chanel and other designers could go straight to the weavers in France and other countries in Europe and tell them what they wanted. But that's impossible now. At least for me."

"Don't give up so easily. Why not go on with this idea that's just hit you and see what happens?"

Before I could repeat that it was useless, a burst of singing filled the room, emerging from the rear, along with the aroma of garlic. In a rich tenor voice someone was singing "Vesti la giubba," and as we both turned to stare, the singer appeared at the rear door. He was a big man, long, lanky, partly bald, with a fringe of faded, gray hair around his head, and a lean body, mostly hidden by the spotless bib apron he wore over his jeans. One hand held a wooden spoon, stained at the bowl with tomato sauce, and with this he conducted himself through a last phrase of the aria, then bowed to us grandly.

Rick shook his head, even while he grinned. "Parker, you've got to quit cooking down here. It's not allowed, and the atmosphere is all wrong. Come and meet Lindsay Phillips. Lindsay, this is Parker Hale, Clara's husband."

The man transferred the wooden spoon from

right hand to left, checked it for drips, and then came into the store to shake my hand gravely.

"Welcome to Sedona, Miss Phillips."

"Parker is part opera star, part chef," Rick explained, "and we're never sure which is uppermost."

Parker's eyes were as faded a gray as his fringe of hair, and they showed no amused response to Rick's words as he studied me. It was not a warming look. I had a feeling that he was prepared to dislike me.

He turned back to Rick. "That's Spaghetti Parker I'm cooking for dinner tonight. I suppose I'll have to take it up to the house. I thought I could just let it simmer back there and give it a stir now and then, while I was helping Clara out. Connie will be in late today. Clara's in the gallery now unpacking some new paintings, and she hasn't noticed yet. She'll be wild."

He went through the rear door and a moment later his wife came into the main shop. Clara Hale was a small, arresting woman, vivid and lively. She was probably in her early fifties—years younger than her husband. Her brown hair, streaked with gray, was bound into a long braid that hung down her back. She wore a shirt with an embroidered Western yoke, a turquoise bola tie, and a straight beige skirt that came just below her knees. Her eyes were her one beautiful feature—large and velvety brown. The sort of eyes that should have worn a loving expression. At the moment they were spitting mad.

She ignored us both and looked around for her husband, who had wisely faded into the back room. "I'll kill that man!" she cried and dashed through the shop like a small but very careful whirlwind that disturbed none of the precious objects that filled the tables. We could hear her voice raised stormily in the rear.

Rick laughed. "They're devoted to each other, though they're both prima donnas. They enjoy these outbursts. I think you'd better wait to meet Clara later, when the spaghetti crisis is resolved. Right now there's something upstairs I'd like to show you."

I gave the thunderbird a last regretful look and followed Rick from the shop. Nearby, a flight of steps done in blue and yellow Mexican tiles rose to an open gallery that rimmed the courtyard at the second story. Set back from a wrought-iron railing, the shop just above Clara's was empty.

Again, Rick used a key, but he paused before opening the door. "I wasn't sure I'd show you this, Lindsay. Perhaps I wouldn't do it now, if you hadn't taken off the way you did downstairs. It's a notion I meant to keep up my sleeve until I could see what might develop. Perhaps nothing will happen, but I'm going to show you anyway."

He opened the door and I went through into a large empty room. There was none of the fine wood paneling here of the shop below. The walls had been painted a soft cream that reflected outdoor light and made it a bright, sunny room. There was no furniture except for a single rough table, on which lay something that made me stop in astonishment halfway into the room.

Resting on the table was a single roll of cloth in a faintly textured weave that was unfamiliar, its color almost duplicating that of the sky over Sedona. The excitement I'd felt downstairs surged back.

I turned to find that Rick's face was alight with an exhilaration that matched my own.

"How could you know?" I cried. "How could you possibly have guessed ahead of time? What sort of magician are you?"

"There's no magic. I knew you were coming, and for a long time before that I'd had a project in mind—without enough knowledge to implement it. You might be the key. Perhaps you could do a dress for us using that cloth. Of course it had to be this shade of blue—the color of an Arizona sky."

I went to the table and stroked my hand over the cloth, sensing its texture, unrolling a few folds so that I could test the weight in my hand.

"It's beautiful. Where did you find it?"

"That's a long story." He glanced at his watch. "I have an appointment, so let me leave you with Clara now and come back later to take you to lunch. Then I'll tell you the whole thing and see what you think."

"I'm not sure I should stay with Clara," I said. Though I didn't warm to the thought of going back to the house to spend the rest of the morning with Sybil.

Rick waited in the doorway. "I expect you and Clara to become friends. I think you'll like each other, and, in a way, she's part of what I have in mind."

"How can we be friends if she holds my father against me? You'd better explain, Rick."

"All right. I'll tell you—briefly. A few years ago your father talked her into investing money in one of his big plans, and she lost every cent she gave him. That was before she knew Parker, or he might have kept her out of trouble. Your father died owing her what he'd taken."

"Then of course she must be paid back," I said. "But she's hardly being fair if she holds this against *me*."

"She's an emotional lady, as well as being a good business woman most of the time. That's what upset her so badly. Not so much losing the money, but because she let Jed take her in. Of course, he always took himself in first of all. That's why his arguments were so convincing. Anyway, she's already been paid back. Jed was my friend, and he did a great deal for me."

I wanted to thank him. I wanted to tell him how glad I was that he'd been my father's friend, but bitterness against Jed rose in me all

89

too easily, and I held back the words. All I could do was try to please Rick, try to make friends with Clara Hale, if that was what he wanted.

"All right, I'll go back to the shop, and I'd like to have lunch with you if you'll come for me when you're ready." I paused for a last look around the big empty room with its single table and roll of bright blue cloth. "Just tell me one thing. Why here? Why did you put that cloth in this empty place?"

He smiled at me again, and the warmth was still there. "I should think you'd guess, Lindsay. This is your workroom. No—don't ask questions now. I'll tell you everything later."

I had to accept that, tantalized as I was. He locked the door and we went down the stairs to the courtyard below just as Parker Hale emerged from the shop called Silvercloud. Carried ceremoniously in his gloved hands was a huge iron pot, and a rich aroma of cooking tomato sauce enveloped him.

He rolled his eyes dramatically upward at the sight of us. "I've been banished! I hope you can soothe my wife and get her calmed down."

He went off toward the parking area, and Rick led the way through the open door of the shop.

4

Clara, spraying a flower scent around the main room of the shop, had a second woman with her. A tall, angular, sun-baked woman, perhaps in her early fifties. She wore her hair in a straight gray cut that looked as though she'd trimmed it herself, and her face was etched with tiny lines drawn in by the sun. At least Parker had left the two of them smiling, so the storm clouds must have cleared.

"Orva," Rick said, "I'm glad to see you. It's been a long time." Though his words were cordial, I sensed a certain reserve in his greeting.

"You know why." Her smile faded. "I thought I might catch you here if I came early. I need to talk to you, Rick."

Rick introduced me to Orva Montgomery, Brian's mother.

"Is anything wrong?" he asked her.

I moved aside, so they could speak together, and stood looking again at the wall plaque of coiled straw. I couldn't move out of hearing, and they didn't seem to expect it.

"Marilla's lessons aren't working out," Orva told him. "The last two times she came to the house she refused to touch her paints or put pencil to paper. She'd been doing beautifully, but now she sits and looks out a window. Or else talks to Brian, if he's around. She's only there because you've told her to come."

"But she loves to draw and paint!"

"Of course she does. Unfortunately, it seems to Sybil that drawing pictures is a waste of time, and she's trying to convince Marilla of this."

Orva Montgomery emphasized her disapproval with a snort that made me look around. I could sympathize, knowing Sybil, and I liked this woman for championing Marilla. I even liked her unbeautiful, though distinctive look and automatically found myself wishing that I could get her out of her straight, tightly belted dress, which revealed bony hip angles too plainly. A softer contour would help.

Rick said, "I'll speak to Sybil," and I heard anger in his voice. His moment of exhilaration had passed, and he was again the dark, driven man who had met me yesterday in Phoenix—a man who carried a burden.

"You do that." Orva was emphatic. "I know Sybil has a thing about wasting time. But I told Marilla that if people don't sit on a rock in the sun once in a while, nothing will ever happen inside their heads."

Rick turned away, fury with Sybil clearly shaking him. I had been there myself. Only this was worse, because the creativity of a talented child was threatened.

Clara had not joined the discussion, and she put her spray aside and moved toward the back room. "So long, Orva. Rick, when you're free, I'd like to show you the new paintings I'm going to hang."

"I'll be right there," he told her. "Thanks for coming, Orva. I'll see what I can do."

When he'd gone back to join Clara, Orva regarded me speculatively. "How about walking me to my car? I'm curious about Jed Phillips' daughter."

Once more I was listening for every nuance, asking myself, *Is this the one?*

"You knew my father?" I asked as we crossed the courtyard beneath a leaning syca-more.

She looked straight ahead as we walked, her profile as angular as the rest of her. "Of course. Didn't everyone? Brian thinks you're like him."

"Your son hardly knows me," I said in surprise. "We've only exchanged a few words."

"He makes up his mind fast, and maybe that's his trouble. Sometimes he makes it up wrong, and then nobody can shake him. How long are you going to stay?"

Before I could answer, a tremendous boom, louder than thunder, came out of the sky, and the earth trembled under my feet. I looked up, startled, and saw nothing but the empty blue.

Orva shook her head ruefully. "Sonic boom.

We get them all the time, though the Air Force planes can go over so high you don't see them. Sometimes the shocks shake our windows and doors, and tumble rocks in the hills where water erosion has made their balance precarious. Probably the pilots can't even see us down here, and there's no use complaining.''

I had a strangely uneasy feeling about the boom—as though Vermilion was stirring. A presentiment, perhaps?

"You were going to tell me how long you plan to stay," Orva said.

"I'm not sure. Not very long, since I have a business waiting for me back in New York."

"Making clothes for rich women!"

I couldn't take offense at her blunt honesty. "We all have to wear clothes. And I can't help feeling that it's better to look well than not. For ourselves, and to give pleasure to others."

I doubt if she paid much attention. Her thoughts were already elsewhere.

When we reached the end of the compound Orva paused, hooking a thumb under the strap of her shoulder bag as she studied me.

"Before you leave, will you come and visit us, Lindsay Phillips? I have a few things your father gave us that you might like to see. Perhaps you can come for supper some night? I'll phone you."

I didn't want to postpone the answers. I wanted to know *now*.

"Why?" I asked. "Are you inviting me

because of a note you mailed to me?"

Orva looked convincingly blank, but that might mean only that she wasn't ready to admit anything.

"Thank you," I said quickly. "I'd like to come. Just let me know when."

She nodded, and hurried off to her car with a rush of long legs and flapping elbows. I watched her get in and drive away without another look in my direction. She could be the one, I thought. Obviously she didn't like Sybil, and her son was a Sybil follower. So what had brought me here might add up to no more than an effort toward spiteful reprisal. Except that Orva Montgomery didn't strike me as a spiteful woman. Outspoken, yes, and honest. But not malicious. I wondered why I'd sensed a certain reservation toward her in Rick. At least I would go to her house for dinner with a great deal of interest.

I walked back to the shop thoughtfully, aware of bright beauty all around me in this place called Tlaquepaque, but aware too of shadows —not only cast by the sycamores but psychic shadows that had their being in me.

It was as though some threat of disaster continued to hang over me, although it remained so nebulous that I couldn't put my finger on the direction from which it came. The feeling grew out of more than the rock that had been hurled at me last night, out of more than Sybil's antagonism—perhaps it was Vermilion's uneasiness that was stirring under the surface. And that I could do without.

The main store was empty when I reached it, and Clara and Rick were still consulting in the rear. This time I didn't even glance at the thunderbird in its circle of straw as I joined them in the long gallery.

The paintings Rick and Clara were discussing stood leaning against the wall, waiting to be hung. Most were Indian pueblo scenes done in those tawny sand and adobe colors that so appealed to me. Emphasis was achieved mainly in the clothing of human figures in the paintings. A woman in a dress of dark indigo blue was cooking bread on hot stones, while a young girl in white knee-length leggings stood watching, her hair arranged in curious butterfly disks on each side of her head.

"That's the way young Hopi girls used to do their hair," Rick said. "Now I'm afraid they want to look and be like everyone else off the reservation. That's natural enough, but I wish *our* standards were higher."

I moved on to study an acrylic of pueblo dwellings built one above another in setbacks, with long narrow ladders leaning against the walls. Ladders that narrowed still more toward the top. On the flat roofs women and children were gathered, some standing, some sitting with their legs hanging over the edge. All were watching the colorful masked dancers who circled in the open space below. I had the feeling that this was a genuine religious occasion and not intended for curious tourists.

The paintings had a marvelous sense of serenity. These people were proud of their traditions, and this feeling of respect for the old ways came through. When I went on to the next section, I received a shock, because the sense of serenity vanished. The following pictures were troubling and haunted.

In one painting children were leaving their pueblo to get into a bus driven by a white man, while behind them, families looked on in sorrow. In the solemn, watching faces I glimpsed the depth of real grief.

Clara spoke at my elbow. "Some of these pictures refer to the past. Years ago, children used to be taken to federal boarding schools, and their parents had no choice in the matter. They might not see them again for a long time. When they did meet again, they might hardly know each other. There were cultural clashes and old values lost. Fortunately, we've moved away from the idea of assimilation, but the psychological effects of that mistake are still with us, as Alice Rainsong believes."

"Rainsong! What a beautiful name! Of course an Indian woman would have painted these?"

" 'Indian' is a very large word. She's part Hopi. Her Anglo name is Alice Spencer, but she likes to use her Hopi name when she can."

"She's very good," I said.

Clara picked up the painting I'd been studying, and her thick braid fell over one shoulder. "Yes, she *is* good. I had trouble prying her loose from these. She doesn't want to sell them, but I mean to give her a proper show anyway. Don't you think we should, Rick?"

"Of course," he agreed. "It's time she stopped hiding her talent. Just the same, I can understand how she feels. Alice puts her heart on canvas when she paints—and her pain. She's reluctant to expose these feelings to strangers."

"Maybe there's some guilt there too," Clara said. "She really belongs to the Anglo world, yet that one quarter of Hopi blood is more important to her than the rest. These aren't sentimentalized glimpses—they're real. I'll get a reporter in to cover the exhibit, since it really must be seen."

"Alice won't like that," Rick said, "but I hope she'll like some other things I have in mind for her."

"She's not one to jump when you snap your fingers." Clara shook her head at him. "Anyway, we have other problems. What are you going to do about *her?*" She was staring in my direction, challenging me and making no bones about it.

Rick grinned. "Smooth down your feathers, Clara. I'm going to leave Lindsay right here with you for now. I've shown her the cloth upstairs, and I don't think she can resist it.

Let's leave her in suspense for the moment. I'll be back to take her to lunch. In the meantime, maybe she can help you hang Rainsong's pictures.''

There was nothing Clara could do without being even more deliberately rude. ''Well, okay,'' she said, when he'd gone. ''If you're going to help, let's get to work.''

The paintings had been lined up in the order in which they were to be hung, and Clara, armed with picture hooks and hammer, climbed a stepladder she had dragged to one end of the gallery.

''Bring me the first one,'' she directed.

That was the limit of our conversation for a while. Once more my thoughts drifted to puzzling about Orva Montgomery. Had I been wrong to suspect her as my letter writer? It was just as possible that Clara Hale was a more likely candidate. She might be testing me in some way, even now. But there would be no telling until whoever had written the notes decided to speak out.

''Have you always lived here?'' I asked when the void between us began to seem oppressive.

''I was born in Santa Fe,'' she said grudgingly. ''My parents still live there.''

Conversation died again, and there seemed no way to break through her crusty exterior. Another fifteen minutes went by in silence as we hung several of the paintings.

I liked Rainsong's work more and more as I

watched it go up. There was one painting that spoke to me especially. It was of Pueblo children in a classroom, with an Indian woman teacher at a desk. The small, bright faces were individualized, and I suspected that the artist really knew her subjects. This, obviously, was not an "Anglo" school.

Clara spoke abruptly, harshly. "I expect your father got what was coming to him."

Her words shocked me out of my reverie. She must have been brooding, stirring them around in her mind for the last fifteen minutes, getting ready to spit them out. I resented such intentional cruelty.

"No one should die the way he did," I told her sharply.

She changed the subject with equal abruptness. "I heard about what happened last night. That rock throwing, I mean. Orva was full of it, though of course Rick never told me. Orva says Brian claims you couldn't recognize who it was you saw out there just before the rock was thrown."

"That's right. It was dusky beyond the light from the terrace, and I couldn't glimpse more than a face and a hand. No details."

We didn't speak again until the last painting was hung. Then we both stood back to regard our work with approval. The display gave a varied picture of pueblo life. Not a flat depiction of what some outsider saw, but a loving, sympathetic, and sometimes bitter record.

"Let's clear up this stuff," Clara said, moving the stepladder. "I hear someone in the shop and my assistant hasn't come in yet. Thanks for your help."

Now and then, when a customer had wandered in, she'd left me, but mostly we'd been uninterrupted at this early hour of the morning. After I'd picked up hammer and picture hooks and put them away in a cupboard, I followed her into the main room. Through the front window I could see visitors crossing the plaza, sitting on benches, looking into the shops. Tlaquepaque was coming to life.

When the shop was empty again, Clara said, "I'll fix coffee. We can have it in my office and still keep an eye on things. There are some books Rick's been collecting for you."

"Collecting for me? Why?"

"I suppose he'll tell you when he gets around to it. Come along."

In a small room next to the gallery were a desk heaped with paper, two comfortable chairs, and a low table, on which books had been piled. She waved me toward one of the chairs and went to the coffeemaker in a corner. The books drew me and I picked one up and leafed through pictures of Zuñi carvings and fetishes. At once my imagination leaped ahead. That blue wildcat might be formalized and adapted in a broad band around a dirndl skirt, or the little mole could furnish an animal motif for a jacket. Lately I'd become interested in decorated

101

jackets. I suspected that just as that roll of cloth had been placed upstairs to tempt me, so had these books been collected. And why not? Why shouldn't I try something for Rick? Ideas might even develop that I could take back to New York.

"I'd like to do a few croquis," I mused aloud.

Clara set my coffee cup on the table. "Croquis?"

"Those are the idea sketches we often start off with. It's odd—when Rick met my plane in Phoenix yesterday, he seemed . . . I don't know . . . preoccupied, distant. As though he wished I hadn't come. And then, just now, when he took me upstairs and showed me that beautiful woven blue cloth, he came to life again."

"You've arrived at a bad time." Clara drank coffee gloomily. "Maybe someone ought to warn you—since Sybil's your sister. It's not any secret. He's asked her for a divorce. But I don't think she'll ever agree. She can be pretty ruthless when she pleases, and blind to anything except what she wants."

The wave of feeling that swept through me was dismaying. It was a mixture of pity for Rick, caught in Sybil's web, sadness for Marilla, and a strange, wild relief for me. Suddenly Vermilion was chattering in my ear: *There's a chance for you now. You always wanted him. Now you can have him. You can get even with Sybil!*

I wouldn't listen. I wouldn't take pleasure in the pain of others. Vermilion was too often the worst side of me, yet I still had the strength to control her, so that she ceased her chattering.

Now, however, a great deal could be explained. Rick's preoccupation, Sybil's hostility, the constant underlying tension I'd felt in their home—all these things must have their base in what Clara had just told me. I hadn't dreamed that events had moved so far toward separating Sybil and Rick, and now I wished myself well away, lest I become a source of more trouble between them. I knew my sister. I knew the weapons she could use when she wanted to be cruel.

I could say none of this to Clara, and my silence didn't stop her. Having started to talk, she went right on, and there was new venom in her voice.

"Of course Rick could always walk out. Only there's the child to consider. He wouldn't want to leave Marilla in Sybil's tender hands. Besides, she holds a few trump cards. She can be damned difficult in plenty of ways if Rick goes against her wishes."

I didn't want to hear any more. "I shouldn't have come at all. Perhaps I shouldn't stay with them now."

"Sybil won't turn you out. She has that grand façade of hers to preserve. Defeat's not something she ever accepts. She's got that much of your father in her. While we're talking—why *did* you come here after all these years?''

We could hear customers moving about in the shop, but Clara merely glanced toward the door, then turned her attention to me. She clearly intended to stand there waiting until I answered.

I set my cup and saucer down carefully, wondering if the question was a smoke screen. ''My father was murdered and I want to know why and who did it.''

She moved toward the shop. ''What do you think *you* can learn that the police haven't been able to pick up? Or Rick either.''

''Perhaps someone around here knows the answer,'' I said.

She gave me another scornful look and went out to the shop, not bothering to reply.

My thoughts continued their inner course, and strangely enough, it was Jed's face that came into my mind, and with it a greater feeling of loss than I'd experienced since his death. A new emptiness, a longing, a *need* to be with someone I could never see again, flowed in to fill the void. I wished desperately that I could talk to my father about this break between Rick and Sybil, and talk about my own half-formed feelings that threatened to destroy me.

And yet—? When had Jed ever been there to help me in an emotional need? Except, of course, when he'd given me Vermilion. But she was something I didn't want to have emerge right now.

Deliberately, I opened my handbag and took out the small sketch pad and soft pencil I always carried with me. To *do* something, to busy myself in the some way, was the only possible answer. On one page I drew a formalized eagle with out-stretched wings, and considered it. Thank God, the familiar absorption could be summoned to occupy me. I needn't think about anything else. Not yet. I realized that I needed to know a lot more about the thunderbird as a symbol before I could use it successfully. Next I drew a long-necked figure in a blouse and skirt, and around the skirt I sketched a design using the blue wildcat from the Zuñi book as a basic motif.

By the time Rick returned to take me to lunch, I had dipped into several books, studied pictures, and filled pages of sketches torn from my pad. Nothing was perfected. I was merely capturing ideas that flashed through my mind. The effort eased me, drew me away from an emotional trap I might tumble into all too easily.

When Rick came into Clara's office, he stood for a moment looking at the littered table, where books were held open by other books, my rough drawings strewn about. He picked up a few sketches and leafed through them.

"These are good. You have a real flair for the imaginative and original. No wonder women like your clothes."

I stood up to stretch cramped shoulders,

wriggling fingers that had held a pencil too long, reluctant to let go of my lifeline of work.

"I've made a reservation for us at Poco Diablo," he said. "I think you'll like it there."

He spoke to Clara on the way out, and as we left I knew she followed us with big velvety eyes that were anything but gentle and warm. I knew that something was troubling Clara, and that I played a part in it. Perhaps more than Rick had told me.

In the truck again, we returned . to the highway and once more I found myself responding to red earth and the starkness of rock, softened by the cottonwoods and oaks that followed the creek. Everything I saw was fresh and new and stirred my imagination. Yet if I were honest, it was the man beside me whose presence made all the colors seem brighter, whose existence gave my life an intensity I hardly dared to accept. What I could accept—might reasonably accept—was only the opportunity to work for him and with him, for whatever length of time I might stay.

When Rick had parked, we walked through the right-angled building of the hotel to a terrace where our table overlooked a rolling green golf course above the floor of Oak Creek. Willow trees grew nearby, and there were flower plantings and a small fountain. Beyond rose steep hills, dotted with luxurious homes, as always wedged in by the pinnacles of rock.

"I like this little valley," Rick said, as we

picked up our menus. "There are some fine homes down there, though these low places can sometimes be flooded, even in this dry country."

I wanted to hear what he had to propose and I ordered quickly. When the waitress had gone, he began to explain what he had in mind, speaking almost hesitantly at first.

"I'm been working with Indian craftsmen here and there—mostly Hopi and Navajo— opening a few markets into a specialized line of women's clothes."

He'd been gazing out toward the green valley below us as he spoke, and now he turned his head to look directly at me. "Maybe I've wanted to get you out to Arizona for a long time, so when you played into my hands I jumped at the chance to invite you here. Destiny, of course! But I'm always willing to help it along." His tone was light, as though he mocked himself, yet there was an underlying seriousness.

"I'd like to help," I said. "If I really can. But I'm still not sure of a lot of things."

As I had done so impulsively that time in New York, he reached his hand to me across the table in what was almost a gesture of entreaty. I gave him mine without hesitation, and as he took it a current as ancient as time seemed to spring between us. I felt it, and I knew he felt it too, and that its intensity startled us both, so that we drew apart self-consciously.

When he spoke again, I could hardly listen because I was so sharply aware of Rick himself. The wind had ruffled his thick dark hair, and his face was eager and alight. Wisely, his words returned to the safety of his own work and interest. Like me, he too had an opiate.

"Indian families in Oklahoma have been making dresses for the Anglo market, using their own distinctive designs," he went on. "We may be able to do something similar here. I have a Flagstaff family in mind that does fine weaving for wall hangings, rugs, and so on. I asked them some time ago to give me something in a cloth that could be used for dresses—and you've seen the result."

He paused, as though considering how he must present this to me.

"You can have any design you like carried out. Your terra-cotta thunderbird, or anything else. My Hopi friends can give you what you want—and more. They're artists in their own right. Our true, conservative Hopi like to follow the old ways, but these women have been educated in federal schools, and while they still respect the old ways, they can be more innovative. They know the native dyes, and if you want special colors and shades, they can find them for you."

He was opening exciting possibilities. How freeing it would be to go my own way, to work for once without the restrictions of the textile manufacturers! I listened eagerly as he continued.

"I'll approach them as I always do through Alice Spencer—Rainsong. This could be a new turn in the road for Lindsay Phillips clothes."

"What do you know about Lindsay Phillips clothes?"

"I know a lot. I've made it my business to know." He was smiling now, teasing me—as he'd done when I was seventeen, so that I melted a little. "If you furnish the designs, my friends will make whatever you like. We can help each other."

I gave up trying to keep the man and his work separate. Even as his ideas stirred my imagination, I could no longer suppress my feeling for *him*. Even more than I wanted to do this work, I wanted to please Rick, and I couldn't quite shut out the sound of Vermilion's glee.

Nevertheless, I made a last effort to be sensible. "Why shouldn't your Indian family do their own designing? They appear to be creative enough. What do *I* know, after all? About their myths or legends, or symbols? I might unintentionally do something offensive out of sheer ignorance."

"Once they've been persuaded, they'll want to show you. You'd work together. You wouldn't be producing silly imitations of Indian costume. They'd be helping you adapt their own great designs. Of course it may not be easy to convince them that you will make a good

109

partner. The Hopi have a great deal of pride, and they've been used too often by the Anglos."

"I'd love to try. I really would. But I'm woefully ignorant about the West."

"You needn't stay that way. There are books and museums. I can send you to Santa Fe, and even to the Desert Museum in Palm Springs. And there's the land itself. All the colors you need are out there, and so are the people. There's so much to feed your imagination, once you get started. And Lindsay, this is work that can grow and benefit a good many people. That's what interests me especially. Not to exploit—to encourage and develop."

"How do you mean?"

"Even today, only a small percentage of Indians go to college. Too many of the women still work as domestics, though these days a few become secretaries or technicians, or teachers. Like everyone else, they have their fine craftsmen and artists who continue to create. When trading posts came in, of course, a great many turned to buying ready-made fabrics. After all, how many white women do you know who weave the cloth for their dresses—though this used to be the custom. These days junk of all kinds is made by opportunists who pretend to produce Indian work. I'd like to see more of the old skills come back. Weaving used to be done in every pueblo, and the men were the weavers in the old days. Alice Rainsong weaves and has a loom, and she's been teaching others. You'd be helping to open a much wider market because of your special skills and knowledge. You're not coming to this empty-handed."

My sense of excitement quickened. This was a far broader canvas than I'd dreamed. Because of Rick Adams, an entire world could open for me. I had only to put out my hand. The very fact that I warmed to the idea so strongly still made me hesitate, however. The electric moment when our hands touched had warned me. It would be all too easy to go on from there. If Rick should want me, need me—how could I not respond ardently? Yet he was still my sister's husband, and Clara's words about a broken marriage gave me no license. This was a time to wait; not to plunge without care, as Jed had always done. There were too many ramifications—Marilla among them. The child must come first with me.

"Generalizations are always dangerous, of course," Rick went on, "but sometimes I think women don't set their goals high enough. They aren't willing to dream the big dreams."

"Men haven't always been willing to let us follow our dreams," I told him sharply.

His grin made me relax a little. "You don't have to attack with me. I had the best of teachers—my mother."

"I don't know anything about your parents," I said.

"My father edited a small newspaper. He

died when I was small, and Mother had to take over. She wrote articles and did very well at it, too. She even had her own radio program in Phoenix for a while. She died much too young. Just the same, she saw to it that I grew up with respect for both sexes. So I'm on your side already."

And he really was, I thought. Though he might not be secure in his marriage, he was secure in himself. He believed in his own abilities, and he was willing to take the risks that big dreaming might entail. Since women were no threat to his ego, he could allow them to dream too—in fact, encourage it. I not only loved him—I liked him very much indeed.

"I *have* followed a few dreams myself," I said more quietly.

"Of course you have, Lindsay. Out here you'll come to life and do work that will satisfy you even more, because of all the wider implications. You may even want to give up New York in time."

Again he smiled, as though he joked, but there was a challenge in his words, and I sensed the force of the man behind them. For all his generous words, Rick would use his own will, his own strong determination, to accomplish what he wanted. He might not always realize a tendency to bend others in a direction he wanted them to follow.

"Besides," he went on, "if Jed were here, he'd urge you to try this. He wouldn't hesitate for a moment to tell you to take the chance."

He had chosen the worst possible words to convince me. If I took this step, it must be because it was right for me, and not because I jumped recklessly into a new adventure, as my father would have done.

I answered Rick a little stiffly. "I'm not free right now."

He misunderstood. "Oh, I wasn't suggesting that you cut your ties to New York. You can go back and forth until you're sure what choice you wanted to make."

"That's not what I mean. I can't be free to move in any direction until the matter of Jed's death is resolved and we know who murdered him. That's my first commitment. That's why I'm here."

"Yes, of course." The somber look was back, and I hated to see his excitement fade. He didn't believe I could find the answers. Yet this was a barrier he wouldn't try to cross.

Our waitress brought my fruit salad and Rick's lamb chops, and I began to eat with no great appetite. I disliked what I'd done to quench enthusiasm—in myself, as well as in him. Though it was true that I must follow through on my purpose in coming here. But the reason I couldn't give him for my hesitation was the fear of my own emotional involvement. With Rick. How strong a woman was I? Was I willing to test myself?

"You seem to have gone a long way off,"

Rick said gently. "I don't want to pull you into something you're unwilling to try."

"Of course I'm not unwilling," I told him, accepting my own challenge. "There are arguments against doing this that I'll have to work out with myself—if they can be worked out. Right now, there's no reason I shouldn't begin in a small way. I can look for answers about Jed at the same time."

Again he held out a hand across the table, but this time it was as though he meant to reassure me, to erase whatever it was that had happened before. "Agreed. I promise not to push you too hard."

I took his hand impersonally, shaking on a business agreement, and I felt pleased with myself and not a little relieved. I was still in charge—of *me*.

A distraction in the dining room caught our attention. Two people were being directed toward a table farther along the terrace—Sybil and her satellite, Brian Montgomery.

My sister saw us. Her look flicked across our table and returned coldly, but then she might have gone by with no more than a careless greeting, if Brian hadn't stopped.

"Hello, Lindsay," he said, cheerfully informal. "Hi, Rick. Has anything new turned up about what happened last night?"

"Nothing," Rick said, and offered no invitation for them to join us. The two moved on to take a table a little distance away, and Rick's look followed them thoughtfully. "Brian's been single-minded for a long while about saving Oak Creek from pollution," he said. "Somewhere along the way he got Sybil converted, and she's taken off and made it her own project. It's the sort of thing she enjoys sinking her teeth into, and of course it's entirely worth doing. I can only give it my blessing."

"This is a new side of Sybil," I admitted. "I'm glad she can take on a cause." Then I was silent again, because Clara's words were sharp in my mind—that Rick wanted a divorce and Sybil had refused him, so that their life together had turned into a stalemate.

I had sensed before this that Rick could be quickly perceptive, and perhaps my sudden silence told him something.

"Clara's been talking, hasn't she?" he said.

"She felt I ought to know, since Sybil is my sister."

"Clara's a privileged friend. In any case, it's hardly a secret. So whatever she told you is probably true."

"Then I may have come here at the wrong time for you both," I said. "Would it be better if I moved somewhere else for however long I stay?"

The quick irritation that I'd seen in him before reappeared. "If I want you to stay in the guesthouse, that's where you'll stay. It's standing empty. God knows, we don't entertain much any more, and besides, Sybil has nothing against *you.*"

I knew perfectly well that this wasn't true, whatever Rick believed. Sybil had always held a grudge against me, and I saw no reason for her to turn into a loving sister now. I'd already seen evidence that she was furious because I'd come. I'd been invited only at Rick's insistence. There was no need to disturb him any further now.

"I'll be glad to stay, if you feel it's all right," I told him. "I couldn't be more comfortable. Once I've been able to shop, and perhaps rent a car, I can take care of my own meals."

"That won't be necessary," he said, still irritated. "We'll expect you for lunch and dinner, unless you're out. *Sybil* will expect you. I'll see to it. And I'll see about a car for you as soon as possible."

"Thank you, Rick. I'd like to get to work right away on some designs. Especially something using that blue cloth. I'll need a few things to work with. The tools of my trade. Perhaps some of them can be borrowed?"

"It's a bargain. I'll take you back to Tlaquepaque now, and you can make a list of what you need. You'll be working in that empty shop for now, though we'll soon put in whatever furniture will make you comfortable."

"Does it belong to you—that room?"

"I rented it some time back. Originally, Clara and I thought we might use it for an extra gallery. When I knew you were coming, this idea seemed more important."

"I'd like to go there now. The feel of the place will tell me what I need to get started."

As we returned to Tlaquepaque, I sensed a truce between us. Rick knew very well that I hadn't agreed to go along with his plans as far as he wished. I wasn't sure I could ever do that. At least emotion that had threatened for a moment to get out of hand had been properly subdued.

When we'd started through the complex again, Rick took a key from his pocket. "This is yours. Now you can come and go as you like. I want you to meet Alice Spencer—Rainsong—soon."

"Does she live in Sedona?"

"No. In Flagstaff. I'll see if she's willing to meet you."

That was a strange way to put it. "Why shouldn't she be willing?"

He didn't answer until we were climbing the tiled steps to the upper level above the store, and he seemed vaguely uncomfortable.

"I'm sorry. I shouldn't have put it like that. You'll understand when you meet her. She's the heart of this entire plan. Rainsong is not only an artist, she's also a gifted weaver herself, and she can help you develop your ideas. Besides, her one quarter of Hopi blood is reassuring. She's very close to these relatives. Deliberately close."

"You mean that she rejects her white blood?"

"Not exactly. She's a complex woman. Perhaps ten years older than you are but, like you, she's still looking for herself. In a way, she's a rather shy person, though sometimes she's angry and not too sure of the direction of her anger. Like you?"

He was being perceptive again, and I clung to the impersonal. "She's a talented artist. Can she make a living with her painting?"

"No, but she's been teaching at Northern Arizona University at Flagstaff. I'll tell you more when I take you to meet her. As soon as we can make plans, I'll let you know."

He opened the door of the upper room for me, and then placed the key in my hand. In a strange way, the gesture seemed symbolic. The opening of a door to which I now held a key—the door, perhaps, to an altogether new life. If I could ever accept all it might involve.

I went into the big room ahead of Rick, thinking absently of the implements of my trade, and what I would need in order to get to work. Rick's sudden exclamation startled me, and I looked around.

Someone had been here. Someone had unrolled a length of the blue cloth, cut it off raggedly with shears that must have been dull, and then, with painstaking wickedness, had cut the turquoise fabric into bits that cast blue confetti over the table.

It was a vicious, mindless act of vandalism.

5

Frozen with shock, I could only stand there staring at this evil destruction.

Rick was already on his way into the rooms at the rear. "There's a window open on the balcony," he called to me. "Whoever it was could have come in here. I'll lock it now."

A window slammed shut and the sound grated across my nerves. I touched the bits of blue cloth, feeling shaken by an act that was so mean and vicious.

Rick returned and saw my face. "Look—you mustn't think this was intended for you. Someone is probably trying to get at me. It could even be—" He broke off, and I knew he was thinking of Sybil. By this time, he would know how vindictive she could be.

But I couldn't agree. *I* was Jed's daughter, and my reason for coming here was known—or could be easily guessed by anyone with a guilty conscience. Someone was worried about *me*. Afraid of what I might stir up. There had been that rock last night—perhaps a portent.

"You're not the target," I told him. "This is an effort to scare me. And whoever's doing it just might succeed. I was frightened last night on the terrace, when that rock barely missed me. But somehow this seems even worse. Rick— how can I stay if it's going to be like this?"

"If you're Jed's daughter, you'll see it through."

Again, that was the wrong thing to say, and I answered heatedly, "Jed always quit and ran! He hated trouble, and he never stayed around for a fight. *Or* a finish!"

"Sometimes he did." Rick's tone hardened. "I've seen him stand against high odds."

"I can't admire him blindly as you do!" I cried. "He managed to cause a great deal of damage to a lot of people in his life. Clara Hale said that maybe he got what was coming to him. If I stay to see this through, it won't be because I loved him without question. I know exactly what he was like and what he did to my mother. And to me. Perhaps it's a debt of life. That's what he gave me."

I'd attacked an idol, and Rick's coolness continued as he spoke. "Shall I take you back to the house now?"

"I still have a list to make—if I stay—and some thinking to do. I might as well look through those books you left for me downstairs. So I'll go back to the shop."

He stood for a moment longer staring at the mutilated bolt of cloth. Then he let me out the

120

door ahead of him and pulled it shut, trying it against the automatic lock. Without another word, he walked downstairs with me, and at the door of the shop I told him I'd call a taxi when I was ready to go back to the house. He needn't come for me. He nodded indifferently and went away, leaving me with an ache inside that I didn't want to accept.

Why had I flown so heatedly into the face of Rick's loyalty to my father? Why did the very mention of Jed's name arouse emotions in me that I didn't want to feel, and couldn't handle? What was I really running away from?

But I knew—I knew very well. I'd taught myself long ago to be self-sufficient, and I'd learned against high odds. To let down my guard, to let other people in, might be to destroy everything I'd built up.

You need me now, the insidious voice in my mind whispered. *You need me to help you get what you really want.*

I could answer without speaking aloud. *I don't need you at all. Leave me alone!*

She wouldn't accept that. *Of course you need me. You'll find out.*

I didn't respond, and she was quiet again.

When I walked into the shop, several people were looking around. Connie, Clara's young assistant, had come in and was waiting on a customer. The moment Clara saw my face, she beckoned me toward the rear. I followed her into her office and sat down.

"Something's happened?" she said.

I told her about the blue cloth, and she shook her head. "That's pretty nasty. Somebody really wants you gone, I'd say. Are you going to take the hint?"

I was rummaging in my bag for notebook and pen. "I don't know. Rick wants me to do a—a designing job. I expect he's told you."

"Then you're planning to stay and go through with this?"

"I'm not sure yet. Probably the wise thing would be to leave at once. I—I've never been a target before. I'm not sure I can take it." Again, I was giving the wrong reason—the only reason that could be stated.

"Smart thinking," Clara said.

"On the other hand, I don't like to run out on Rick."

She shook her head despairingly. "You're not much like your father, are you? He could make up his mind in seconds." Suddenly she grinned at me. "And in twenty different directions in one day."

She returned to the shop, and I began to make jottings in my notebook. I would need tissue for patterns, unbleached muslin for draping and pinning a toile, good shears, of course, a yardstick, pins—the usual implements of my trade. A dress form could be borrowed. If I stayed, of course I would buy my own.

If I stayed.

A half hour went by before I recognized that

I was no longer concentrating. Wherever I looked I seemed to see the jagged bits of blue cloth that had been left so spitefully for me to find. And I could see Rick's face—remote and cool because I was disappointing him.

Since I felt too tense to sit still, I jumped up and went to a shelf, where several decorative sculptures were displayed. One in particular caught my eye.

Carved out of a chunk of Sedona's red sandstone, it stood about a foot high. At first glance it looked like some of the red rocks I'd seen since I'd come here—those tall, weather-worn cliffs that rose on every hand. But as I looked closer I saw that several standing human figures had been carved side by side into the stone. Tall figures that were part of the rock, their heads and faces detailed, while the touching bodies faded into crevices of stone. I could count five heads, all with strong, clearly defined features, all grim and forbidding, yet different from one another. The central face in particular seemed touched by the red light of sunset, so that it glowed more than the others. Due, perhaps, to the curious effect of polishing on that one face? The eyes looked at the sky—and knew what was there.

A sense of awe touched me and I jumped when Clara spoke from the doorway. "You've found Marilla's favorite—the Fire People. What do you think of them?"

"Marilla's? But she couldn't have—"

"No. I only mean that she thinks of them as hers, out there in the rocks. The real ones. Jed only copied them."

"You mean my father did this piece? But I didn't know he'd ever sculpted anything. How could he have a talent like this without everyone knowing?"

"Oh, you needn't get the notion that he was a great sculptor. You can't be a great anything without applying yourself. He played around with it, and he could be pretty good at times. But only accidentally. He never worked at anything long enough to develop his talents because he got bored with whatever he was doing, if he did it for more than five minutes. This piece was a fluke. The way once in a blue moon a new writer can turn out a single masterpiece, and then never repeat—because he doesn't know how he did it. Marilla's Fire People out there in the rocks are pretty impressive, and I guess they caught his imagination." Her words carried unveiled scorn.

"I don't understand. If you disliked him so much, why have you kept this?"

"Because I respect the art, even though I learned to detest the man. I suppose it was meant to repay me for some of what I lost in that damned scheme of his."

How angry she was—this small, lively woman, with the big dark eyes and surging emotions. She made me uncomfortable with

124

her judgments, even though there was justification in her anger against my father.

"This sculpture might even do that," I said. "Pay you back, I mean. It could be a valuable piece."

"That's not the way value is made. There needs to be an artist's reputation behind it. And that's not achieved by one piece."

I'd had enough of emotion—my own and others', and because my knees were feeling surprisingly uncertain, I sat down. "I'll phone for a cab," I said. "I'd like to go back to the house now."

"Here it's *the* cab," Clara said dryly. "We're not a metropolis. But don't bother. I've already called Parker, and he'll drive you to Rick's. Have you finished the list of what you need?"

"More or less."

I showed her my jottings and she read them through, nodding. "Leave this with me. You may need to shop in Flagstaff for a few of these things. I'll see if I can find some of them at home."

"Don't bother," I said, "I was only killing time. I'll probably leave in a day or two."

Clara looked around. "Here's Parker now."

Her husband, looking loose-limbed, cheerful, and slightly ruddy of face, came through the store and back to where I waited. As before, I had a feeling that his eyes held a certain suspicion of the world around him in spite of his easy smile.

Clara gave her husband an affectionate look. "Don't let him talk your ear off, Lindsay," she warned me.

"You ready to go, Miss Phillips?"

"Yes—thanks for the lift."

We went out to where he'd left his car, and before we'd driven far, I began to sense that at this moment Parker's cheerful exterior covered a surprising anger. Perhaps an anger as great as his wife's.

"I'm making you a lot of trouble," I apologized. "I'm sorry. I really meant to call a cab."

"Don't worry." He was curt. "I'm not going out of my way. I've been *summoned.*"

I didn't know what he meant, and as we drove toward town he glanced at me. "When Mrs. Adams whistles for us, we jump," he said dryly. "She's giving a dinner for you Saturday, as you probably know. And she wants me to prepare it."

I'd forgotten about Sybil's dinner. I dreaded it now, with my new knowledge, and so much else hanging over me.

"Do you do this often?"

"Now and then. Why not? Since it's what I do best, I might as well work at it professionally. It's not out of the goodness of my heart, you know. All the same, this time I'd like to tell her where to get off. And I don't much care if you let your sister know how I feel."

So here was someone else who despised Sybil.

She certainly wasn't winning any popularity contests. But then—she never had.

"You'd better tell her yourself," I said. "Surely you don't have to do this dinner just because she expects it."

"If I don't do what Sybil Adams wants, she'll make it even tougher for Clara," he admitted. "And she's already doing quite a lot in that direction."

"How can she? Rick depends on your wife. She's his partner, and even in the short time I've been here I can see how valuable she is. Rick's talents lie in another direction."

"Rick's okay," he said, and let it go at that.

The familiar question had to be spoken. "Did you know my father—Jed Phillips?"

He answered readily. "I never ran into him. Which is just as well, from what Clara's told me."

I searched for a question that might cool his anger. "Where did you and Clara meet?"

He didn't answer at once as we drove through the village toward the hillier section of West Sedona. Then he gave me another quick look, as though he gauged my reaction and decided to be frank. Unnervingly frank.

"My past isn't much of a secret around here. I'd turned into a lush by the time I came to Santa Fe. Emily, Clara's mother, makes a job of rescuing the needy. And I sure was needy by that time. She used to be a nurse, and Clara's father is a doctor, so they brought me home, and Emily got me dried out. Anyway, I was nearly back on my feet when Clara came down to visit her parents. The rest, as they say, is history. How's that for a thumbnail story of my life?''

I couldn't deal with his self-derision but at least he had relaxed with me, and he seemed to expect no comment.

"How long are you going to stay?" he asked.

Everyone seemed to want to know that, and I still had no answer.

"I'm not sure," I told him. "Not long, probably."

His quick, sidelong look was searching. "You know something, Miss Phillips? I'll bet you've been upset ever since you got to Sedona. You've got the look about you of a firecracker waiting to go off."

So he too had watched me, and rather perceptively at that. Nevertheless, I didn't think he was the one who had written the note to bring me here.

We'd reached Rick's street, and there was no need for me to respond to Parker's firecracker accusation. Whether or not it was true, I didn't want to consider. I had to hold on to myself.

Parker rang the front doorbell and Consuela came to let us in.

Almost at once, Sybil appeared from another part of the house. Again, she wore a light suit of natural beige that had a couture look about it. I could recognize the details of hand stitching. So far, I'd never seen her in slacks, even though her lithe body was made for them.

"I'm glad you've come, Parker," she said briskly. "Now we can start on plans for my Saturday night dinner party. As I've told you, Lindsay, the dinner's to be given for you. Rick wants it."

Her look was coolly speculative, and I knew she was planning something more than a dinner, and that the idea was not wholly Rick's. If I knew my sister, someone was likely to be hurt, and I had a strong suspicion that it would be me. It was best to put a stop to this at once.

"I've wanted to tell you," I said quickly. "I'm not sure yet whether I'll stay. I may leave tomorrow."

She gave me a long, studying look. "I'm not surprised. I told Rick I didn't think you'd stay for this rather wild idea of his. Nevertheless, I hope you'll postpone leaving for a couple of days, at least. I've been phoning friends who want to know Jed's younger daughter. We mustn't disappoint them, must we? It's only till day after tomorrow."

I was aware of Parker's laconic attention.

"I'll decide soon," I said.

Sybil was clearly displeased. "This is really too bad of you, Lindsay. And of course you'll break Marilla's heart."

That startled me. "What do you mean?"

"She has plans for you on Saturday, when she's home from school. She's arranged to take you on Brian's jeep trip into the back country. His mother runs those tours now, you know. Is it really so important to leave at once?"

It was growing more important by the moment, but I wouldn't tell her why. The last thing I wanted her to guess was that my feeling for Rick was stronger than it had ever been. During this present strain between my sister and her husband, a new focus on me might present her with exactly the ammunition she'd want to use.

"There's a chance," I said, keeping my tone light, "that if I stay much longer I might very well stay altogether and try to do this designing assignment Rick has told me about."

That disconcerted her. She wouldn't want me here for more than a few days. As always, Sybil needed to set the scene dramatically when she had something up her sleeve, and that obviously was what she planned with this dinner. I was reluctant to stay and find out why it was so important to her.

"Well, about that," she went on, "of course you'll need time to consider. A few more days will give you breathing space. Then you can make up your mind more sensibly. You don't always think things through very well, Lindsay."

The familiar put-down—and the quick rise

of anger in me. I'd thought a good many things through in the years she hadn't known me. So this time I meant to have none of her diminishing tactics. She had helped me to make up my mind.

"I've decided," I said. "I'll go to Phoenix tomorrow and catch the first plane I can for home."

She turned smoothly to Parker. "Would you mind having a look at the menu I've left for you in the kitchen? I'll be with you in a minute."

Parker glanced at me before he turned away, his look faintly mocking—perhaps of himself as much as of me.

When he'd gone, Sybil motioned toward the sofa. "Do sit down and stop fidgeting, Lindsay. We need to talk. I'd wanted to surprise you, but now you're forcing my hand. You see, I've invited someone to the dinner. Someone you really must meet—a relative of yours. In fact, a member of your *real* family. You've always wanted to know about them, haven't you?"

I froze, staring at her blankly. She laughed, and I remembered the sound from my childhood. Even as a young girl, she'd laughed like that. Her speaking voice was musical—her laughter always harsh, splintering into notes that had an ugly ring.

"Oh, don't get the idea I'm doing this because I want you around." The laughter was gone and her tone had turned low and deadly.

"Do you think I haven't seen the way you look at Rick? Do you think I don't know how quickly you'd reach for him if you could. You've always wanted him. Only this isn't going to happen. I've my own ways, and don't think I won't use them. First you're going to stay and do what you haven't done in your whole life, little sister. You're going to face the truth about yourself. About who you are and what you've come from. *If* you have the courage. Though of course I won't be surprised if you turn and run."

I managed to find my voice. "*Why* did you write inviting me to come here? Rick could never have made you send that letter if you didn't want to."

She continued to watch me, her smile bright with malice. "Of course he couldn't have. When your letter came, I began to make some plans of my own. You see, I'd learned about your family only recently."

I could understand now. Understand very well. My sister's greatest pleasure had always come from the act of *hurting*. Too often in the past I'd been her helpless target. Not anymore. Undoubtedly she had learned some unsavory things about the other side of my family, and she meant to enjoy every moment of this revelation.

I got up quite steadily and walked out of the room. Later, though I couldn't remember crossing the bridge to the guesthouse, I found myself in the bedroom, where I put on a robe. My hands were shaking so that I could hardly tie the cord. When I lay down on the bed, I pulled a blanket over me to stop my shivering.

The telephone stood within easy reach. I had only to pick it up and make a plane reservation. Yet I waited, and in that moment of desolation I was open again to Vermilion. The whispering came quickly and clearly. Almost as if it emanated from somewhere in the room outside of me.

You have to stay. You have to know.

"I don't want to know. I'm afraid!" I spoke the words aloud.

There's more than that. You need to fight Sybil — pay her off. It's in your power now to do that.

Again I found myself answering aloud. "I don't need that. Not anymore."

Determinedly, I sat up and reached for the phone, and as I did so my hand encountered something on the table beside it. Something small and delicate and beautiful. It rested in a film of the red dust that seemed to permeate everything in Sedona whenever the wind blew.

I saw that it was a tiny unicorn made of clay. Unfired, unglazed, brittle clay, and very fragile, I picked it up with care and balanced it on my palm. A child's work—Marilla's undoubtedly—done with an exquisite feeling of grace, of motion. The little thing looked at me with a gentle, benign gaze—as though it might cavort

133

off my hand at any moment and go charging away, flinging that slanted horn in the air as it tossed its tiny head.

I'd left the door open and when I turned at a sound, she stood there watching me—small and alert, and as ready to fly at the slightest rebuff as the unicorn on my hand.

"Come in, Marilla," I said. "You made this, didn't you?"

She had just come home from school, and her books were still on her arm. Dropping them into a chair, she came toward me.

"It's for you. I didn't know what else I could give you. I wanted to make up for—for being mean to you last night, when I brought you Grandpa Jed's cane. Maybe I really did know it would upset you."

"This is very beautiful," I said. "Thank you, Marilla. It's a lovely present. Have you shown it to Mrs. Montgomery, your art teacher?"

She shook her head and soft curls danced. "Oh, no! Nobody knows I make up imaginary animals. Except Grandpa Jed. He showed me how, with the clay. My mother would say it's foolish. She likes me to do sensible things."

I winced. "And your father? Has he seen this?"

"No! Please don't show it to him, Lindsay."

"I won't if you don't want me to, but I think he'd be delighted."

Her eyes wouldn't meet mine. "My mother doesn't like me to be dreamy," she said. "There really aren't any unicorns.''

Anger was rising in me—a fury against my sister that was greater than any I'd ever felt. Nevertheless, I answered quietly.

"Perhaps she just means not being dreamy at the wrong time. I don't think much would ever be accomplished if there weren't dreamers.''

"That's like what Grandpa Jed told me one time.'' She had brightened and now she took a cushion from a chair, dropped it on the floor and sat cross-legged, looking up at me. "He said the most fun he knew was to make up exciting dreams.''

"He certainly knew how to do that,'' I agreed.

"Yes! He said all the best and most wonderful things in the world came out of dreaming.''

And some of the worst, I thought, though I didn't say it aloud. Not for anything would I erase the rapt expression on Marilla's face as she went on.

"He said carrying out dreams was the hard part, and not nearly so much fun. He said it was fine while he was getting things rolling. Then after a while he started to get bored.''

I held up the little unicorn. "He was wrong. This is the best part of dreaming—when you make what's in your mind come true.''

"But sometimes dreams just fall apart when you try to make them real.''

"That's part of it too. You should see my

wastebasket! But then when something begins to happen on the paper—or in the clay—there's hardly anything in the world more exciting. In the end, if there's a unicorn, you have a better reward than money, or becoming famous, or anything."

Marilla's eyes were shining. "That's the way it was! Only when I finished, I didn't know if it was any good. You're the first person I've shown it to."

"It's very good. Perhaps Mrs. Montgomery can fire it for you, if she has a kiln. Otherwise, it will dry to powder and fall apart."

"It's yours. You can do what you like with it."

"Why don't you want me to show it to your father?"

"He might laugh, and then I'd feel awful. And Mom says not to bother him when he's so busy."

"I think he'd have time for this. Do you really mind if I show it to him?"

She tried to sound indifferent. "I don't care."

I wondered if Rick had any idea that he inspired such anxiety in his daughter. I knew that he worried about her, and about Sybil's influence, although he might not be fully aware of Marilla's hidden fears and hero worship. Or of the subtle damage Sybil could do.

"I was in Clara Hale's shop today," I went on, "and I saw the Fire People that my father sculpted. It's a very fine piece."

Once more she brightened. "Wait till you see the real Fire People on Saturday. Brian is going to save places for us in the jeep when he takes out a tour. We can sit right up front with him. He promised."

I hesitated and then spoke gently. "I'm not sure I'll be here on Saturday. I've told your mother that I may be leaving."

"What about the dinner she's planned?" Marilla cried. "Mom said you'd be here for that."

"There are reasons why I shouldn't stay," I told her.

She regarded me sadly. "I didn't even get to see Vermilion." She went to a window and stood looking out toward the house. After a moment she beckoned to me. "Come here, Lindsay."

When I went to stand beside her, I saw that Sybil and Rick were on the terrace behind the house. Rick's back was toward me, but I could see Sybil clearly, and if ever body language meant anything, she was an angry woman.

"They're fighting again," Marilla said. "Sometimes they scare me."

I'd turned away in dismay, when my phone rang and I went to pick it up.

"This is Orva Montgomery," the voice said.

"Yes," I answered. "Brian's mother."

"Clara tells me you may be leaving soon. If that's true, I'd like to see you first. It's rather important. What about supper tonight? Will you come if I send Brian for you?''

So she *was* the one! I was sure of it now. The writer of those two notes would never let me get away without revealing her purpose.

"I'd like that," I said. "What time shall I be ready?"

"Let's say five o'clock? Then we'll have time to talk. It will just be early supper. I'm no Sybil."

"Anything at all will be fine. I'll be ready. And thank you."

"You can think about thanking me later," she said and rang off.

Marilla had left the window and was moving listlessly toward the door.

"Mrs. Montgomery has invited me for supper tonight," I told her. "Do you mind if I take the unicorn to show her?"

"I don't care." Again, she spoke indifferently, and I had the feeling that she was deliberately dismissing me from her life. Perhaps she had connected me with my father, whom she loved and missed. Perhaps she expected more of me than I could give. I was sorry to disappoint her, and I felt guilty about it. Had I made the wrong decision, after all?

"Would you like me to stay through Saturday?" I asked.

But I had already lost her, and she wouldn't trust me now. "I don't care," she repeated, and went out the door.

I wished there had been some way to reach her. If I stayed, perhaps I could manage that on Saturday's jeep trip.

Now my meeting with Orva Montgomery lay ahead, with whatever disturbing revelations it might bring, and I must hurry to get ready.

As I started for the bathroom to shower, someone knocked on my door. I opened it to find Rick standing there, and I stepped back to let him in, once more on guard. Against myself, as much as against him.

"I can drive you to your plane tomorrow, if you're really bent on leaving," he said abruptly.

So he'd been talking to either Clara or Sybil. I let my breath out in a long, despairing sigh. "I've never felt so torn and undecided, Rick. A little while ago Sybil said some things that I don't know how to deal with."

"You mustn't let her drive you away. At the same time, Lindsay, if you stay it has to be your own choice."

"I know. Rick, Sybil says she's invited someone who's related to me for dinner Saturday night."

We'd stood near the door talking, and now Rick came past me into the living room to sit down wearily. "I was afraid she'd try something like this. A long time ago Jed told Orva about you. Orva's never said a word until recently, when she let the truth slip out with Sybil. Never mind. Sybil will play out of her dramatic scenes, and that gives us time to forestall her."

"Is it my mother she's invited?" I asked.

He answered me gently. "Your mother died when you were born, Lindsay. That's why Jed took you home to New York as a baby. I've always thought he should have told you that much, at least. His wife didn't want you to be told, however."

A surprising, almost devastating relief flooded through me. For as long as I could remember, the age-old question had hovered over my life: why had my real mother given me up? Why had she let Jed take me from her? But I'd never expected to feel such relief at the answer. The flood of emotion brought with it a kind of healing. Nothing that Sybil had planned could hurt me now.

"I'll stay through her dinner," I said.

"By that time you'll be armed—because I mean to tell you the whole story first. I've intended to. I just wanted you to be ready. I'd planned to take you to Flagstaff tomorrow to see Alice Spencer, and if you stay then I think we should still go. I'd like you to see what's possible in this idea of mine before you leave."

"I'm willing to go," I said.

His look was kind, and I turned away because kindness might undo me completely. When I spoke again, I tried to sound casual.

"Brian Montgomery is coming in a little while to pick me up. I'm invited to his mother's for supper tonight. Will you please tell Sybil I won't be with you."

"To Orva's?" There was something uneasy in his voice.

"Don't you like her?"

"I do like her. I don't always trust her. She's fine with Marilla, but she's also capable of conniving."

I picked up the small unicorn and held it out to him. "Your daughter has a very special talent."

He held the tiny animal carefully, wonderingly. "Marilla did this?"

"Yes. She was afraid to show it to you because she thought you might laugh at her."

His smile was rueful. "So I have a daughter who thinks I can't see unicorns?"

"She thinks you're very busy doing important things."

"No one should ever be too busy when a unicorn drops in. I'm sorry she thinks that. It's my fault, and I'll tell her how much I like this. I'd hoped you'd make friends with her, Lindsay."

When I reached out to take the unicorn from him, he held my hand lightly.

"You're not in this alone, you know. We'll work it all out somehow."

I wasn't sure just what he meant. To tell me that I was not alone was perhaps the most threatening thing of all, and I couldn't answer. Perhaps he saw more in my eyes than I wanted him to, for he let my hand go and went away across the bridge.

For a moment longer I stood in the doorway, watching, and then hurried to shower. When I looked in the long mirror through misting water, it was as if Vermilion stared back at me, and her mouth was curved in a mocking smile.

6

Brian arrived promptly at five. He seemed relieved to find me watching for him near the door. We drove off immediately, and I sat holding the small box that Consuela had found for me, and into which I'd nested Marilla's unicorn in tissue paper.

When we were well on our way, hurrying from whatever it was we fled, Brian said wryly, "A good getaway! Sybil has a talent for thinking up new things for me to do, and I'm trying to get back to my book."

His words surprised me, since I'd regarded him as a willing satellite. When I made no comment, he went on quickly.

"I'm not being critical. Your sister does a great deal of good and she's taught me a lot. A remarkable woman. Though sometimes I think she's made of steel. Also, she has more time to put her energies into whatever interests her. I need to be about three people right now."

"Don't we all?" I said. "What's your book about?"

He was willing enough to talk. "I'm doing a study of Oak Creek Canyon—the rock formations, the plants and animals, the back country. The back country interests me especially. Out there everything is still pretty wild. There are too many houses coming into Sedona, too many people. I'll show you what I mean—at least a taste of it—if you come with us on Saturday. I suppose Marilla's told you? Your father liked to get out there too. He had a thing about those rocks, and he could almost make *me* see spirits in them."

"My father had a great imagination," I said.

Brian glanced at me again. "You didn't like your father very much, did you?"

That came too close to wounds that hadn't healed.

"Did *you* like him?" I countered.

"I did for a while." His answer was short, and after that he gave his attention entirely to his driving.

Orva's house was a short distance away, located on one of the roads that climbed toward the Coffee Pot, but not on the cliff's edge like Rick's house. It was smaller, and built of concrete bricks tinted to look like adobe.

The living room centered about a stone fireplace, where piñon logs burned invitingly, giving off a pleasant scent. I found it a warmer, more restful room than the great living room at Rick's house. A number of paintings of Indians decorated the walls.

Unlike those I'd helped Clara with in the shop gallery that morning, these paintings were crude, the work of a gifted amateur. One oil of a masked and costumed figure dancing caught my eye.

"Did your mother paint this?" I asked Brian.

He nodded. "She did it from life. She used to teach on a Hopi reservation years ago. Sit down, Lindsay. Ma's in the kitchen—I'll tell her you're here."

A moment later Orva came to greet me. Standing beside her muscular son, she seemed thinner and more angular than ever. Her short gray hair flew about in wisps, and there were beads of perspiration on her nose.

"I'm glad you've come, Lindsay. May I call you that? Everything's ready, if you don't mind eating early."

The dining room was gracious, with paneled walls and glass doors that looked out upon the view. There were always the rocks to be seen, and I was discovering that they could be different under changing skies, and with the shifting of sunlight and shadow.

Brian sat at one end of the oval table, with Orva at the other, and I sensed between them a liking and understanding that nevertheless seemed to carry a slight edge to it, as though some disagreement, scarcely suppressed, was ready to show itself. Sybil? I wondered.

Supper was a fresh green salad sprinkled with sunflower seeds, and buckwheat pancakes filled with a white cheese that had been mixed with raisins and nuts. Not the thin blintzes of New York, but pancakes you could bite into. The sauce was clear and slightly thickened, with a hint of honey and lemon. Brian brought me a glass of cold milk.

"This sauce is a trick of Parker Hale's," Orva said. "The pancakes are mine. I used to feed them to your father when he came to visit us. Of course, though he always stayed with Rick and Sybil when he was in town, he didn't get along well with his older daughter, as you probably know. So he would come here for meals whenever I'd have him. He'd sit right where you are now and finish off as many servings as I'd feed him. Don't know where he put it all on that big frame of his. He never gained a pound."

I tried to shut out the picture her words built in my mind, bringing my father too close again.

"Jed brought me that," Brian told me, and nodded toward a corner of the room.

I looked at the Indian drum standing against a Mexican serape that draped the corner. It was tall and cylindrical—a black drum, with a red spot in the center of its rawhide top. The drumhead was tightened with thongs that ran down the sides in a crisscrossing pattern, and symmetrical stripes were painted red and white, with scallops of pale blue around the top.

"That's what they call a barrel drum," Brian said. "It's made from a hollow cottonwood log, and it's typical of Indians in the Southwest. Maybe the tone isn't as vibrant as the cedar drums of the North, but the Southwest tribes can still make them talk. This one's a Pueblo drum—from Oraibi—and Jed taught me some of the medicine."

I found myself staring at the drum with its single padded stick set across the drumhead, as though I could see my father holding it in his hand.

"Medicine?" I asked.

"Sure. I've seen a Hopi sit before his drum with that same dreamy, absorbed look that drummers can put on anywhere, so that what comes out in sound can be an almost mystical experience. Some drums are for religious ceremonies, some for dancing. On a personal level they mean a release to the man who plays them. Jed knew that, and he got me interested. He said there was always a spirit power in the drum—the medicine of life."

"Those blue scallops are the rain symbol," Orva said. "When we're through, Brian can show you."

Emotion came too close again. Too close for comfort. "I'm sorry, I really don't want to hear it."

The words sounded terse, but Orva seemed to understand. "I can guess how you feel. We didn't always love Jed either. If ever there was a man who wasted himself —"

"Sometimes he wasted other people,"

Brian said sharply.

"That too," she agreed.

"I guess the worst time"—Brian was staring out through glass at the rocks—"was when he brought us all to Vegas for that last party— which was only a scheme to get money for a new plan. The time when he died. I haven't forgotten the way Sybil told her father off that night. Rick was sorry for him and wouldn't criticize him, ever—so Sybil was the one who quarreled with him. Not that I could blame her. Though, as it worked out, we never did get the details of what he was going to propose. He said he'd tell us the next day—so as not to spoil our fun that night, I suppose. Only he didn't live long enough."

There seemed a rising tension in his voice, as though some deep bitterness he harbored against my father had welled to the surface.

Orva spoke quickly, with a clear intent to cover whatever her son might be feeling. "You can imagine how that party upset Clara—once she knew there was another scheme coming. She'd already been rooked by him, and it made her pretty mad that he'd try it again."

I still wasn't ready to hear details about that time in Nevada, and I changed the subject quickly. "Tell me about growing up in Sedona, Orva. Was it very different from now?"

She allowed herself to be diverted. "We were smaller, of course—mostly apple orchards in the old days. We could keep out the bulldozers then, and some of the real old-timers were still alive. Sedona was named for a woman, you know. An early settler—Sedona Schnebly. I remember it as a very good life, though I was hardly an early settler."

"How long have you known Rick and Sybil?"

"I knew Rick when he was a little boy. I even had him in some of my classes then. That's how I met your father—when Jed stepped in to help Rick after his father died. I suppose you know that Jed put Rick through the university?"

I hadn't known that. But Jed had always been generous when he was in the money.

"Of course we met Sybil through Rick when he married her and brought her here to live. I've thought ever since that she was bad luck for him. I hope I can speak frankly, even if she is your sister."

Brian moved restlessly, as though he didn't want to listen. He got up to clear the table, while Orva brought in plates of homemade pumpkin pie, and poured cups of strong black coffee, which turned out to be made from a sort of bean that wasn't coffee.

The interruption didn't shift Orva in her course, however. "You might as well know, Lindsay, if you haven't already guessed, that there's very little love lost between Sybil and me. I was fond of Jed at times—when I wasn't being angry with him—as I'm fond of Rick, so I hated to see what was happening. Sybil—"

This time Brian broke in determinedly, though his tone was light and faintly mocking. "Don't mind Ma, Lindsay. She's an intolerant and prejudiced woman!" The edge between them was sharper than ever, for all that he grinned.

Orva responded quickly. "Sybil's got you under her thumb, and you never see what she's up to."

"She's up to accomplishing some things I could never do by myself," Brian said. "She's plenty persuasive when she sets out to be, and she knows how to play on emotions. She can stir people up enough to get things done. I'd follow her for that alone. Don't forget that I'm the one who feeds her the factual stuff she uses in her arguments."

"Do you think she gives a damn about ecology?" Orva's voice grew heated with indignation. "Jed was right about her. I'm sorry, Lindsay, but all Sybil ever wants is to prove that she's better, stronger, smarter, and more powerful than anyone else. What's more, she's on her way to doing it. And it helps a lot to have Rick's money behind her. *Power*—that's the name of her game. And it was your father who told me so. Sedona, Flagstaff, Phoenix—they're only the beginning. That's what he said, and he wasn't being admiring. She'll be in papers all across the country—for her good deeds! Just wait and see. Her picture will be in magazines, instead of just the local papers. She'll be interviewed on national television."

"Sometimes I feel sorry for her," Brian said. "All that single-minded drive must come out of a lot of insecurity."

Again his words surprised me. I'd never looked at Sybil in that light. I knew too much that Brian didn't—especially about what she was doing now to Marilla.

"I want to show you something," I said. "Excuse me a minute."

I left the table and went to fetch the box with Marilla's unicorn. Orva, cooling down as quickly as she'd heated up, watched with Brian as I unpacked the little creature and set it on the table before me.

"Gosh!" Brian said.

Orva picked up the unicorn, turning it about in her fingers. "This is Marilla's, isn't it? Sybil doesn't deserve a child like her. I didn't know Marilla had done any work in clay."

"She said my father showed her how," I explained. "Could it be fired, do you think?"

"I have a kiln out in back. I'll take care of it. It won't last too long otherwise. I wish I had more to give Marilla as a teacher."

"I showed this to Rick," I said, "and he was surprised. Marilla's shy and afraid of criticism, so she hides the things she does. But I think he'll talk to her mother now."

"Jed was the one who opened up her mind and her feelings," Orva said. "And he loved her more than he could his own daughter." She broke off abruptly, remembering that I too was

151

Jed's daughter, and set down the unicorn, blinking angrily.

Pain struck through me again. *I* had been a small girl once, and I too had been the recipient of Jed's brief affection and encouragement. Before he got bored and went away.

"What Jed had," Brian said soberly, "was the knack of stretching people to their limits. He could push down barricades because he never accepted limitations for himself or anyone else. I wish I'd never found him out at the end. I wish—" He broke off gloomily.

I could understand exactly what Brian meant. No one ever forgives the magician who reveals himself as human, and I wondered what my father had done to so disillusion Brian.

A silence filled with unhappy thoughts and memories settled on us, and Orva ended it by pushing back her chair.

"Leave the dishes," she said. "Get along to your book, Brian. I want to talk to Lindsay."

The time had come, and as I followed her from the table I wasn't sure I was ready. When I looked back, her son still sat staring at the unicorn. Bearded men could mask their emotions better than most. Facial lines, mouths, were lost, so that only the eyes gave them away. When Brian sensed my attention and looked up, I saw a sadness in him that I hadn't glimpsed before. He was far from being the mere follower that I'd first considered him.

Orva led me into her small study, where a

battered wooden desk—probably a teacher's desk, left over from long-ago classroom—held a stack of children's drawings and watercolors. Books piled upon books burdened the wall shelves, and she picked up a stack from a chair so that I could sit down. But there were evidences of her Jeep Tours business as well—steel files and a big ledger. And on the walls photographs of open safari jeeps in rocky settings.

"Things grow," she said. "I can never figure out what happens when my back is turned, but when I return there's always more of everything everywhere."

She sat down in the modern leather chair behind her desk. A chair that appeared to flaunt its superiority over the rest of the furniture, and which I suspected must have been a gift from Brian. Orva's tastes ran more to the old and trusted.

There was a moment of silence, and Orva's eyes seemed filled with a barely suppressed excitement that made me thoroughly uneasy. With one finger she traced patterns in the prevailing red dust on a corner of the desk, and began with no preamble.

"I want to talk to you about Sybil. If you're really leaving, then it doesn't matter as far as your own comfort goes. But it does matter that you know something I've never told anyone else. Especially Brian. If you decide to stay— and in spite of what Clara told me, I have a feeling that you're still not sure of anything — if you decide to stay, then I think you must be put on your guard. Sybil is a dangerous woman. The fact that you're her sister doesn't change that."

She seemed to become aware of her finger tracing in dust, and stopped to wipe it clean with a piece of tissue.

"Gets into everything!" she said, and then went on with what she wanted to say. "Brian makes allowances for how Sybil got the way she is. Maybe that's something Jed was responsible for too. I think she's always resented you because you were the one he loved best. But in the end we all have to be responsible for ourselves, for our own actions, no matter what has made us that way. Not that we always succeed! In Sybil's case, it's getting worse, and it's the terrible things she can do now that matter."

I sat very still, with my hands clasped in my lap to keep them from nervous movement. We were coming to the reason that had brought me here.

"Perhaps Sybil has changed in some way," I said carefully. "Perhaps she's become a woman who's in control of her life and herself."

"That's exactly what she's not. Because she always wants most what she can't have. And she must punish those who hold it from her. She hasn't had *Rick* for a long time."

I had to stop her, though I kept my tone

154

even. "I'm not sure that's my business, but I'm very sure it's not yours."

Orva spread her hands on the drawings before her, splaying her fingers. They were long, thin hands, brown from the sun, with nails that indicated earth digging without benefit of gloves. They were strong hands that pressed into the papers, as though to restrain her impatience with me.

"What is bound to affect Brian is certainly my affair."

"Perhaps you don't do your son justice. I suspect he can take care of himself."

She slapped one hand on the papers with a quick violence that startled me. "Let's not play games, Lindsay."

"All right then—let's not. You're the one who brought me here, so perhaps you'd better tell me why."

She made no denial and excitement was alive in her eyes. "How much do you know about the night your father died?" she demanded.

"I know only what Rick told me, and what little I've heard since I came here. He was apparently throwing one of his extravagant parties to bolster his latest scheme, and he invited a number of Sedona friends to attend. But why did any of you go, when you knew him so well?"

"Have you forgotten how persuasive he could be? Sybil gets some of that quality from him, when she chooses to use it. He was indebted

155

to us all—as he admitted readily enough. He deluded us into thinking it was a party to pay us back a little for past generosity. We could easily have gone to Scottsdale, which is a lot closer, but he made one of his grand gestures and chartered a plane. In Arizona we can be a little snobbish about Vegas, but it was always Jed's town. He was so beautifully plausible. Of course when I look back, I marvel at how we swallowed it all and did as he asked.

"There were six of us. Clara, Brian, and me. And Rick, Sybil, and Marilla. We had rooms on the same floor, and Jed proceeded to give us a very good time. He was in one of his highs that night. Keyed up and abnormally excited. Oh, I don't think he used drugs of any sort. He didn't even drink more than moderately. He didn't need to. His particular highs came out of those crazy ideas of his. To be fair, I don't think he ever meant to cheat anybody. He believed in all of it himself. Every time it happened, he believed. That's how he always sold his victims—out of his own strong convictions. And afterwards, when everything collapsed, he was desperately sorry."

I remembered that—the way he'd always taken the blame, poured out regrets that came too late to help anything.

"Then it was someone who didn't appreciate the purity of his motives who struck him down," I said wryly. "Anyway, it's over now. It's finished. So why did you want me to come?

Why did you write those notes?"

She evaded the direct question. "How can it be finished when whoever killed Jed is still walking around unpunished?"

That was what I'd felt too, but I had to play devil's advocate. "And will probably never harm anyone else. My father attracted lightning once too often. If you brought me here to tell me about that Las Vegas party, it seems pretty extreme."

"All right—I wrote those notes. And I mentioned Sybil, didn't I? Brian told you about the quarrel she and Jed had after dinner that night. Jed tried to put her down once too often. He was usually a kind man, but he knew what she was doing to Rick, and he tried to have it out with her. They got to baiting each other, and he told her off. After all, she was his daughter. She lost her temper and slapped him, and he shook her so hard she had bruises on her arms the next day. Brian stopped it. He got pretty mad at Jed himself. Rick wasn't there when it happened because he'd gone to take a phone call. The rest of us were there, except for Marilla, who had fortunately gone to bed. So we saw what happened."

Orva paused, the veins standing out on the backs of her hands as she pressed them down, smudging one of the pencil drawings under her fingers. There was more to come, and I sat tensely, waiting.

"By the time Rick came back, Jed had left.

Rick got Sybil quieted down, and we went to our rooms. Sometime after midnight Sybil walked down the hall to Jed's room. No one knows this but me. Not even Sybil knows that I opened my door and looked out just as she was leaving Jed's room and hurrying back to her own. I couldn't sleep after all the excitement, so when I heard doors open and close, and someone moving about, I was curious.

"I got out of bed and opened my own door. Sybil came out of Jed's room fast and ran back to her own. She was fully dressed, as she'd been for that rather grand dinner. I didn't see her face because she was moving away from me. Believe me, I shut myself into my room in a hurry and went back to bed. Whatever was going on, I didn't want to know any more about it. It wasn't my quarrel. Not then. I didn't learn until morning that Jed was dead."

"Why didn't you tell what you'd seen right away?"

"Because of Rick. Because I'm fond of Rick, no matter how much I dislike Sybil. I thought Jed probably invited what happened to him, and if I talked about what I'd seen it would only stir things up in a horrible way."

"Are you accusing Sybil of our father's murder?"

Her hands relaxed their tension and dropped into her lap. "That's for you to do," she said. "That's why you're here. Because you're the only one close enough to Sybil to find

158

out the truth."

"And you're doing all this to save your son from my sister?" I was incredulous.

"I would do more than that, Lindsay, but my hands seem to be tied."

"You could still tell Rick."

"After keeping still for more than a year? I'm not sure he would even believe me."

"Why should I?"

"No reason. Except that you grew up with Sybil."

I closed my eyes, not wanting to remember. But the pictures were all there. Sybil holding those sharp-pointed scissors of hers, threatening me, when I'd been no more than three. Sybil pushing me off a high swing when we were riding tandem. Sybil lying to our mother, blaming me, to get herself off. She had always been able to convince Mother, when she never could with Jed. But none of this would help me now.

When I opened my eyes and looked at Orva, she was still watching me intently.

"There's nothing I can possibly do," I said. "It's too late."

"Just think about it, Lindsay—and then run away if you dare."

If I ran, it would be from more than Orva Montgomery.

From another part of the house a sound reached us, and I raised my head, listening. It was soft and whispery at first, like the stroking of a drumstick over taut rawhide as the player sought his rhythm. Then the sound grew stronger, more resonant, until it filled the house. The beat was clear now: *Boom, pause—beat-beat-beat.* The last three beats were quick, and then the simple rhythm was repeated. Over and over—Jed's Indian drum.

I looked at Orva and saw that she leaned back in her chair, smiling as though some battle plan had been successfully launched.

"A tom-tom?" I asked.

"The Hopi don't use that white man's word. Brian really has learned to play it, hasn't he? Sometimes I've heard the drums talk like that in the pueblos. Though I never knew what they were saying."

What this drum was saying made the skin prickle at the back of my neck. The message was somehow anticipatory, as though the steady, monotonous beat was building toward some climax—some explosive climax.

"How can you stand it?" I said.

She continued to smile. "Just listen."

The sound had risen in volume, the rhythm quickening until it seemed to burst the confines of the house, vibrating outward to echo against red peaks, calling to the old, old land.

Now the rhythm changed to something still more insistent, more primitive: *BOOM, beat-beat; BOOM, beat-beat,* over and over again, a sound of warning, an arousal of dark emotions, of mounting passions that must find release.

It was more than I could bear to listen to. I had to make it stop before it got into my blood and caused me to do—whatever it was that was forbidden. If I listened too long, it would make me feel more deeply than I dared. It was a sound that might cut me free of all the past and send me down some new and reckless road.

I stood up quickly. "I'd like to go back to Rick's now," I said.

Orva nodded, understanding more than I liked. "Yes, I know. I can feel it too. Makes you want to kick over the traces, doesn't it? Maybe run away from everything that's sensible and safe. I'm glad I'm too old for it to reach me anymore. But sometimes that sound makes me wonder if I really know my son."

As though my insistent thoughts had reached out to touch the man who played the drum, he changed the rhythm to something less insistent, beating it out more softly and without accent, then building to a sudden climax that ended on a last loud *BOOM*.

Whatever it was that gripped me, let go, and I looked around as Brian came to stand in the doorway. An ordinary young man with a fair, curly beard and a pleasant smile. Not at all a prophet of danger and doom. A peacemaker. Or at least that was what he claimed.

"What was the drum saying?" Orva asked her son.

His eyes looked a little sleepy, as though he had gone somewhere far away and hadn't fully returned as yet.

"I can't always tell," he said. "My hands know more than I do. The drum is like Jed—always depths beyond depths. I wonder if anything really lies at the promised end?"

"Will you please take me back to Rick's?" I said. "I'm very tired. I expect I'm still on New York time. Forgive me for running, Orva," falsely polite.

"Of course," she said. She knew one reason why I was running, but not all. Mainly, perhaps, I ran from a burden of responsibility that I wasn't ready to accept.

Brian went to back out the car, while Orva came with me to the door.

"Catch up on your sleep," she said. "I believe I'll make a phone call now."

Something in her voice alerted me. "You're going to call Sybil?"

"Why not? It's time to carry the attack of nerves a little further. In the end, I think she'll betray herself."

"What else have you done?" I demanded.

When she grinned at me impudently, the sun lines in her face deepening, she could look disarmingly innocent. I knew she wasn't innocent at all.

"Oh, nothing much," she said. "Just a little note to Sybil to let her know that you were coming out to investigate your father's murder. That was all—I left it at that. Hasn't she said anything?"

So this was what lay behind some of the hostility I'd sensed in my sister? Orva's scheming outraged me, but I couldn't express what I felt. Not yet.

As I waited for Brian, she came close to me and patted my arm. "Don't look like that. In the end, you'll thank me, you know. I'll see you the day after tomorrow at your sister's dinner. Has it struck you that it's rather curious—that dinner? Except for you and Parker, and of course the absence of Jed, the guests will be the very same ones who were gathered in Las Vegas when your father died."

I ran down the steps toward the car and got in without looking back. I didn't know whether or not she watched as we drove away.

A full moon sailed high over the great rock formations, silvering their edges, making deep shadows of the crevices. The landscape seemed wilder by night—as though darkness brought turmoil to those red peaks. A turmoil that matched my thoughts.

I was grateful for ordinary lamplight shining in the windows of Sedona as we drove along. There was still a normal world around us.

"You're shaking," Brian said. "My mother has upset you, hasn't she? They were really a pair, you know—she and Jed—when it came to imagination and weird schemes. Not that Ma could ever match your father. Sometimes she gets carried away by some notion that doesn't have much connection with reality. So don't take her too seriously."

Sometimes I wondered how much *he* was in touch with reality. This notion of Orva's might have more connection with what was real than her son understood, no matter what fantasy she might indulge to bring about a confrontation with Sybil. For an instant I thought of telling him what his mother had done, but quickly backed away. I didn't know him well enough, and I mustn't forget that he was one of Sybil's followers.

When I said nothing, he let the matter go and didn't speak again until we were in Rick's driveway. Then, like his mother, he put a light hand on my arm.

"Thanks for coming, Lindsay. I'm looking forward to taking you and Marilla on that jeep trip Saturday. The kid's counting on it, you know."

"I'll try to come," I said. "I can't leave until I've found out who killed my father." I heard my own words with a certain relief. It didn't matter to whom I'd spoken them. They reinforced what I'd said to Rick, and I was glad of the commitment. It didn't matter that this was no longer my entire reason for staying.

Brian's hand tightened on my arm. "Hey, wait a minute! That's a pretty cold trail. I don't know what my mother opened up with you, but you'd better not follow any of her wild clues—if she gave you any. I'm keeping more of an eye on things than she thinks. I know how she feels about Sybil. Though Ma doesn't always see things in the round."

"And you do?"

"Nobody does," he said shortly, and came to open the door on my side of the car.

The front entrance of the house was only a step up from the drive, since no basement had been dug into this deep rock. I stood on the terra-cotta tiles of the entryway and watched Brian's car disappear. Lights were on inside, but the house seemed very quiet and I felt a strange uneasiness about going through its empty spaces. Had the telephone been ringing? Had Orva's call been answered?

Even more, I disliked crossing that lonely bridge to the island of the guesthouse. Tonight I didn't want to feel isolated. So much that might be more terrible than I could face had been planted in my mind.

Another car stood on the apron before the garage, and as I raised my hand to ring the doorbell, someone got out and came toward me.

"Wait, Lindsay. Don't go inside yet."

It was Rick. His voice came out of the darkness with that same deep timbre that I remembered. I paused uncertainly.

"Come and get in the car," he said, and I heard the anger in his voice. Yet in the same instant I knew that it was not directed at me.

The drum wasn't silent after all. It was still

beating in my blood.

I walked over to the Mercedes and got into the passenger seat.

7

My sense of direction wasn't clear, and at first I didn't know where we were going. The rocks looked different with their heads in the moonlight. It was an alien landscape and more disturbing than ever.

Not until I saw ahead the lighted bell tower of Tlaquepaque did I realize where we were. Beside me, Rick was quiet, though tension showed in his hands on the wheel, in the set of his head—a tension that seemed to draw me into it, making me a part of his deep anger.

We left the car in an almost empty parking area and walked once more into a world of perfect beauty and harmony. The central plaza was empty except for couples strolling through now and then. Farther on, in one of the upper galleries, a restaurant was open and we could hear voices, but most of Tlaquepaque drowsed in the moonlight, a quiet and enchanted place. Over all rose the slim pencil of light that was the bell tower shining through the trees.

In the courtyards Spanish lanterns shed a

soft glow. We found a green iron bench and sat down in the shadow of a sycamore, its branches flung above us scattering spangles of moonlight. Nearby, a fountain splashed softly, and on one of the galleries a guitar strummed an old romantic ballad about Mexico. The words were sung softly, as if for the singer's pleasure, or that of his lady. Somewhere, I could hear the rushing sound of the creek far below.

We sat so close that I could sense his warmth through my thin dress, and yet we were not touching. It was a moment of such heightened sentience for me that I knew when the rage began to flow out of him, when he began to let all his torment float away. If he moved now, if he touched me, I would be in his arms and no voice of reason would stop me. Yet his words startled me.

"I think I'm in love with you, Lindsay. I wanted to tell you this—away from the house."

I sat very still and waited, lest I break the spell of the moment.

He went on softly. "Perhaps I've always been a little in love with you, even when you were only seventeen and we were friends. I didn't have the good sense to listen then, to wait. What I felt for Sybil was too demanding and strong. It got in the way. Then when I met you later in New York and saw the woman you'd become, I wanted to know you better. I also knew that it wasn't any use, that it was too late, and I went back to Sedona. When your letter came, I was eager to see you again, and I began to make plans to try to keep you here a little while."

I started to speak and he put a hand on my arm, silencing me.

"The plans I worked out are good ones, and they're genuine. There's a valuable role for you to play out here. It was because you were coming that I began to develop them seriously. And I tried to make the break with Sybil that should have been made long ago. I even began to fool myself with hope."

I put my hand over his where it lay on my arm. "You don't need to tell me this. I know how hard it is for you."

"I don't think you do, exactly. That doesn't matter. I want you to understand how I feel, though I won't ask about your feelings."

"You don't need to. You already know."

He moved away from me on the bench, so he could look into my face. I could see the shine of moonlight in his eyes, the gold of it touching his dark hair.

"Yes, I do know," he said gently. "I don't want you to commit yourself until you're very sure. That's why we must talk. I don't want to hurt you—yet if we go on, there's nothing but hurt ahead. There's no sure commitment I can make, with things as they are. I can't promise anything, Lindsay. You have to understand that."

"I do understand," I told him warmly. Just

the same, he was right—I didn't really. And perhaps he didn't either. There were all kinds of commitments—large and small, and I was ready to make the largest, and accept the smallest, if that was the way it had to be. I had never thought I could feel like this.

"I *want* you to stay," he went on. "But you'll have to do it with your eyes open. Sybil will cause trouble. I had something of a show-down with her a little while ago, though all that came out of it was her promise to injure me in any way she could. Of course I didn't bring you into it, but she's already guessed how I feel. That's why I came to offer you a lift to Phoenix tomorrow if you want to go. You'd be better out of it."

"I'm not going," I said.

He cupped my cheek gently with one hand. "I don't know the answer. Not yet. I'll try to find one. I promise you that."

Again I sensed his rising anger, frightening in its strength, carrying a current of purpose that I began to dread. I didn't know what he might do against Sybil.

He stood up abruptly. "Let's go back," he said.

Reluctantly, feeling a little dazed, I let him pull me to my feet. It was difficult to return to the reality of this dusky plaza, with only the moon and a few lamps to light it. I looked around, trying to quiet the thudding in my blood. No matter what he'd said, a commitment *had* been made by both of us, and it was only a matter of—days? Hours?

For the first time, I realized that the nearest shop on my left was Silvercloud, and I walked toward its windows, trying to get myself in hand.

The Indian mask stared at me through the glass, its white teeth glimmering in the moonlight, slitted eyes watching me. Rick came up beside me, and as I was about to turn away, something moved in the dim interior of the shop.

"Rick," I said, "There's someone inside."

We both stared intently through the window, but the faint stirring of shadows was not repeated.

"Is Clara working at this hour?" I asked.

"I doubt it. And if she was, she'd have turned on more lights. I'd better have a look. I've got my key."

I followed him into the shop, and just as we stepped inside a sound came from the back as if something was knocked over in the darkness at the rear. Rick flicked switches, and the shop blazed. As he ran into the back rooms, I stood among the counters, remembering the cruel act of vandalism upstairs, as well as the rock that had been thrown at me across the terrace.

With a strange conviction that had little to do with reason, I believed in that instant that everything which had happened was connected. My father's death, Sybil walking an empty corridor that led to his room, Orva's machinations, even the desecrated blue cloth upstairs—and now this. Some connecting thread drew it all together, and no matter what I did, I could not escape being a bead on that thread. Even Brian and his drum were part of it, beating out a rhythm that warmed the blood and lulled the defenses.

When Rick came back, I started as though I'd been in a trance. He didn't pause, however, but rushed outside and was gone for a while as he searched the vicinity. The effort was fruitless, however, and when he returned he explained.

"It's the same sort of entry as upstairs," he said. "A window at the back has been forced. What we heard was a chair being knocked over. Whoever it was could lose himself easily in the courts and passageways until he could get outside. I'll phone Clara to come and see if anything is missing."

While he made the call to the sheriff's office and then to Clara, I waited tensely. Such mischief seemed all too ominous, promising worse. Rick returned to say that Clara had gone to bed early but she would dress and come as soon as she could.

It took a good half hour for her to arrive, and Parker came with her. A deputy followed shortly after—a woman officer who made notes in her book as Clara moved about the shop noting everything with a practiced eye. She had put on Levi's with a zippered windbreaker, and her long hair was free of its braid, caught back with a ribbon. Rick and Parker and the officer went to examine the window at the rear.

"The jewelry counters are locked," Clara mused aloud. "And as far as I can tell, nothing seems to have been disturbed on the shelves or show tables. I'll check my office."

When the others returned, we followed her into the small room where I'd waited earlier that day. Oddly enough, I was the one who discovered what was missing. Perhaps because my memory of it was still so sharp and recent.

"Jed's Fire People isn't here," I said. "Did you move the piece, Clara?"

She went to the shelf where the sculpture had stood. "It was right there when I left today. That *is* what's been taken. But why would anyone take *that?*"

No one had the slightest idea of the answer, Clara least of all. It seemed oddly fateful that something Jed had made was the only thing missing.

When the deputy left, Rick said he would have stronger locks installed right away. "You're sure nothing else has been taken?"

Clara shook her head. "As far as I can tell. I'll check more carefully in the morning. Lindsay, are you really going home tomorrow?"

I wondered if there was a hopeful note in her voice. "No," I said, "not tomorrow." And then I repeated what I'd told Brian. "First I want to know what happened to my father. Clara, may I

173

come and talk with you soon? I mean about that night in Las Vegas when he died?"

She looked startled. "I suppose—if you like. Though there's nothing else I can tell you. All that ground's been gone over again and again. All the questions have been asked."

"Yet something hasn't been answered, has it? There're things no one has ever brought out."

Clara stared at me, but Parker was watching her, and he must have seen the smudges under her eyes.

"Let's go home," he said. "You've had enough for tonight."

We locked up and walked again through the moonlit plaza, but now the enchantment was gone, and only a sense of heaviness and loss remained for me. Rick was still a mystery, and he had moved away from me. I had no idea what the future held for us.

On the drive home, he had little to say, and I wondered if he would always be something of a stranger to me, however well I might come to know him. Was the mystery, perhaps, even a little of his attraction? When we'd met in New York I'd thought of him as a Western man. The impression had grown. He was like his own red rock country—secret, knowing more than was ever revealed, yet at the same time strong and never to be shaken.

When we turned into the drive, lights were on in the house, and lamps burned on either side of the front door.

"Come in for a nightcap," Rick said. "It will help you sleep."

I wasn't sure I wanted to come in. My nerves had been scraped raw throughout this long day. I couldn't take much more, and I was afraid of my own breaking point. Nevertheless, I moved toward the front door as Rick put the car away, but as I reached the step, I came to a stop.

"Rick!" I cried. "Rick, look!"

He was beside me in a moment and we both stared at the object that rested on the bricks of the front step. It was Jed's red sandstone sculpture—the Fire People. Whoever had taken it from the store had brought it directly here and left it in this conspicuous place while we talked to the police and Clara searched her shop.

"I'll take it inside and return it to Clara tomorrow," Rick said.

"But what can it mean? Why should a thief bring it here?"

The door was pulled open suddenly, and Sybil stood on the threshold, her fitted green robe flowing about her, and her fair hair as beautifully combed as ever. She too was staring at what Rick held in his hands, and her reaction was extreme.

"Why are you bringing *that* into the house?" she demanded.

"There's been some mischief," Rick said, walking past her. "Someone stole this from the store tonight and left it on our doorstep."

Sybil's control vanished astonishingly. "Take it away! Get rid of it! I've always hated that thing. I knew from the beginning that Jed made it only to spite me."

I remembered what Orva had said about a war of nerves that might cause Sybil to betray herself. It looked as though the war was already under way.

"I'll leave it in the trunk of the car," Rick told her. "Wait for me, Lindsay. I want to talk to you about tomorrow."

He carried the Fire People outside, and I followed Sybil into the living room, aware that she was close to the cracking point.

She made a last effort to control her voice as she spoke. "I've talked to Orva on the phone. She *is* a little crazy, you know. All that nonsense about getting you here. But don't think I'm not aware of why you really came. And I want you away—at once. Never mind the dinner, or anything else! Pack your things and get out!"

I asked a single question. "You *were* in Dad's room that night in Las Vegas, weren't you?"

She was so angry that I thought for a moment she might strike me. It was as if we'd slipped back in time to when I was a small girl and a bigger, stronger sister could indulge her cruelties without any fear of reprisal. For just an instant I was afraid, because I knew she was capable of anything—including Jed's death.

"Did you hear me?" Her voice rose shrilly.

"I want you out of my house immediately."

"I'll leave in the morning," I said, and moved toward the terrace door.

"You'll do nothing of the kind!" Rick had returned and he'd heard her words as he came down the room. "You forget this is my house too, Sybil. Lindsay is welcome here."

She answered him sharply, though she managed to bring down her voice. "My lawyer called me today. If you go ahead with divorce proceedings, Rick, I'll make you regret it. God knows, I don't want you as a husband, and I'll be happy to have you leave this house whenever you like. I mean to go on living here, and Marilla stays with me."

Again I moved toward the door, not wanting to hear any of this.

Sybil stopped me. "Wait, Lindsay. You need to listen to the rest. You're forgetting something too, Rick. If you take one more step I'll go to Parker. I'll tell him about you and Clara, and that will fix this silly idyll of theirs nicely. Parker's very old-fashioned."

"It's not a good idea to threaten me," Rick said.

"But that's what I'm doing! Don't you think I know what's going on between you and Lindsay? I'm no fool. It's been pretty easy to go over the bridge and into her bed whenever you please, hasn't it? That's going to stop."

A dark flush had risen in Rick's face and I could see the tightened muscles around his mouth. I came back to sit on the edge of a chair, not daring to leave now. Because if she pushed Rick too far . . .

"I only wish it were true," he said grimly.

Something about his tone must have warned her that she could go no further. She whirled about and stalked out of the room, leaving devastation behind her.

Rick poured us each a brandy and brought me mine. I felt torn, lacerated—and furiously angry.

"You shouldn't have been subjected to any of this," Rick said.

"I knew her before you did," I reminded him. "I know what she can do."

"I never knew her at all. I don't think anyone ever has. Lindsay, I want to tell you about Clara."

"You don't have to tell me anything."

"I'd like you to know. Clara has a generous heart and a hot temper. There was a time some years ago when we were both lonely, and we were working together. She knew what Sybil was like. For a little while we comforted each other. It was nothing more than that, but I'm fond of her and I owe her a lot. I don't want to see her hurt. Sybil knows this, and she's right about Parker, I'm afraid. I'm not sure how he would take it if he knew that I was a man in Clara's life—however briefly. Not when she works for me now. But, even more important than that, I can't allow Sybil to harm Marilla, as she surely will if she's not stopped. I may have to call off my lawyers."

My anger against my sister had never been so great. I was Rick's ally now, wholeheartedly. "She's got to be stopped," I said. "There'll be a way. Orva told me today that Sybil was in Jed's room the night he died. Orva saw her come out of his room."

Rick waited, questioning.

"It was Orva who sent me those notes," I said. "But she doesn't know anything—not really."

The torment in Rick's face made me utterly sad, yet there was no comfort I could offer him.

"Are we still going to Flagstaff tomorrow?" I asked.

He answered without spirit. "Yes, Alice Spencer is expecting us. But I can cancel the trip if you want to go home to New York. I won't blame you for leaving now."

"Let's go to Flagstaff. If Alice is part of your plans, then she's part of mine too. I'd like to meet her. We have to go on with our lives somehow. Sybil isn't invulnerable, and there'll be a way. Though I'll move out of this house as soon as I can."

"Thank you, Lindsay," he said, and I heard the pain in his voice.

I didn't want his thanks. I wanted only what I couldn't have.

"I'm going to bed," I told him and stood

up as weariness surged through me.

"Right—you're nearly out on your feet."

He saw me across the bridge to my door and left me there quickly.

When I was in bed, I lay on my back and stared at the ceiling, unable to sleep. I fought to put the ugly scene with Sybil out of my thoughts, and tried to slip back in time to those tender moments beside a fountain in Tlaquepaque. Rick had said that he loved me. That was all that mattered. That was the thought I must hold on to. I must not think of Sybil's vengeance.

Perhaps these gentler imaginings helped me at last to fall asleep, and the early night hours slipped away.

Then, quite suddenly, I was wide awake again, with all drowsiness gone, and a vivid picture uppermost, insinuating itself into my consciousness. A totally irrelevant memory of Brian Montgomery beating an Indian drum that my father had given him. With a maddening insistence the rhythm of the drum echoed through my mind—over and over, unendingly.

And Vermilion was there. *Listen. Listen to the drum!*

I was never going to sleep with this pounding in my head, and at last I got up and went into the kitchen, seeking hot milk. But instead of taking the carton from the refrigerator, I stood at the counter beside the sink and let my fingers tap on stainless steel.

The sound wasn't right. I took a wooden spoon from a rack, and without even smiling over my own compulsion, I tried Brian's drum rhythm on the steel. It didn't work. There was none of the resonance that taut rawhide over a hollow log could give. A drum had its own individual voice. The metallic sound was flat, and there was no *soul* to speak out to me.

Nevertheless, I found the simple rhythm of the drum. *Beat, pause,* and then quickly, *beat-beat-beat.* Always the emphasis on the first beat, with an instant's pause, followed by three beats. Over and over, hypnotically.

I broke the spell by trying other combinations that Brian hadn't played. I followed the first beat with a single, lighter beat. Then I tried it with four quick ones. It was never the same. My senses were confused, not satisfied, and I returned to the first rhythm until I seemed to float upon the sound, with nothing real about me.

Then, almost of its own accord, the rhythm changed to the quicker, more insistent beat that Brian had played toward the end: *BOOM, beat-beat; BOOM, beat-beat.* Somehow a call to action, to arms, to war—to love?

I seemed to become a part of the sound, as Vermilion was a part of it—so that it burned through me, throbbing with every pulse of my blood. In the cool night, I felt unbearably warm, and I flung down the spoon and ran into the outside air.

On the deck there was no wind. The coolness of the mountains was on my face, relieving the beat of my blood a little. Mushroom lamps shed a dim radiance on the terrace. Lamps that probably burned all night. In the darkness against the terrace rail I saw another light—a tiny red glow that could only be the end of a cigarette. I had never seen Rick smoke, but I knew he stood there now, staring up at dark rock shapes, unable to sleep, as I too could not sleep.

Vermilion glittered in my mind, urging, pushing. This time I was strong enough to erase her—to wipe her out of my consciousness completely. This choice was mine, and only mine.

I stood for a moment longer, watching, while the echo of Brian's drum thudded through me. Then I ran inside to pull on a coat and hurried across the bridge in my slippers. He heard me coming and turned. I didn't hesitate. The moon had long since set, but the lamps and the glow of his cigarette guided me as I ran directly into his arms. The last I saw of the glow was when he dropped the cigarette to the tiles.

He held me with the hunger of long emptiness, and yet with a touch that was gentle and tender. When he kissed me I knew that nothing else mattered. Together we crossed to the guesthouse, and at the end of the bridge he stopped, looking up at the sky.

Air that had seemed quiet a moment before

rustled through the canyon and there was a stirring of leaves, a sighing.

"The wind comes up at dawn," Rick said. "You can see the sky is lightening a little."

I understood. He was giving me time to draw back before it all became irrevocable. Except that it was already too late for that. I put my hand on his arm and drew him toward the open door.

8

When I woke up it was bright morning and Rick was gone. I had a faint, sweet memory of his kissing me one last time and then slipping away before the house should waken.

I'd slept deeply until nine o'clock, when I'd come wide awake with all my memories happy ones. For a little while longer as I bathed and dressed, reality could be held away. All the questions, all the insurmountable problems, could wait while I moved about bemused, reliving the lovely hours of the night. Vermilion was there again, ready to gloat, but I could laugh at her. She'd had nothing to do with last night.

I'd never dreamed that a man with so much darkness in him could be so loving, so careful of me. Yet so exciting. And of course he was all I'd ever wanted. Afterward, I lay in his arms with my head in the hollow of his shoulder, and we'd talked for a long while, not wanting to waste in sleep the precious moments of getting to know each other. Sometimes we'd even laughed a little—as we'd done when I was very young. Strange to find there was still the possibility of laughter in our lives.

Today on the drive to Flagstaff I would be alone with him for as long as we were gone, and this I looked forward to. I didn't want to think of Jed, or about what Orva had told me, or of Sybil's vindictiveness last night. I didn't want to remember my father's carving left on the doorstep—because someone knew it would frighten Sybil? Yet as I came more fully awake, everything crowded back and the doubting began.

Rick and I could not easily have each other, and I wouldn't know until I saw him again how he would feel by daylight about what had begun so recklessly on the terrace last night. For the first time the other side of the coin became all too clear in my mind. Had we allowed Sybil to goad us into each other's arms too soon, and might this not drive us apart?

As I dressed I took special care, wanting to please Rick, wanting him to *like* me. My silk blouse was the color of a poinsettia, and I tucked it into slim-tailored beige slacks. Then I tied back my dark hair that was so unlike Sybil's, with a ribbon of the same poinsettia shade, and was ready. Clothes, as always, were my armor.

Vermilion spoke clearly in my mind. Last night I had held her back, but now she seemed free of my will. *You'll need weapons today, as*

185

well as armor. You mustn't let him get away.

Be quiet, I told her. *I won't hold him with tricks.*

This time she wouldn't obey. *This is your chance to beat Sybil forever. Don't fluff it. Play your cards properly. Let me in and I'll help you.*

But I no longer wanted to pretend to be Vermilion—I only wanted to be *me.* I must be the one Rick came to love, if that was ever to be possible. This was no game, to be cleverly played and scored.

I spoke out loud "Go away! There's nothing I want from you."

Her laughter sounded sulky as she faded out, and I was thankful for her silence. Vermilion had become my make-believe friend because she indulged me in all that was self-seeking, self-promoting. At least I could see this now, and sense the division between us. I was almost ready to let the gap widen, to let her fall into the void where she belonged. Soon, soon, I must take this step.

I turned my thoughts quickly away, lest I stir her up again, still troubled by this mystery of her being that lay deep inside me, and fearful to test this, in case I might not yet be ready to be free.

When Rick came, I saw at once that the black mood was upon him again. He had shut himself away as completely as though last night had never been, and I dared not presume by so much as a touch or a word on what had happened between us. There was to be no privilege of intimacy—that was clear. And this could only mean that he regretted.

When we were well away from the house, he told me as he drove what was wrong.

"Sybil knows where I was last night. She was waiting for me when I left you this morning. She was sitting in the living room waiting. She got up very early for her, and she went to my room and found my bed empty."

I made a small sound of dismay.

"I'm afraid I've played into her hands," he said dully. "What happened was right, Lindsay —you mustn't think anything else. Though that may be small consolation now. She has to be stopped from the moves she plans. She has to be stopped—somehow."

"Be careful," I said. "Oh, Rick, do be careful."

He reached out to cover my hand with his. His touch was light and it lasted only a moment, but it told me he loved me and he hadn't forgotten. His deepening rage had nothing to do with me, yet it frightened me nevertheless. Sybil might push him too far, and I didn't think he was a man one could push for long with impunity. I was glad we would both be away from Sedona for part of the day.

The drive north through the canyon was spectacularly beautiful. We crossed the bridge over Oak Creek, and for a while followed steep red cliffs that rose straight from the water. When we left the canyon behind, we climbed a switchback road through tremendous forests of white pine, and the air grew purer, rarer.

Just as my first glimpse of Sedona's red rocks had been something to remember, so was my first view of the San Francisco Peaks—those dead volcanoes that formed a backdrop for Flagstaff, with the city set out in neat grid precision below the mountains.

Our long silence while Rick drove had helped a little. He could speak more easily now.

"Those are the highest mountains in Arizona, and there's usually snow up there," he told me. "The Hopis believe that those who die with pure hearts will go to be with their ancestors on those snowy peaks."

I watched the long strip of mountains as we drove toward them and thought of the legendary spirit home they represented to those who had lived here before the white man came.

But as we neared the city, the coming meeting with Alice Spencer began to take on more reality for me.

"It might help," I told Rick, "if I could understand why Alice was hesitant about seeing me. Had she known my father?"

"I'll tell you a little about her," Rick said. "Her Indian great-grandparents lived at Oraibi, northwest of Flagstaff. There's a place named Black Mesa that reaches three fingers toward the south—First, Second, and Third Mesas. Old

Oraibi is at the tip of Third Mesa, with New Oraibi in the valley below. Old Oraibi is the oldest continuously lived-in settlement north of Mexico. The word Hopi comes from Hopituh, which means the Peaceful People, and they have a culture and a heritage that's very ancient. You'll be learning about them.''

There seemed a strange intensity in his words, as though the information he was giving me had some particular portent that I didn't understand. I listened as he continued, and my anxiety about meeting Alice Spencer grew.

''Alice's Hopi grandmother came outside to marry a white man. So Alice's mother was half Indian. Then her mother in turn married an Anglo, which diluted the blood still further. Something which Alice resents. She'd rather be three quarters Hopi and really belong to those she regards as her people.''

''I'm glad to know about her,'' I said, feeling oddly formal now, as though Rick were a stranger I'd just met. ''You haven't answered my question about whether she knew Jed.''

Rick went on as though he hadn't heard me. ''Alice has been a full professor, teaching Indian subjects at the university in Flagstaff. As I've told you, she wants to use her talents by working directly with her people.''

''Did she know my father?''

We had left the highway at an intricate cloverleaf and were on the edge of the city— with the great peaks looming close. Rick slowed

189

the car and pulled over to a curb.

"I'd meant to wait for Alice to tell you herself—if she chose to. Perhaps I'd better prepare you. A few years ago Alice had a young protégée in one of her classes. Though the girl had no family, her mother had left her a little money when she died."

Rick paused, and I waited for him to go on, somehow dreading what was to come. I was right to be fearful.

"Lindsay, this may be hard for you. The girl was in the car with your father when he had that accident in San Francisco. She was the woman who was killed."

I felt cold with shock. I had never wanted to know about the woman. I had been sad for my mother's sake, and fiercely angry as well. I hadn't wanted to read about the woman who had died, or know about her. Now, suddenly, she had an identity, and she had evidently been dear to Alice Spencer, whom we were going to see, and who was so important to this plan of Rick's.

"Alice must have hated my father," I said.

"She's never talked to me about what happened. And she *has* told me to bring you to see her. It's better to go through with this and put it behind you, Lindsay. Alice is a woman with a great heart—you can tell that by her paintings."

"She has a great anger in her as well. That also shows in her work. Of course I'll go. Just drive slowly, please, so I can have a little more time to get ready."

Rick did as I asked and we followed the streets of Flagstaff at a leisurely pace until he pulled the car to the curb before a one-story gray house, uninspired in architecture, with bright planters of geraniums and begonias on the front porch.

"Here we are," Rick said, and reached over to touch my hand. I sensed his concern and was grateful.

"I'm all right," I assured him. "This is just one more thing tied to Jed that I must deal with."

"You'll deal with it. And more when you have to."

He sounded grim again, and I braced myself as I got out of the car. Together we went up the walk to the front steps.

Alice Spencer appeared at the door to greet us and I was aware of a woman who was beautiful in a quiet way. Large dark eyes were framed by long lashes, and she wore her black hair short and softly curled. Delicate turquoise earrings dangled from her ears and her sand-colored shirtdress made a perfect background for an exquisite necklace of silver and turquoise in the squash blossom design.

As she extended her hand and I took it, I could sense her intensity and knew that she was as uneasy about this meeting as I. For an instant I thought I had seen her somewhere before, then the impression vanished as she moved and spoke.

"The day is lovely, so let's sit out here on the porch and talk. I'm glad you've come, Rick, and that you've brought Lindsay Phillips. I want to know more about what you're planning."

She had a quiet assurance about her, a certain authority that perhaps came from her years in a university classroom. There was no way in which I could feel comfortable, however, and as we sat down in rustic chairs, I could think only of Jed and the accident in San Francisco. It seemed too much to hope that this attractive woman would not hold my relationship with my father against me.

Rick was watching, reading me again. "Before we talk about anything else, I think we ought to clear the air. Alice, I've told Lindsay that your young protégée, Celia Brooks, was killed in a car accident when Jed was driving."

"Yes?" Alice Spencer waited, her expression grave. I had no idea what she was thinking, or how she felt toward me. I only knew I had to speak, had to apologize in some way.

"My father hurt a great many people," I said. "I'm terribly sorry about your friend."

She seemed to stiffen a little, as she spoke quietly. "Jed was trying to help Celia because I'd asked him to. I should have know better. I should have remembered—" She broke off, sighing, and then went on. "He was completely

192

shattered by what happened that rainy day. Not just his body in the hospital. His spirit too. He didn't care about his own injuries, once he knew that Celia was dead.''

I heard deep sadness in her voice over the loss of this young girl whom she'd tried to help. She seemed to be blaming herself more than she did Jed. Nevertheless, the dark eyes that watched me were appraising—perhaps judging *me* in some way.

The years of bitter resentment against my father seemed to press in on me. Years that had made the accident just one more count against him. I had never let him talk to me about what had happened, protective as I was of my mother. I'd known he would make excuses, perhaps berating himself for his own failings, wanting to be forgiven. Only this time the result of his actions had been far worse than usual.

"He really did suffer over what happened," Rick said.

I could only answer him dryly. "I know. He always suffered.''

Alice continued with the same cool reserve. "Jed was ready to help whenever he was needed—which is why I asked him to look out for Celia in San Francisco and see if he could open some doors for her. She had a notion about working in the theater, and he knew a lot of people in show business.''

It was strange to realize that Alice's coolness toward me grew not so much from what Jed had caused, but because I'd judged him harshly. This was something I couldn't deal with.

Rick must have glimpsed my confusion, for he turned to the matter that had brought us here. Clearly, he and Alice had discussed some of this before, and now my role as a designer was being considered. While Alice's manner toward me was not particularly warm, she seemed to accept what Rick was suggesting.

"You're what we need," she told me. "I'm good at a loom myself, and I can teach others. But I couldn't design a dress in a way that would appeal to the fashion market. The Pueblos have a heritage of fine weaving, though it's dying out in most places. The Hopi are still making textiles, and these days, of course, the women weave too. I want to see this continue and develop."

She took us inside to show us her loom, on which cloth with the zigzag pattern of formalized lightning was appearing. I had brought a few of my sketches and she examined them with interest. I liked the way her face could light with eagerness, and animation could come into her voice and manner as the coolness fell away.

"This is all wonderfully promising," she told Rick. "I'm eager to get started. How do we go about it?"

"Perhaps you could come to Sedona?" I suggested hesitantly. "Rick is fixing a workroom for me there, and once I have the materials and my tools, I can begin seriously. I'll need a lot of advice right away."

"I'm sure Alice will come," Rick said, and she nodded.

"This can be good for everyone," she agreed. "Pueblo life is hard. There are rules and standards to live by, and the individual is never as important as the group. Today many have moved out to work at regular jobs—for the Santa Fe Railroad, in motels and hotels, even as owners of stores. There can still be psychological problems connected with the past, and there's some alcoholism—though not as much with the Hopi as with other tribes. They're pretty well adjusted, and I hate to see the old talents lost."

Alice spoke with regret, and I could sense in her the same depth of feeling that I'd glimpsed in her paintings. Though I wanted to like her, I still felt her reserve toward me, even when she warmed to Rick's burgeoning ideas.

Next she took us into her studio, where a canvas stood on its easel, a worktable was strewn with paint tubes, and there was an odor of turpentine.

"I saw your paintings at Silvercloud in Sedona," I told her. "They're very moving."

"Silvercloud," she said, and turned from the painting she was studying to look at me rather strangely.

"You remember, Alice," Rick said quickly. "That's the name Jed suggested for our shop in Sedona.''

She nodded. "Yes, of course I remember. It just startled me for a moment." But she didn't say why, and we returned to sit on the porch for a while longer as further details were discussed. She promised to come to Sedona soon to work with me. When she'd seen what I wanted to do, she would return and talk to the family she had in mind.

I couldn't let go of the thing that concerned me most, and I broke in to ask her a direct question. "How did you come to know my father?"

Her response seemed strangely "Indian." She was silent, with her eyes cast down, and Rick answered for her lightly.

"You forget, Lindsay—Jed knew everyone."

A moment of strain seemed to have passed safely for Alice with his words. Clearly she wanted no more questions, and she rose with the grace that was natural to her.

"Excuse me for a moment. I'll bring tea and something else I've fixed for you especially."

When we'd returned to the porch, and she had gone into the house, I questioned Rick. "Why did she react as she did when I asked how she'd met Jed?"

He shook his head. "Not now, Lindsay. This isn't the time. I'll tell you later."

Once more I felt impatient with this holding back, but in a few moments Alice returned with a tray that she set down on the porch table, and I tried to put my frustration aside.

"I've made *piki* especially for you, Rick," she said. "And I thought Lindsay might like it too. I learned how one time when I visited Oraibi. Though I think it's better when hot stones are used."

She poured a fragrant herbal tea, scented with orange peel, and served us the layered bread made of blue cornmeal that I found delicious. Rick talked of his plans and as always I realized how much all this meant to him.

Away from Sybil, he could seem warmly alive again—an eager, vital, creative man. Watching him, I knew how much I wanted to help in any way I could, whether there was a future for me with him or not. Already I was a part of his life, even though, in spite of last night, he had not fully let me in.

A short time later we parted with Alice and went out to the car for the drive home. When we were on our way, I made no further effort to control my impatience.

"Tell me, Rick, tell me what you're holding back from me!"

"Wait," he said. "Just a little while longer. Time moves fast enough as it is. At least Alice liked you. I'm glad of that."

I wasn't sure he was right, but my main concern now had yet to be answered, and the very fact that Rick held back from telling me suggested depths I might not be prepared for.

We drove through the streets of the city,

past buildings of Coconino sandstone, and very quickly we were on the highway heading for home. Which would mean further encounters with Sybil, and difficult decisions to be made. Rick had said I needn't move out in a hurry— but move I would.

My waiting came to an end when we were once more driving through Oak Creek Canyon and nearing Sedona. Rick found a place where he could leave the car, and we climbed down to where the creek flowed between rocky banks, and canyon walls rose steeply above us. Noonday sun reached into deep recesses, erasing the shadows, while cooling blue water ran at our feet. Great flat slabs of rock edged the water.

"They call this Slide Rock," Rick said. "In summer there're always swimmers and sunbathers here. But it's empty now—a good place to sit and talk."

Above us, the broad, slanting rock plunged toward the water, and I looked up at painted cliffs. "Look! There are heads in the rock— faces—almost like sculptures. Are these the Fire People?"

"No, Marilla's friends are a long way from here. These are what she calls People Rocks. You'll see them everywhere—all carved by nature. Come on up, Lindsay, there's a ledge at the top where we can sit."

I let him pull me up the steep slant and sat down beside him, uneasy now that the moment was nearly here. The quiet was that of any wild place, with a few birds talking among themselves and water murmuring below. The rock was warm beneath my hand.

"Do you like Alice?" Rick asked.

I'd known that what he had to say would be connected with Alice Rainsong. "Very much. At least, I wanted to. I'm not sure she was willing to let me like her."

"She couldn't be sure about you, either. Lindsay, there's no way to tell you except simply and directly. It's way past time."

I put my hand on his arm and he covered it with his own as he'd done in the car. "It's Jed, isn't it? Something else my father has done?"

"Alice Spencer is your sister. Your half sister, just as Sybil is, because—"

I couldn't grasp what he was saying right away. "You mean because Jed was her father?"

"No, Lindsay. Just listen to me. You and Alice had the same mother. Your mother's Indian name was Silvercloud. *Her* father was an Anglo-American, her mother Hopi. She married Alice's Anglo father, who deserted her before Alice was born, and was never heard from again. When Jed came into her life he became something of a father to Alice, and she was devoted to him. He bought them that little house in Flagstaff. If circumstances had been different, I think he would have married Mary Silvercloud. But that was never possible."

"So he just hurt my stepmother by staying away," I said bitterly.

"You can see your stepmother only through your own loving eyes. You see her the way you want to see her. But you can't possibly see her with Jed's eyes. I'm not judging. I never knew her well. I did know Silvercloud long ago when I was a small boy. She was beautiful and loving. Alice looks a lot like her. She was a highly intelligent woman with a great deal of courage and generosity. Alice adored her, and it was terrible for her when you were born and her mother died. She was only ten. Terrible for Jed too, when he lost her. There was a Hopi family in Flagstaff who took Alice, but Jed always looked after her, even though she wasn't his daughter by blood, and he saw that she got a good education. You he brought home to his wife, who must also have had courage and generosity."

And very little fight in her, I thought sadly. Though the very fact that she had been submissive had given me a home and a loving mother. I didn't think I could be as generous in like circumstances.

"Why was I never told?"

"Your mother was against telling you when you were small. Jed wanted to bring you out here and tell you himself, have you meet your sister. I'm sorry if I've done this badly, but it's long past time for you to know."

I looked across the creek up to more high red cliffs, with blue sky and white clouds above. Arizona! Then I looked down at my own arms browning in the sun. In what way did my mother's blood show in me? I thought with growing wonderment that my real mother had been half Hopi. On the Indian side she had come from a culture that went back a thousand years and more into the past on this continent, where Jed's people were newcomers. Some of me belonged to that history. Some of me belonged to the true Americans.

Whatever I was feeling must have showed in my face and reassured Rick.

"It's going to be all right, isn't it?" he said.

I could only smile at him, though tears welled up in my eyes. "I can't take it in all at once. A little while ago, part of me was a blank because I had no way to fill it in. The half of me that came from my real mother I couldn't know about. Now there's something, where there was nothing before. I know a lot of this will be troubling because it will be strange, and sometimes it may even be shocking, because I'm not used to it. I don't know anything about my mother's people on the Hopi side. Now that I know it's there, I can learn. I can really learn, if Alice will help me."

Rick's arm was about me and I raised my head. I knew that everything I longed for with him would have to wait. What had happened last night was a page out of time and that had somehow slipped in too far ahead. There was still Sybil, and my heart sank a little as I thought of this other sister.

"We go on from here," Rick said, and there was a promise in his words.

On the drive into Sedona I thought for the first time in hours of Vermilion. I'd heard not a word out of her through all this revelation. Had I really subdued her at last? I hoped so, because I would need to be stronger than ever now.

When we reached town, Rick drove first to the shop at Tlaquepaque.

"I'll stop long enough to return Jed's sculpture to Clara," he said. "I never got to call her about it."

I had forgotten about the Fire People in the trunk of the car, and when he parked and took it out I went with him to the shop. Just before he reached it, I thought of another question that had to be asked.

"This is what Sybil knows, isn't it, Rick? I mean, about the relationship between Alice and me?"

"Yes. This is what she meant to spring on you at her dinner. She could never understand that it might not devastate you—as *she* would expect it to."

I felt a certain relief as I followed Rick into the shop. At least Sybil's supposed "weapon" had been blunted. Though she would never understand why.

Clara's eyes widened at the sight of what Rick carried in his hands. She came with us back to her office. I tried to dismiss any thought about her and Rick. That had no relevance now.

"Where did you find that?" she demanded, taking the sandstone sculpture from him and examining it carefully for any damage.

"Whoever took it from the store went directly to leave it on our doorstep," Rick told her.

Clara could look rather sly at times. "Did Sybil know it was left there?"

"She saw it when I carried it into the house, and she was upset."

"I'm not surprised," Clara said. "You may not know it, but Jed put a sort of voodoo on that piece as far as she was concerned. I think you were away, Rick, the time when Marilla persuaded her mother to come with her to see the 'real' Fire People. We all went out there on a picnic. Brian took us in a jeep and brought his mother along. This was before I'd met Parker. Jed was at his best that day, and he had fantastic stories to tell about some of those rocks. Things he made up as he went along, of course." Clara reached out to touch the central figure in the carving. "He had a name for this fellow, you know. He called him the Shining One, and he told Sybil that *he* was watching her and she'd better be careful or he might freeze her into the rock too."

"That doesn't sound like anything that would throw Sybil," I said.

"I'd have agreed," Clara went on. "But Jed had a way of getting under her skin. He never really liked her, you know, even if she was his daughter. He gave her the carving because he wanted to frighten her."

This was still another count against Jed, I thought. He had been capable of deliberate cruelty.

Rick was shaking his head. "I've never known Sybil to be superstitious."

Clara agreed. "You're right. It takes imagination to be superstitious. But Jed kept insisting that the Fire People would always search her out and watch her. Couldn't she *feel* them watching? He got through even her thick skin. So she put the thing out of her sight as fast as she could by giving it back to Jed, who gave it to me. What Sybil doesn't understand makes her uncomfortable. So I expect her old feeling about it came back when it was left on your doorstep. Retribution, and all that kind of thing."

"I don't know," Rick said. "More likely, it was the idea that someone wanted to get at her through the carving that upset her. I wonder if she knows who it might be?"

I had gone to stand closer to Jed's carving, and I could see that he really had given the face of that awesome central figure a special shining look as it gazed at the sky. There was an eeriness about it that disturbed me—because when he chose, Jed could be as cruel as he could be generous and kind. And he had meant this as something that would haunt Sybil.

When we left the store and drove back to Rick's, I was relieved to find that she was out.

204

A showdown of some sort was certainly coming, and I needed to be ready for it. Nevertheless, I was glad for the postponement. There was too much that I needed to explore and understand before I could be ready to face my other sister.

Marilla was still at school, and Rick had made an appointment in the afternoon, so he drove away as soon as he'd left me at the house.

For once, I was glad to be alone. In my bedroom I stood for a few moments looking at myself in the mirror—searching as I'd done when I stared at my arms after Rick had told me. Her Indian heritage showed in Alice's beautiful face—in the very modeling and breadth of her cheekbones. It didn't show in mine. My hair was black, my eyes greenish like Jed's and the shape of my face was like his, to the very cleft in the chin. What traces did blood heritage leave in the flesh, the spirit, the genes? A quarter part of me was Hopi. Yet only my familiar self looked back from the glass—that self which had grown up in New York and knew nothing at all of the great red rocks outside my Sedona windows. Or of a pueblo called Oraibi.

Yet something seemed changed. At this moment something about me seemed softer, gentler, more ready to be loving—and I knew why. "Oh, Rick," I said, and turned away from the mirror.

When I'd found another book about the Pueblos, I sat down and began to read with new involvement. I wanted to learn about a people whom I'd scarcely known existed, whose problems I'd never considered—who were now my people.

As I read, Rick's face sometimes came between my eyes and the page, and I wanted to fall into a reverie about last night. I dared not. Rick had not been entirely unloving today, but he had held me away.

An hour or two later, I put my book aside, knowing that I'd barely touched the surface. It was time now for me to go over to the house and see if Sybil had returned. I wanted to confront her as soon as I could. Since she no longer had anything to hold over me, I must make her tell me about that night in Las Vegas.

As I went outside I saw movement on the deck, and Brian came around to meet me.

"I just wanted to check about our jeep trip tomorrow," he said. "Is it still on?"

I'd forgotten about it. "As far as I know," I told him, and wondered if this was his real purpose for being here.

"What's up with Sybil?" he went on. "Do you know?"

"What do you mean?"

"She came over to see Ma this morning. I was out, so I didn't talk to her. Ma seemed upset afterwards and wouldn't tell me what it was all about."

"I haven't seen Sybil. I drove to Flagstaff with Rick this morning."

Brian didn't seem interested in our trip. "Sybil's not around, though I had a sort of appointment with her this afternoon."

"I'm afraid I can't help you." I wanted to end this and be alone.

He saluted me ruefully and went away over the bridge. I crossed to the main house and questioned Consuela. Neither Rick nor my sister had come home as yet, and there were no messages.

Sybil was gone all afternoon, but no one became concerned about her absence until dinnertime, when she had neither appeared nor phoned. Calls to friends gave no clues, and around ten o'clock that night Rick reported to the sheriff's office that his wife was missing.

9

I slept badly that night, missing Rick and haunted by thoughts of Sybil. Unhappy, tormenting thoughts. Knowing her as well as I did, I suspected that this "disappearance" meant only that she was up to something new in her war against Rick. And against me. My sister had always been capable of shrewdness and cunning that could wound and damage. I knew very well that more trouble was coming.

Last evening Rick hadn't seemed especially worried about Sybil's absence—at least not outwardly. Perhaps he too was suspicious of this sudden vanishing. Or perhaps he simply didn't want to alarm Marilla, because he didn't phone the sheriff's office until after she had gone to bed. On the phone he admitted frankly that his wife might have gone away on her own and would probably be heard from the next day. Though strangely enough, her red Spitfire was in the garage, so someone else must have driven her. Disappearing without leaving word was unlike her, so he wanted to report it.

I got up early remembering that this was the morning we'd planned to drive into the back country so Marilla could show me the Fire People. Undoubtedly, this would be called off now. As soon as I finished a quick breakfast, I went over to the house.

Rick and Marilla were breakfasting on the terrace, since the morning was already warming. Marilla had left most of the food on her plate. This being Saturday, there was no school, and she was still in pajamas and a short terry robe.

When I said, "Good morning," she didn't look up. Rick pulled another chair to the table and poured me a cup of coffee. Suddenly, intensely, I felt that Vermilion was there, watching, listening.

She'd left me alone for some time, strangely subdued. This disappearance of Sybil's would appeal to her, and I heard the faint whisper: *Maybe she's gone for good.*

I rejected both the idea and Vermilion herself, and spoke to Rick. "Have you heard anything?" I asked.

He shook his head, his eyes on his daughter, who obviously knew by this time that her mother had gone off without leaving any word.

"I don't want to go on the jeep trip," Marilla said, clearly continuing an argument. "Not now. I don't feel like it."

"Look," Rick said patiently, "there's nothing you can do around here. I'll stay by the phone, in case there's any word. I don't think there's anything to worry about. You and Lindsay need to get your minds off this until your mother shows up."

"I don't want to go," Marilla repeated. "I'm scared of that place."

Rick showed his surprise. "You're always begging Brian to take you out there."

"That was when Grandpa Jed used to tell me stories about the Fire People. Mom says it's a bad place, and I shouldn't go there."

I tried to help Rick, knowing how important doing *something* could be at a time like this. "Ever since I heard from you about the Fire People, I've wanted to make the trip to see those cliffs." This wasn't exactly true, but perhaps it would serve. "I can't go if you won't be my guide," I added.

Marilla looked uncertainly at her father.

"It's okay to go," he told her. "When your mother comes home I'll explain to her."

She gave in and got up from the table. "All right. I'll go put on some jeans."

She ran off and Rick looked at me with a question in his eyes. "You're still all right?"

"Of course." That wasn't true either, since I wasn't sure anything would ever be "all right" again.

Consuela came out to the terrace, and Rick signaled that we were through. "Bring your coffee," he said to me. "I want to show you something."

Cup in hand, I followed him into the house and down the length of the living room to where the painting of *The Blue Corn Maiden* hung.

"Alice Spencer painted this," he said. "She did several from snapshots, from memory, and out of her imagination. It's a picture of Mary Silvercloud that she gave Jed, who kept it here. Her mother—and yours."

I looked again at the figure in the blue dress and long white leggings. The young woman's face had drawn my interest when I'd first seen those great dark eyes, the slash of black brows, the lips parted breathlessly. Now I knew why I'd had a sense of recognition when I first met Alice. The resemblance was there. I'd thought of ceremonial drums when I'd seen the picture, and now that seemed all the more likely. By this time I knew something of the spell of a drum, and Alice's brush had given the face, framed by the square-cut black hair, just such a listening look. To believe that the young girl in the painting had become my mother seemed a remote and unlikely thought. To me, she was a costumed stranger, and I didn't know how to bridge the gap emotionally.

"I ought to feel something," I said sadly, "but I don't. I want to reach her, to know about her. I want her to become real for me. How do I manage that?"

"It will happen," Rick said. "Give yourself time. Alice is part of the answer."

Perhaps for me she was the whole answer,

yet I had sensed her coolness toward me, and the way she had held back—perhaps protecting her own pride, her own private feelings about *her* mother. Feelings she might not want to share with me.

Rick drew me away from the portrait to where I could look at the frieze of carved heads that had been placed along a high shelf. I remembered that Marilla had told me they'd come from Oraibi—a name that had meant nothing to me then. I sipped coffee and studied them.

"Your great-grandfather carved those heads." Rick's tone was gentle, careful.

I stared at the brightly painted carvings, and their black eyes seemed to look back at me, their multiple red mouths sneering a little. My great-grandfather on Mary Silvercloud's side had been a full-blooded Hopi Indian and his hands had carved these strange heads.

"It's not in the nature of the Pueblos to do unusual things," Rick said. "The old way is to feel that the family, the clan, is everything. Whether it's pottery, or basket-making, or weaving, the old patterns are used in the same way down the years over and over. One doesn't look for individuality, though that old man did. He wanted to carve heads that were of absolutely no use to anyone, and that no one had ever done before. What's more, he wanted to do *them* over and over."

"How old was he when he carved these?"

212

"In his eighties. This—drive—came on him late in life. He's ninety-six now, and his hands hurt him, but he still carves a little."

"He's still *alive?*"

"Yes, indeed. I've met and talked to him, and so did Jed. No one talks about senility in the pueblo. He is allowed to do what makes him happy. Unlike some of our own old people."

Before I could find anything more to say, chimes rang, and Rick went to open the door to Orva Montgomery.

She came in with her usual long-legged, slightly uncoordinated stride and barely paused to greet us before she flung herself into a chair. Today she wore corduroy pants and a man's shirt with the sleeves rolled up. Sloppy, but comfortable.

"Brian's gone to get a jeep ready," she said. "I couldn't come as long as he was watching me, and I didn't want to talk about it on the phone when he was listening. He knows that Sybil came to see me yesterday morning. I didn't tell him everything. She was mad and looking for a fight, though I didn't give it to her. She rather frightened me." ·

"What did she come for?" Rick asked.

"To tell me her plans for the dinner she wants to give tonight."

"What's dinner got to do with anything?"

"Exactly what I'd like to know. She's been so bent on having us here together. Do you realize that she's inviting only those who were in

Las Vegas the night Jed died? Except, of course, for Parker, who's cooking the dinner. And you, Lindsay. I told her straight out that I'd seen her coming from Jed's room that night. She didn't seem to care. She just wanted to make sure I'd be here tonight and bring Brian. She said she was going to lay everything right out, and that maybe this would shut me up and make me stop writing idiotic notes. She said one of us already knew what happened that night—and we might get a new version."

A flush had come up in Orva's thin cheeks, and when we remained silent—mostly, I think, because we were shocked—she went on doggedly.

"I guess I'd put her on the spot with my suspicions. I wrote those two notes, Rick, as maybe you know. I got Lindsay to come out here because I wanted to stir Sybil up, and I think I have. But now I'm not sure of the result. So I thought you ought to be forewarned about what she means to do. It might be a good idea, Rick, if you get her to call this off for tonight. It might even be dangerous to go ahead."

"Why do you think that?" Rick asked.

"I just think you'd better shut her up before she goes through with it. I'm not going to do or say anything else to upset her. Ever since Lindsay came, it's been out of my hands."

"Sybil didn't come home last night," Rick told her. "We haven't heard from her, so I

214

don't suppose there'll be any dinner party. Perhaps you've hit on a possible answer. It could be that she suddenly realized that she shouldn't go through with this, and simply went off for a while."

"Sybil doesn't run away from things," I said.

Rick nodded. "I was just thinking of possibilities. She'd be more likely to bluff her way through. Anyway, there's no use in speculating until she shows up and tells us herself."

Orva rose, setting thin elbows akimbo. "I'd better be going. I haven't told Brian all of this because he's a fool when it comes to Sybil. Anyway, I've said my piece here, and I've plenty to do."

She went off as quickly as she'd burst in, and as the door closed after her Marilla returned carrying two straw hats. She held one out to me. "I borrowed this from my mother's room. You'd better wear it, Lindsay. The sun gets awfully bright out there and there's no roof on the jeeps. Brian said he'd pick us up, and I think that's his car coming now. Are you ready?"

I thanked her and put on the hat. I'd dressed in slacks, with a short-sleeved blouse, and walking shoes, so I was ready. Marilla ran to fling herself into Rick's arms, and he held her tenderly for a moment.

"Don't worry," he said. "Just think about Jed's stories."

We reached the door as Brian rang, and went

outside to stand for a moment on the walk.

"There's been no word?" he asked Rick.

"Nothing. Have you any ideas?"

"No, I haven't. She never said anything to me about going off."

In the morning sunlight he looked browner than ever, his hair and beard more sun-bleached. But I never knew exactly what he was thinking.

Rick watched as we drove away, and I looked back, wishing I could have stayed with him—even though he didn't especially want me just now. Like everyone else, he too was a stranger. Under the laughter there must always have been a sense of darkness. Now it seemed to have surfaced for good. Only for a little while had I seen him lose it.

As we drove toward town, with Marilla sitting between us, Brian spoke to her. "Don't worry, kid. Your mother will show up. If anybody can take care of herself, she can." There seemed something a little hard in his voice, and I glanced at him, thinking again that he wasn't as wholly devoted to Sybil as his mother thought. If Sybil had been using him, perhaps in his own way he had been using her to accomplish what he couldn't do alone.

Marilla said, "I know where she's gone. That's why I didn't want to go there today."

I turned to her in surprise. "What do you mean, Marilla?"

She only squirmed a little, as though

sorry she'd spoken.

"You'd better tell us," Brian said quietly.

She hesitated before answering him. "Yesterday, after Lindsay and Dad went to Flagstaff, Mom said she guessed she'd have to have a talk with the Fire People. She said she had something to settle. So maybe that's where she went. But then she never came home, and I'm scared."

Brian put an arm around her as he drove. "I expect she only meant that carving of Jed's somebody left on your doorstep."

I was startled. "How did you know about that?"

He put his hand back on the wheel and stared straight ahead. "Sybil phoned me yesterday before she came to see my mother. She thought I ought to be out of the way when she talked to Ma. She told me what had happened with that carving, and that someone was trying to get at her. She even asked if I knew anything about it."

So Sybil had been suspicious of Brian too?

"And did you?" I said.

He glanced at me over the top of Marilla's curly head and spoke quietly. "No, Lindsay, I didn't."

I had no idea whether his seeming sincerity hid anything more ominous.

Nor could I tell whether Marilla had accepted his explanation. The little girl stared fixedly at the road, and who knew what fantasies she might be concocting in her mind?

I felt increasingly uneasy. There had always seemed a certain eeriness connected with Jed's Fire People, and it might be disturbing to see the real rock faces, even though I was curious about them.

In town we drove to a parking space where three jeeps waited. Two were filling up with passengers, and Brian led us to the third. When he'd seen Marilla and me into the front seat, he went back to his car and opened the trunk. To my surprise, he took out the Indian drum I'd seen at his house and brought it to the jeep, placing it behind us on the floor of the car.

"We're in luck, I think," he said. "I've fixed it so the other jeeps will take the tour parties, and we can probably have this one to ourselves."

When the two jeeps went off loaded, we got aboard our own.

"You can hold on to the overhead rail, Lindsay," Marilla cautioned when we were moving. "You'll need it when we get off the pavement."

I did indeed. Away from Sedona, we left the highway to jounce over a dirt road into the rough growth of the canyon floor. Vegetation grew thick and green, with reddish earth showing underneath, and always the rim of red rocks standing up all around. Some of the growth was scrub oak, Brian said, and a species of manzanita, low and spreading. There was Arizona white pine too, though they didn't grow tall out here.

"Some of these trees can live to be a hundred years old," Brian told us, "and they'll never grow any taller."

I was glad to see that Marilla had cheered up a little since leaving the house. Perhaps she'd forgotten her anxiety about taking this trip.

Brian was mostly silent unless I asked a question, and I had a feeling that he was still thinking about Sybil.

With no roof over us, the sun was hot and bright, but it felt good to be warm in this natural heat. There were places in the rough growth where dead trees stood up starkly, their bony arms pointing. Some had been split to the heart, yet sprigs of green showed here and there on branches that seemed otherwise lifeless.

"Lightning can explode a tree," Brian said, "but it doesn't always kill. These pines resist fire to some extent, so even when there's a storm and lightning strikes, it doesn't always start a blaze."

We jolted along the "road" that wound haphazardly between stunted trees, until the way ended before a high outcropping of rock burning yellow-red in the sun. The rocky horizons had moved farther away as we reached the center of this flat valley. The humped rock looked rather like a beached whale flung onto dry land, with high cliffs cutting into the sky beyond.

"Now we're getting near," Marilla said.

I heard the rising anxiety in her voice and knew what she meant. *Near to the Fire People.* Ever since she'd first told me about the cliffs my father had discovered, I'd had a curiously fateful feeling about them, and it had increased after I'd seen his carving. Yet, inexorably, we drew closer, and I could sense Marilla's growing fear of something that might lie ahead. I wanted to reassure her, in spite of my own misgivings.

Earlier, I managed to hold Vermilion back. Now she was growing strong again, and more insistent. She wanted out. *Her* excitement was my excitement, though I tried to hold that particular door tightly shut.

The two jeeps that had gone ahead were on top of the huge rock, their passengers already moving around with their cameras.

"Hold tight!" Brian warned.

Our own jeep tilted at an alarming angle and then roared its way up the steep side, big tires gripping the rock. We crossed the broad expanse at the top and came to a halt near the other cars. It was good to get out and stretch, though I was more apprehensive than ever, and Vermilion's eager muttering didn't help.

"Watch youself near the edge," Brian said. "Sand makes the stone slippery, and water erosion constantly wears down the surface."

I stayed safely on the flat top, while Brian reached into the back of the jeep and brought out the big drum.

"What's that for?" I asked, my uneasiness growing.

He answered casually enough. "Just a little atmosphere. Sometimes I play it out here where it belongs. Usually the Hopi heat the rawhide at a fire before they use a drum, since moisture makes the sound go flat. But the sun's done that for me." He heaved the drum under one arm and started toward the far edge of the rock. "Come along, you two. Better hang on to Marilla, Lindsay. She's part goat, so don't let her get away."

Marilla, however, showed a reluctance to climb down the rock. She hung back when I started after him down crude steps in the stone, and he stopped at the bottom to look up at her.

"Coming, kid?" he asked.

Still hesitant, she descended the steps, and we followed Brian in single file along the valley floor. Ahead of us, the nearest line of cliffs stood up like tall Egyptian statues carved in yellow-red rock. Under the high sun the color wasn't as fiery as it could be under less brilliant light. These, I knew, were not the Fire People. I had a feeling I would recognize Jed's rocks at once.

Very quickly we were out of sight of the jeeps, picking our way on foot over chips of red stone as we approached the base of the cliffs. The sun beat down on us and the smell of juniper and pine was spicy hot, as though the very vegetation burned.

Blocking our path before we reached the cliffs stood a small forest of blighted trees, grotesque in their deformity, charred where lightning had destroyed them. No sprouting of hopeful green touched these bare limbs. It was as though some unseen hand had set down this barrier of dead trees to give us warning: *Come this far, but no farther.* Vermilion was like a quivering inside me and I shivered as I followed Brian into the trees. When a reaching gray arm caught my hat and lifted it from it from my head, I cried out in startled dismay.

Marilla ran to retrieve it. "The tree did that on purpose," she said slyly. "It's worse the closer we get, you know. I mean, the rocks and the trees, and even the birds—they don't want us here. You can hear one of those scrub jays scolding us now. They have to protect the secret place, if they can."

"Just the same, I'm going on," I said, and she came with me, suddenly walking close, as though, for all her teasing, she feared to be left behind alone.

Brian had reached the base of the cliffs and was scrambling up over loose shale, mounting a slope toward a thin crack in the rocky face.

"Watch it," he called back to us. "This stuff's slippery, but we're not going very high, so you needn't worry about falling." He seemed to disappear into the cliffs as I looked up at him.

My shoes were already smudged with red

dust. The soles were sturdy and until now they'd clung securely to rock surfaces. There was no solid footing here, and I stepped with care, sometimes sliding backward, using my hands to pull me up wherever something solid offered.

When I looked back at Marilla, I saw that her eyes were filled with the excitement of dread.

"This is the secret way!" she cried. "Grandpa Jed found it and he showed it just to a few of us. He found another way too—a way up over the cliffs, though it's dangerous, so he told me never to use it. Mom only came here once, because she hates this place."

Now that she was close, the urge to go through seemed to possess her and she lost all hesitation. Nimble as some small mountain creature, she scrambled up to the crack ahead of me and turned to wave a triumphant hand before she disappeared, just as Brian had done.

A feeling that verged on panic seized me. My feet seemed locked to the stony earth. Not for anything would I climb into that black crevice— and vanish like the others. It was almost as though something atavistic stirred in me, warning me away. Vermilion was growing stronger by the moment, beginning to excite me, so that I had to struggle inwardly to resist her.

Staring up at the cliff, I saw that at some time in the past erosion had opened several fissures in the stone. The one that served as the way in was partly closed at the top, due to a slippage of the worn rock. It looked so narrow that almost any jar might close it completely.

Then, as I hesitated to trust myself to that slanting crack, a sound reached me, muffled a little by the rampart of the cliffs. A sound I knew all too well—the thudding of a drum. On the back of my neck the hairs rose, and I felt cold in the hot sun. I wanted to cry out, "No, Brian, no!" but I knew I could never be heard beyond the rock barrier and the rising beat of the drum. This was a beat that was different from what I'd heard before. Or from the sounds I'd tried to make with a wooden spoon on steel. It seemed oddly irregular, confusing the senses, promising and refusing, all in the same instant.

Instinctively I knew that the most comfortable beat would be one that matched the human heart, the pulsing of blood in the veins. This beating of Brian's drum ignored the natural pulse, yet was wholly insistent, as if calling me back to my own origins. Unsettling, demanding, as though a part of me knew and recognized—responded. The Indian part of me?

I *had* to go on. The Fire People waited beyond the barrier, and that was where some destiny seemed to draw me. I had no will to resist.

The muffled beating continued to summon, to demand, and I pulled myself up through the shale, clinging to any outcropping of rock, grasping at the juniper's prickly growth. The crack, as I neared it, seemed wider than I'd thought, but it was still black in its depths, since rock had fallen in upon itself, and no sunlight seeped in from above. When I stepped through onto the narrow, stony floor of the gap, I could see light ahead—deflected light because the passageway turned in a zigzag path. On either hand the sides reached into darkness overhead and seemed to lean inward. I could see now that there must once have been a slit all the way up, where the erosion of great storms had worn it through. I had the horrid feeling that the slightest tremor would pitch those precariously balanced sides together, crushing me in a monster vise.

The thought made me hurry toward the light. With my hands pushing against rock walls on either side, as though to hold them apart, I felt my way. This wasn't a cave I had entered, but indeed a passageway that led past two turns into brilliant sunlight at last.

"Come on!" Marilla called to me impatiently. "How pokey you are, Lindsay! Hurry up!"

I squirmed through the last narrow gap and stepped into the relief of open air and the blaze of sun that fell into this pocket in the mountain. Marilla smiled and held out her hand, pulling me into the open.

"It's okay," she said. "Mom didn't come here, after all. There's nobody but us. Isn't this a wonderful secret, Lindsay? No—wait! Don't look up yet. Look all around and get used to it first. And listen to Brian's drum."

She was like her own unicorn, I thought, and tried to smile. Part of the time she was lost in make-believe, reveling in unreality. I couldn't feel reassured as I looked around slowly, with no wish at all to raise my eyes to what awaited me.

There was a mysticism in Brian that I'd only glimpsed before. His drum had taken on new and mysterious reverberations, and the echoes of the rock-enclosed space played them back like a hundred drums as the volume rose. The potency of the sound was terrifying. I couldn't bear it—my head would split.

"Stop!" I called to him. "Brian, please stop!"

He stopped instantly, the padded beater with its beribboned end quiet on the rawhide, his hand silencing the vibrations. He had found a slab of stone a little way from the entrance crack and was sitting upon it, with the drum upright between his knees.

"What *was* that rhythm?" I cried. "What does it mean?" The rock walls took my voice and clapped it back and forth in dying echoes.

Brian wore the same lost look that I'd seen before, and there was wonderment in his voice as he spoke. "I'm not sure. My hand seems to know exactly the beat that's wanted. This wasn't anything I've ever tried before. Jed always said this was a haunted place, and I'm beginning to believe it."

I turned away, not liking the look in his eyes.

A large clearing had been left at the heart of the great rock butte, like an oval jewel of red and green, mounted in stone. Its floor slanted unevenly and was rough with shale, the irregular rock cliffs rising all around.

"Now you can look," Marilla said softly.

I raised my eyes slowly to the heights at which she was staring. There they were—as I had known they would be—but far more awesome and intimidating than I'd dreamed. Not even Jed had been able to capture them in his small sculpture as they'd stood here for—a million years?—staring out at eternity.

Above me stood five immensely tall figures carved as if in cinnabar and clothed in long robes, the folds of which were lost in shadow-lined stone. The five heads were etched as clearly as though a sculptor's mallet had been used in gigantic scale. Four of them seemed to me like Indian faces, belonging to the land, to the mountain, and they looked grandly out, far beyond our puny selves. The fifth figure—the central one—the one to which Jed had given the greatest prominence in his carving, was the Shining One.

Its face glowed with blinding firelight as the sun moved up the heavens, spotlighting stone that was smooth and brilliant. Deep eyes looked only at the vaulted, burning blue, and they knew—*everything.* The sense of something beyond the human was overwhelming, and I couldn't move. I could only stare, awed speechless, not a little frightened.

Marilla was still excited. "Grandpa Jed said this was a sacred place—that it belonged to *Those Who Have Vanished*. You know something? He always used to ask permission before he came through the doorway. Maybe it's wrong for us to be here—we didn't ask, did we?"

"I didn't know about asking," Brian said. "I paid homage with the drum, so I think it's all right."

I found myself shaking my head. "No! It's not all right. Something is wrong. Something is terribly wrong!"

Brian and Marilla watched me as I began to move about the space, not looking up at that face now, not tempting the sky, just moving and searching because of a strong current that seemed to flow through me. *She* was pushing me—Vermilion. I walked about, seeking, searching—for what I didn't know, though I dreaded discovery.

When I did find it, it was as though I had been aware all along of what would wait for me here. From where I stood, farther down the oval, I could see what was out of Brian's and Marilla's sight, and what I saw left me sick and trembling.

"Brian—look! Up there!" My hand was shaking as I pointed. "Look behind the first rock figure!"

Pale green shone against red stone, and was

smeared with red dust. I held Marilla back as Brian ran in the direction I pointed. He knelt on the shale, half-hidden by scrub growth. For a long moment the secret place was intensely quiet, with no haunting memory of a drumbeat, but only a strange, high, humming sound.

Marilla clung to me, and we both looked up at a far silver airplane moving against deep turquoise. An entity from another, younger world. Not until the plane was out of sight, leaving the ruled line of a vapor trail behind, did Brian stand up and return to us.

"It's my mother, isn't it?" Marilla whispered.

He touched her shoulder gently. "Yes, honey. You have to be brave now. Can you be very brave?"

"That means she's dead, doesn't it? But why would my mother come here? She hated this place—just as she hated *them* because they made her afraid." Her voice rose, and for an instant her eyes moved upward to the five faces carved in rock that seemed even more fiery now.

I held her tightly, trying to hold on to myself as well. "Marilla, honey, there are things we have to do now. Brian will tell us."

He glanced at me, and then he too turned his eyes upon the high, shining, central face, and said something very strange. "It was destined. It had to be." That mysticism again.

"Brian!" I cried. "Don't talk like that! We must get Marilla back now. You must take us in."

He seemed to return from very far away. "We'll go back to the jeep. I've got a two-way radio there, and I can call for help. Someone will drive you and Marilla home. I'll have to stay until the people from Search and Rescue come. An ambulance can't get in here, so I'll need to show them the way to bring in a stretcher. It's best if you go straight back to the house and tell Rick before someone else reaches him."

Brian picked up his drum, and it made a hollow boom as he lifted it and started back toward the thin, leaning gash that had brought us into this place of death. He slipped in first, and I pushed Marilla up after him. Before I followed, I stood for a moment longer in the open, once more finding the courage to look up at that shining face that stared so mercilessly into the heavens.

"I know who you are," I said softly, and my voice echoed mysteriously against the cliffs. I didn't know what my words meant. Perhaps Vermilion had spoken them. I was afraid of her now—afraid of what she was thinking.

It was true that I'd never loved my sister, but I'd never wished her dead. *Had I?* Almost beseeching, as though I asked the very cliffs for help, I looked again toward where Sybil lay. Horror and regret—and my own sense of guilt—whipped through me.

As I stood there, my eyes picked up a tiny

gleam of metal among red chips of rock. A small object lay halfway to Sybil's body, sparkling in the sunlight.

I stumbled across shale to pick it up and saw that I held a key in my hand. A meaningless bit of metal. When I looked again toward where my sister lay, I was close enough so that I could see her feet and legs extending down the slope on which she had fallen. So dreadfully without motion! The sleeping were never as quiet as this, and the sickness of realization swept through me. She shouldn't have died in this lonely place, with no one to hear any cry she might make, or to help her in her suffering, if she'd died slowly. My sister, whom I'd never known— never wanted to know.

Yet behind my strange, tearless grief and shock lurked something else, something I couldn't even think about yet, which Marilla had already begun to question.

10

I brought the key home with me, but it wasn't until later that I remembered it. Too much intervened before that time.

Brian had reached someone on his radio, and he drove us back to the highway, where a car came shortly to pick us up and take us home. Then he returned to wait for the Search and Rescue team, and to talk with the Coconino sheriff when he came.

I still felt shattered and was trying to pull myself together when Marilla broke the news to her father the moment we entered the house. She ran to him with a torrent of words pouring out, and he listened while she sobbed in his arms.

"I must go wherever they've taken her," he told me over her head. Then to his daughter, "Hush now, darling—I'll be back as soon as I can. In the meantime, stay with Lindsay."

Marilla's sobbing broke out more stormily than ever. For a little while, in the place of the Fire People, she had clung to me for comfort.

Now she repudiated me completely.

"I don't want to stay with *her!* She never liked my mother, even if she was her sister. Mom told me so. Mom told me how mean Lindsay was when she was little. Once she even threw a pair of scissors at Mom!"

I'd put my hand on Marilla's arm in entreaty, but now I took it away. Sybil's poisons were still working.

"Shall I phone Orva?" I asked Rick.

He nodded. "I'm sure she'll come. I'll have to hurry. Marilla, you must try to help now. There's no use saying wild things you'll be sorry for later."

He released himself gently from her clutching hands and went out to his car. The moment he was out of sight, Marilla stopped crying, staring at me with a malice that broke my heart and seemed all too terrible an echo of Sybil.

"You wanted her dead, didn't you? You *always* wanted her dead!"

Had I? Had this child seen through to an ugliness I'd hidden even from myself? Had I always exonerated myself by turning whatever was unpleasant over to Vermilion?

Before I could telephone Orva, she forestalled me by arriving with a squeal of brakes, slamming the car door, and rushing past Consuela into the room.

"Brian phoned me," she said breathlessly. "I thought I might be useful here." She looked at Marilla, who had thrown herself on the sofa face down. "Would you like to come to my house for tonight?" she asked.

The child relaxed a little, though she didn't raise her wet face from her arm.

Orva turned to me. "Brian told me you found your sister. I know you've had a shock, Lindsay. Will you be all right alone for a while?"

"Of course," I said. I couldn't put into words any of the clamor that was swirling through me.

"You go out to the car, honey," Orva said to Marilla with quiet authority. "I'll be with you in a minute. I want to talk to Lindsay."

A little to my surprise, Marilla got up and walked out of the room without objection.

"I'll see if I can quiet her," Orva said. "You look pretty sick yourself. Brian said that Sybil was trying to climb one of those rock columns that Jed called the Fire People. How could she—those cliffs are practically vertical! Besides, how did she get out there anyway?"

Orva looked as grim as Rick, and she was stating the question that must be surfacing in all of us.

"I don't know anything definite," I said.

"No, of course not. At least this will make everything easier for you."

I heard her with a sense of outrage. Nothing would be easier, and her words were callous. My face must have answered for me, because she went on.

"People like Sybil don't change just because they're dead," she said wryly. "The wrongs they started can go on causing trouble for a long time to come. So don't start blaming yourself. What she had in mind was wicked—even her dinner tonight. To repeat Jed's dinner party and bring out everything that happened in Vegas—a cruel exposure for someone. Well, now she won't get the chance."

Her words startled me. Had Sybil died to prevent her from bringing off her plan?

"Anyway," Orva said, "don't worry about Marilla. She can stay with me as long as she likes. Take care, and I'll see you later."

She went away with her curiously rangy gait, her angled elbows reminding me of some bird that was always awkward on land.

Outside, I found a table with an umbrella, where I could sit in the shade. The terrible beauty of the red rocks looked down on me, but there were no faces out there—no one shining face that saw only some terrible destiny. I let my eyes rest on the deep green wash below, where cottonwoods grew, and other growth that needed moisture.

It seemed a long while ago that a stone had come hurtling over this very rail, surely aimed at me. Yet it was Sybil who had died. And was it only yesterday that I'd learned the truth about myself—that Alice Rainsong was my sister? And in what distant lifetime had Rick held me in his arms? I didn't dare think about that.

Everything receded now, paling beside the cruel fact of Sybil's death. New York belonged to another planet. Some instinct told me that with Sybil's death a greater obstacle than ever would come between Rick and me, though I didn't understand then what this new barrier would be.

What was immediate, what was so dreadfully *now,* was the moment when I'd stood in that pocket in the cliffs, that moment when I'd gone to pick up the key and had glanced briefly again in Sybil's direction. That one quick glance had been enough to photograph in my mind what I'd scarcely been conscious of at the time. Now one such detail returned to strike me with shocking force.

Her feet had extended toward me where she lay, and I had seen her shoes. They were white and had been smeared with red dust. They were also flimsy high-heeled sandals that would have been totally impractical for hiking in the back country. If she had known where she was going, she would never have worn shoes like that.

The very fact proved that someone had taken her there. Someone who had contrived her fall?

Consuela appeared, bringing a tray with coffee. There were tears in her eyes as she served me. At least she could cry for Sybil, and that was more than I could do. Horror was still too close and frightening for tears.

All around me the quiet seemed intense. I started at every slight sound, longing for Rick to return with word of some sort. As always, waiting was endless. My mind could take too many anxious, torturing turns, and questions only seemed to multiply. Nor was there anyone I might call to learn the answers.

When the sound of chimes finally rang through the house, I jumped up in relief and ran to the door myself. To talk to someone about anything would be better than this lonely, anxious vigil. But I was disappointed when I saw that my visitor was Parker Hale.

He greeted me cheerily and breezed into the house carrying a large hamper in his hands.

"Hi, Lindsay. Sybil's expecting me. I'll just take this stuff out to the kitchen, and you can let her know I'm here."

I stood staring at him, realizing that he knew nothing about what had happened. He had come to prepare dinner for tonight. Now he saw my face and realized something was wrong.

"What is it?" he asked, sounding petulant. "Don't tell me —"

I broke in on his words. "Sybil is dead."

It was his turn to gape, not believing me.

"Brian and I found her when we took Marilla out to see the Fire People. Sybil must have been climbing out there when she fell."

Parker put his covered hamper carefully on the floor and then threw himself with less care into the nearest chair.

"You'd better tell me," he said.

I gave him what details I could while he

listened morosely. When I finished he mopped his damp face with a handkerchief.

"I'd better call Clara right away."

I nodded toward the phone and he went to dial. I didn't listen because a curious thought had come to me. It was an urge so strong that I couldn't put it aside, no matter how shocking and foolish it might seem. Rick would probably be angry and the others indignant—perhaps one of them frightened—yet I knew I had to go ahead. Perhaps there was a way to discover why Sybil lay dead, and perhaps even what she had known about Jed's murder.

Vermilion was suddenly there, whispering. *Now you're getting smart! Do this—it's the only way,* and I knew the source of my impulse.

Had I been foolish to think that I could now take charge of my own life? At this moment Vermilion seemed to separate from me as though she might take over. And I could no longer fight her—because *I* wanted this too.

Parker was still on the phone with Clara. I held out my hand. "Let me talk to her for a moment."

He looked dazed as he handed me the instrument.

Clara's voice went on excitedly, still speaking to Parker. "What do you mean—she's dead out there near the Fire People? She hated that place!"

"But she went there, Clara," I told her. "It's true."

"My God!" Clara said, and was silent.

I continued as she listened. "Parker is here with whatever he's brought for the dinner party Sybil meant to give tonight. Do you see any reason why we shouldn't go ahead with the dinner?"

I looked at Parker as I spoke and saw his astonishment. There was a brief pause before Clara exploded.

"How can you possibly go ahead, when Sybil—when—"

"Do you mean you won't come?" I asked quietly.

"There won't be any dinner. Rick won't allow such a thing. Oh, I never liked Sybil, but this isn't—" She choked and broke off. I waited until she could go on again. "Exactly what would you be celebrating, Lindsay?"

"I don't think what Sybil planned would have been a celebration either. But if you'll come, and if Parker is willing to go ahead and cook dinner, I'll ask Orva and Brian, so they'll be here too, as Sybil intended."

"My God, you *are* crazy!" Clara repeated. "Let me talk to Parker."

Parker had been listening and he raised his shoulders in a vast shrug as he took back the phone. "So what does it matter? I don't mind cooking, if that's what Lindsay wants. Though I expect Rick will cancel this idea the minute he gets home."

I couldn't tell what Clara said. Parker

grinned sardonically as he hung up. "She'll come. Why do you want to do this, Lindsay?"

"I'm not sure I know. Not exactly. Perhaps I'm just acting on a hunch, the way my father used to do."

"Well, I suppose we all have to eat somewhere tonight. So it might as well be here. Though I'm not enthusiastic about this."

He picked up the hamper and went out to the kitchen, where Sybil's cook had been given the day off. I sat listening to the rattle of pans with Parker's usual operatic accompaniment.

Was it really because of Vermilion that I'd just done what I had? What might we be asking for if we went ahead with this dinner? I could hear her in my mind: *Answers. Answers are what you're looking for! Stay with it, Lindsay.*

From my shirt pocket I took out the key I'd found in the clearing and considered it thoughtfully. Then I went to the front door and put it into the lock. It slipped in easily and turned. As I was trying it for the second time, Rick's car pulled into the driveway. He was alone, and I waited as he came up the walk looking haggard and grave. There was so little comfort I could offer him now.

"I'm sorry, Rick. I know how awful this is for you. And how awful for Marilla."

"Come inside," he said, and then noticed the key I'd drawn from the lock. "Have you found yourself a door key. Good."

I followed him inside nervously. I didn't

want him to discover Parker in the kitchen until I'd had time to explain. At least Parker was quiet for once, but how was I to tell Rick what I'd suggested, and get him to accept such a plan? It seemed more and more important to me to go ahead with this.

"The key must have belonged to Sybil," I said and handed it to him. "I found this a little way from where she lay. I'd forgotten about it until just now. Does it being there mean anything?"

He took the key and turned it in his fingers. Then he lowered himself into the nearest chair and stretched out in weariness. "This isn't Sybil's key," he said. "It belonged to Jed."

I dropped down beside him. "To Jed? How do you know?"

"See this notch? Jed had a way of marking his keys with notches like this so that he could identify them by touch in the dark. You know he was always a night owl, and I gave him his own house key, since he stayed here at times. This appears to be the same one."

For an instant that strangely atavistic feeling that had touched me in the place of Fire People flowed through me again. However, it wasn't Jed who had returned to punish Sybil.

"How could it have been dropped there?" I demanded. "How could it possibly—"

"It could have fallen out of someone's pocket. One of the men from the sheriff's office found some loose change on the ground as well.

The key could have been dropped at the same time. I don't think Sybil would have had it. Someone else lost it there."

"They *do* think she was murdered, don't they?"

"No one's saying. The Coconino County coroner will decide the cause of death. There are already some doubts and they're expecting someone down from Flagstaff to help out. But, Lindsay, why do *you* think this?"

"I saw the high-heeled sandals she was wearing. She'd never have gone hiking in shoes like that!"

He shook his head wearily. "If they come to that conclusion—murder—I'm likely to be the first candidate for a suspect. It's no secret that Sybil and I have been having rows. She's been talking about it all over town. And I expect others have too."

I hated the possibility of such suspicion. He touched my hand and I turned my fingers to twine in his. We sat for a moment in silence, gaining what comfort we would from this slight touch.

"Whatever happens, I want to keep you out of it," he said, and I knew that circumstances were already changing everything between us.

A fresh burst of operatic sound came suddenly from the kitchen, and Rick tensed. "Parker? What on earth is he doing here?"

There was nothing to do but blurt out everything. "He's getting ready for the dinner that was planned for tonight. Sybil's dinner party. Rick, I—"

"And you didn't stop him?" Rick got up and started for the kitchen.

I flew after him. "Wait, please! Let me explain. I told him to go ahead. Clara is coming, and I was going to call Orva and Brian to let them know the dinner is still on."

He didn't tell me I was crazy, as Clara had, but his look was hardly approving. "I'll stop this immediately. This is no time to give a party. What's come over you, Lindsay?"

He was reacting just as Clara and Parker had warned he would—as any sane person would react. On this particular matter I didn't feel altogether sane. *Make him do it!* Vermilion was shrill.

"It's not a dinner *party*," I told him. "It's an—an inquisition. That's what Sybil meant it to be. An opportunity for revelation. Orva thinks she was going to tell us what happened when she went to see Jed in his room that night in Las Vegas. She only invited those who were there, plus Parker and me, and of course Alice. We can't know just what she planned, but we can ask questions."

I must have sounded convincing, for Rick was listening intently, and I hurried on in spite of his ominous expression. "If that was Jed's key I found, and it was dropped by someone else, and not by Sybil—"

Rick made the same connecting link in his

mind and shook his head. "It's too long a shot. It could be innocent enough, and even Sybil could have dropped it there."

He was quiet for a moment, considering, while *"Celeste Aida"* soared out of the kitchen.

"Sybil thought something would come out of this dinner," I repeated urgently.

"All right, Lindsay. I don't know what good it will do to go ahead. If Sybil knew something, she's not here to carry through. But it's possible that if we meet and talk over Las Vegas together, something may come out that hasn't surfaced before. Something that might have a bearing on the present."

I remembered something. "Sybil told me she was inviting a relative of mine. Was it Alice Rainsong?"

"Yes. I called Alice an hour or so ago to tell her what has happened. She said that Sybil had invited her tonight. Now she's driving down anyway."

"Why does she still want to come?"

"Because you're her sister," Rick said quietly.

"I don't think she even likes me."

"There's trouble, and a family sticks together."

How strange to realize that, except for Marilla, this woman whom I hardly knew, this gifted, part Hopi woman, was now my only family.

Rick glanced at his watch and stood up. "I

have some things I need to do. Arrangements to make.''

As he'd done so short a time ago with Sybil's father, I thought. My father, my sister. Again there was that sense of unreality that comes when death is sudden and impossible to accept.

Rick continued, impersonal and more formal with me than ever. That touch of his hand might never have been. ''Can you take care of Alice when she comes?''

He was leaving me to handle this meeting with my sister alone—the first since I'd learned the truth—and while I felt uncomfortable, I recognized that this might be the best way.

When he'd gone I walked out to the kitchen, where Parker was working busily, humming to himself as he whipped up some sort of creamy concoction for a dessert. Sybil's death was not bothering him very much.

''Has Rick canceled everything?'' he asked, beating eggs expertly with a wire whisk.

''No. We're to go ahead.''

''Depressing,'' Parker said. ''It's a terrible idea.''

''Why do you think that?''

''Aside from being inappropriate—which I'd have thought Rick would consider—it's not going to work, is it? Sybil had something special in mind, and she's not here to carry it out.''

''She told you that?''

''Hardly. Clara and I were talking about it. It seemed too pat a performance—this dinner.''

"Perhaps it's a good idea for us to get together and talk about everything openly, before the police move in on us," I said.

The whisk paused in the air, foamy yellow, and he gave me a questioning look. "The police are moving in?"

"They'll be making an inquiry, of course."

"I suppose they have to," he said gloomily.

"There'll be one more guest. Alice Spencer is coming from Flagstaff."

"The Indian woman?"

"My half sister," I said. "It turns out that I'm as much Hopi as she is."

Parker didn't seem surprised. "Clara's said she always thought there was something between Jed and Alice's mother. I only met Alice once, but I know her a little through Clara. She's a fine person."

For once he sounded warm and approving, which surprised me. He was even regarding me in a kindly fashion.

"I'll go call Orva now, since it's already after four," I said. "What time shall I say for dinner?"

"Early. Let's get it over with. It's hardly a festive occasion."

"How about six-thirty?"

He nodded and returned to his humming concentration, switching to *La donna è mobile*." He really had a good voice, and he knew his opera.

"When you were young, Parker," I asked,

"did you ever think of a singing career?"

"Sure, I thought about it."

"Then why—?"

His grin twisted down at the corners. "No character, I suppose. Too much alcohol. I could manage better with my other talent—cooking."

I returned to the living room and dialed Orva's number. She answered after a couple of rings, and I explained about the dinner.

While she didn't approve, she took a different tack. "Why stir up things, Lindsay? Sybil's motives were always pretty twisted, but maybe she had someone running scared. There's no point to following through on that now, and, as I say, you can't tell what you might stir up."

"Perhaps it's necessary to stir up a few things. You used to think that yourself. Will you and Brian come?"

"I guess nobody would dare *not* come. As though there might be something to hide. And I'll tell you one thing—Sybil Adams would never have gone out to that place unless somebody forced her to go."

"Who would do that?"

"Jed, of course. Jed still owed her one, you know."

Her words shocked me because they were spoken so earnestly. I thought of the key in Rick's keeping. However, I didn't mean to be led down this particular road.

"If you're trying to scare me, it's not working," I said. "I'm not superstitious."

"Too bad. You could do with a little scaring."

I hardly waited for her good-bye. I might have my own peculiar voice that I listened to on occasion, but I didn't want to open the door to anything else.

As I stood by the phone table, undecided as to what I should do next, I heard a car coming up the hill. When I went to look out a front window, I saw that it was another four-wheel-drive pickup truck, with Alice.

Once more, the door chimes sounded, and Consuela, always hovering watchfully, ran to answer. A moment later, Alice Rainsong came into the room, carrying a small suitcase.

Today she was dressed casually in Levi's and a tan shirt, her lovely face showing little expression as she stood looking at me down the long el of the room. The planes of her face were broad, and her dark eyes looked at me impassively from between heavy lashes. Indian, I thought.

"Hello, Alice," I said. "I'm glad you've come."

She continued to stand just inside the door, and I sensed that she searched for something in my face, just as I had in hers.

"There are a great many things unspoken between us," she said gravely, formally. "In time, perhaps, we'll say them, but we need to be strangers first. In spite of the blood tie. It's a tie that may be troubling until we become accustomed."

I liked her frankness, and I wanted to tell her that it was a tie I was proud of. It was true, however, that we were strangers, and intimacy must come slowly, if it ever came. I couldn't say this to her yet—not until it could be spoken from the heart without self-consciousness.

"I'm sorry about Rick's wife," she said, coming into the room. "What has happened is very terrible."

I noticed that she didn't refer to Sybil as my "sister."

"Please come in." I knew I sounded stiff and I couldn't relax with her yet. "Rick hasn't told me where your room should be, but I know he wants you to stay here."

"He said I might share Marilla's room for now. We're good friends, and a cot in her room will be fine."

"I have a whole guesthouse to myself. You can certainly share that."

She shook her head gently. "The time isn't right. Later, perhaps."

At least I was relieved that she wouldn't be in Sybil's room. All Sybil had left behind was still there.

I hurried into words. "Marilla is staying with Orva tonight, so I'm not sure which room . . . You know the house better than I do."

"I've been here with Jed," she admitted. "I'll show you."

She picked up her case and led the way into

the bedroom wing. All the doors were open, and I glanced into the rooms as we went past. First Rick's bedroom, done in desert shades, with an Indian rug visible. Sybil's next, all pastels, tailored and very neat. She'd never gone in for frills. Marilla's room looked as though chaos had struck, and I suspected this might be its usual condition, except when her mother was watching.

"I'll hang the few things I've brought in Marilla's closet," Alice said.

I thought of Parker in the kitchen, preparing dinner, and knew that she must be warned.

"I should tell you," I began, "we're going ahead with the dinner Sybil planned. Just Clara and Parker Hale. And of course Orva and Brian Montgomery. You know them all, I expect."

Alice nodded. "They were all guests of Jed's in Las Vegas, weren't they? As well as Rick and Sybil."

She was sensing intuitively the point Orva had made.

"I asked Rick to go ahead with this," I told her. "There are questions about Sybil's death, and perhaps about Jed's that we need to consider."

"A sad, driven woman, Sybil."

Her words surprised me. "Driven, perhaps, but what do you meant by sad?"

"That's only an impression I had. I never knew her well."

Alice had carried a few things to Marilla's

closet, and I watched her hang them up. I didn't want to talk any more about terrible, sad things. I asked a question, somewhat timidly.

"Will you tell me about our mother?"

"What would you like to know?" She slid hangers along the rod without turning, and I sensed a deep quietness in her.

"Anything, I suppose—everything! It's strange to be so ignorant, but this was always kept from me. Rick says Jed wanted me to know and would have told me eventually. My stepmother didn't wish it. All I was ever told was that my father had brought me to New York from Arizona."

"It's hard to know where to begin," Alice said, and I sensed a reluctance in her to share something that might still be painful. Yet I had to go on—for both our sakes. In the open, pain could be dealt with.

I sat down in a small armchair and settled myself into waiting. It was easier to talk in the midst of Marilla's lively clutter than in that vast and somehow impersonal living room.

"Did she ever live in a pueblo?" I asked.

"As a child she did. But you need to understand something here. These two women —our mother and grandmother—weren't typical. Hopi women are honored and they get a lot better treatment from their men than they'd be likely to find with chauvinistic white men. There isn't much intermarrying, and I don't know why they turned away from

251

their own people.

"Anyway, our grandmother's Anglo husband died and she returned to Oraibi when Mary Silvercloud was very small. Mother was only half Hopi, and she was a rebel as a young girl. She had lived outside and she didn't want to settle for the old ways. Though they *are* good ways and still work for those who believe in them. Trust, honor, integrity, working for the good of all—these are Hopi beliefs. Christians might find some resemblance. Though you won't see the struggle for success that's usual in the Anglo world. They don't compete with each other and they counsel living in peace. Difficult concepts for a competitive world to understand!"

Concepts. That was where the great difference lay, I thought. Customs could easily be learned and accepted, but basic concepts could make a great, instinctual difference. Alice, and perhaps Jed too, had been able to cross the line back and forth and live in two worlds. I could never step across as easily, though Alice might be able to help me stop being an "outsider."

She went on. "While the Hopi weren't warriors like the Plains Indians, they'd defend themselves when necessary. The early pueblo was like a fortress built on top of a mesa, with only one trail hacked out of rock leading to the top. It was pretty impregnable."

"I suppose the Spaniards were the enemy they had to fight?"

"Their worst enemy was the Navajo. They still call Hopis by the name "Moquis"—the dead ones. Which meant in the past that they would like to kill them on sight. Nobody really got through, however, until the Spanish priests came along and the Hopi began to accept some of their ideas. But they never gave up the old altogether, and wise priests know this even now."

"How did your mother happen to leave?"

"Somehow, she met my father and ran away with him. Her family would never have approved. They didn't like him, and they were right. I was still a baby when he left her. After that I only remember—Jed. It was Jed who bought the house where I still live in Flagstaff."

Alice's dark eyes looked far away, and I saw the shine of tears. She was not as impassive as I'd imagined.

"I loved him when I was small," I said. "Later, I could only resent him and feel angry about the way he behaved."

"I know. I've been through all that. I suppose it's always hard to accept flaws in those we care about."

Flaws? That was too kind a word to use about Jed. I changed course.

"Alice, were you ever in the place of the Fire People?"

"Jed took me there once. I was only twelve and I felt afraid. I knew about the Old Ones—the Ancient Ones who came *before*. He told me he'd found some evidences of them there, but he didn't want archeologists coming in to tear things up, so he only showed the place to a few of us. He said it belonged to the Fire People—and to the Shining One, the One who looked at the sky."

"It still does. I saw that face in the rock this morning. Before I knew that Sybil was—there."

"It's not a place where an enemy should go." Alice's voice was low and there was an oddly rapt look on her face, as though she saw again something she'd glimpsed as a child.

"We don't know how Sybil came to be there," I told her.

She was silent, offering nothing.

"I don't know what will happen at dinner tonight," I went on. "Alice, do you ever feel an inner prompting that makes you do something that your mind tells you isn't sensible?"

Her face lost the rapt look and she smiled at me. "So! You have it too? The gift from our mother. It's not very strong in me, but there are times when I think it stirs. It brought me here today."

"How strange. I'd have thought it came to me from Jed. He was always the one in my life who could touch the stars. And the clay as well."

"Then you have it doubly strong. You must listen to it and never deny, because it may lead you to wisdom. Perhaps with you it speaks through your friend—Vermilion?"

I felt shocked again—almost violated. Vermilion was *my* secret, perhaps even a rather shameful secret, and I'd never shared her with anyone but Jed, who had, after all, helped me to create her. To others who didn't understand her power, she might seem a childish invention, and even now I didn't want her to be laughed at. Or perhaps I didn't want *me* to be laughed at.

Alice saw my face. "Of course Jed and I talked about you many times. I always wanted to know about—my sister. For me, it made you seem more real—that you had this friend. Though if I were a true Hopi, I think it would frighten me badly. Voices and vision are something to be superstitious about."

"They're only in my head," I told her.

"I know. We've both been lonely, sister."

The simple way in which she spoke the word caused my sense of violation to dissolve. Suddenly I found that I could talk more naturally to this woman whose blood I shared.

"I'm afraid of what may happen now," I confessed. "Of what may happen to Rick. Something evil has moved into our lives."

"Into my life too," she agreed. "Sometimes trouble seems lighter when there's more than one to carry the burden."

In her words I sensed her strength. I had seen anger in her paintings. Now I knew that she could be calm and filled with fortitude as well. I felt a stirring of new affection for Alice Rainsong.

11

Once more I dressed carefully in a gown of my own design. A pale taupe print with tiny stylized blossoms in lilac and white. I needed all the courage I could find tonight. As I fastened carved ivory teardrops in my ears, an idea came to me. If I was going to startle anyone at the table into a betrayal, I would have to do something really shocking. Now, quite suddenly, I knew what it could be.

Before I left the guesthouse I picked up the object I must take with me, and then stood for a moment watching the house across the bridge.

The evening was too cool for a table to be set on the terrace. Through the great glass windows I could see Consuela arranging a centerpiece of chrysanthemums in a ceramic bowl. When she went out of the room, I hurried across. As I dropped what I carried into the shadow of a bush just beyond the rail, a faint sound of inner laughter echoed through me.

I tried not to listen. It seemed as though Vermilion grew more tangible as a presence with the crises deepening around me, and I didn't like that. When fantasies grow so strong that they can be confused with what's real, so that the dreamer loses a sense of the difference, it can be dangerous. I tried to persuade myself that I still knew the difference very well. And I *had* rejected her more than once lately.

We sat down to dinner promptly at six-thirty, with everyone there except Brian. Orva said she'd left a note asking him to join us when he could. Marilla was visiting a little girl next door, so Orva must leave early to pick her up. Clearly, she didn't want to be here at all, in spite of her enormous curiosity. Probably she could weave fantasies as skillfully as Jed—or I—but I suspected that she didn't always know how to live with them.

We were solemn and subdued that night. Rick seemed more distantly removed than ever. Though the only empty chair at the table was Brian's, we all sensed another empty place. The questions about Sybil hung ominously over us, and the shock of her sudden death weighed upon us all.

Clara spoke into a long silence. "What *is* this going to be tonight? Are we holding a séance?"

What we were doing might not be so far removed from just that. I wondered whether Sybil, and perhaps Jed too, might not hover near us in the shadows.

At least, Clara's question had broken the first restraint, and now both Orva and Clara asked questions of Rick. He answered curtly at first, then began to resent the questioning about Sybil's death, so that when Clara pushed him too hard, he grew increasingly sharp.

"Lindsay will tell you, since she was there."

Consuela had served our watercress soup, while Parker hovered between table and kitchen, an eye on his broiling steaks. Everyone looked at me. I could only shake my head helplessly.

"You all know about as much as I do," I said, and wondered silently if someone at this table knew a great deal more.

It was Clara who challenged me. "*About* as much? What do you mean by that?"

She looked quite stunning tonight in moss green, long and flowing, with a belt of hammered silver medallions, her thick, graying braid looped about her head in a style of her own. I'd never seen her look like this before, and I found myself watching her with new eyes. Now she and Rick were merely business associates and friends, yet I sensed that Parker didn't like Rick. I wondered if jealousy might be part of that feeling. When he was at the table, his eyes seemed to follow his wife in a strangely watchful way.

When I didn't answer, Clara repeated her question. "What aren't you telling us, Lindsay? You're the one who wanted us here tonight—so why don't you go ahead with whatever you have in mind?"

I was all too sharply aware of Rick's sardonic

look—as though he dared me to bring something out of this dinner. I couldn't very well say, "Vermilion wanted me to do this." Having pushed me, she had subsided, and I was left with little to go on. So I played the only card I had—except one. Rick had returned the key I had found, showing no inclination to turn it over to the police, and I'd brought it to the table with me, wrapped in a handkerchief. Now I took it out and placed it beyond my soup plate.

There was a sudden silence, while all attention centered on the key.

"I found this today," I told them. "I found it near the spot where Sybil fell. Rick says it belonged to Jed. He doesn't know how she would happen to have it. Do any of you?"

Orva reached across the table and picked up the key. "That's right. Jed used to mark his keys like this. So what?"

She passed it along to Parker. He turned it over once or twice, then handed it to Alice. He was clearly more interested in the dinner that was his responsibility than in what we were discussing. He had not shown any sorrow over the death of Sybil Adams.

Alice, too, confirmed the marking on the key, and it was passed around the table, returning at last to me.

"Does anyone know why Sybil had such a disturbed feeling about the Fire People?" I asked. "She seemed really frightened when that carving was left on her doorstep. I don't think she'd have gone out to those cliffs of her own free will."

Only silence met my question, and Rick watched me coldly. I tried a further challenge.

"Do you all know about the high-heeled sandals she was wearing? She'd actually been walking out there in those unsuitable shoes. They were stone-scuffed and powdered with red dust when she was found. So who brought her there? And how?"

Again no one answered.

"You have a theory?" Rick asked. Tonight he was a man I hardly knew, and wasn't sure I wanted to know, in spite of the aching void inside me. Somewhere I had lost him, and I didn't know how or why.

Of them all, Alice Rainsong sensed my discomfort the most keenly. She drew attention gently away by speaking to Orva.

"Did Brian say where he was going when he left this afternoon?"

Orva seemed startled, but she didn't evade a question that no one else had thought of asking. "He said he had to go to Jerome."

I could hear the whisper in my mind: *Watch them,* and I looked quickly at each in turn.

Alice's head came up as though the name of Brian's destination had startled her. Parker was looking only at Clara, and he seemed more sad and thoughtful than anything else. Clara stared at her empty soup plate. Of them all, Rick seemed the most surprised.

"Jerome!" he echoed. "That's where Sybil went a few days ago."

"I know," Orva agreed. "Brian drove her there." She spoke calmly, yet I heard uncertainty in her voice, as though her son's actions had puzzled her.

"What is this about Jerome?" I asked. "Why does the idea of Brian going to Jerome seem upsetting?"

"Maybe I can answer that." Brian himself had come around the house by way of the outside walk and stood at the terrace door, watching us. He still wore his jacket with the Search and Rescue insignia on the pocket. His hair was tousled from driving in the open. As always, his curly beard seemed to hide any real expression of what he might be thinking. Only his eyes regarded us in challenge as he came through the door to our table.

"I drove back to Jerome today, because Sybil told me to go," he said.

Everyone was silent, and he went on, outwardly calm. "Lindsay, your sister told me that if any sudden accident overtook her I was to go to Jerome and start asking questions."

"But you already went there!" There was a wail in Orva's voice, as though something had frightened her. "You told me that you drove her there just a couple of days ago!"

"That's right—I did. I played chauffeur,

the way I always would when she snapped her fingers. Do you care if I sit down?'' He came to the empty chair next to me, dropped into it and glared around the table. Now he was letting his anger show. ''How poisonous can you get—throwing a party at a time like this? *Her* party!''

''We're trying to sort out whatever we know that might help us find the truth about her death,'' I said.

''My steaks!'' Parker cried, and jumped up to race for the kitchen.

''Well—go on!'' Orva said to her son. Her long face looked drawn and thin.

Consuela, observant as always, served soup to Brian, then brought our salads.

''There's nothing to tell, Ma,'' he said. ''I took Sybil to one of those old houses, where miners used to live, and I left her there. She didn't ask me to come in with her. I walked around for a while and had a look at the museum. When I went back she was waiting for me in the car. She seemed excited—or maybe it was elated—but she didn't tell me anything. She only repeated what she'd said before—that if anything ever happened to her, I should go back to that house and ask questions. So that's what I did today.''

There was an interruption as Parker returned bearing a platter of sizzling steaks and placed them before Rick.

Orva's voice cut through the distraction.

"Never mind the food! What did you find out?"

Brian scowled. "I found out—*nada*. Zilch. An old woman lives in that house—a Mrs. Jessup. One of the few old-timers left in Jerome. When I got there today she had a doctor in her room, and he wouldn't let me talk to her. She's probably dying, by the look of her. I don't think you'll get much at that end. I couldn't."

Rick sent plates of steak down the table and I picked up my knife and fork with no eagerness for food. As we began to eat, Orva suddenly sputtered and put down her fork.

"Parker," she said, "is this the same menu that Sybil told you to prepare for tonight?"

He looked faintly embarrassed. "Well— almost. I made a few changes because what she asked me to fix was pretty dull. So I made watercress soup, and stuffed the potatoes with chives and cheese. And I've made a dessert instead of the ice cream she wanted."

"What kind of ice cream?" Orva demanded. "What did she ask for?"

Parker wrinkled his nose. "Plain vanilla. With *store* cookies! Not even a sauce."

Orva stared around the table. "Don't you see what she tried to do? This is the very same hotel dinner that was served us that night in Vegas! Except for Parker's touches, it's the same. Don't you see? She wanted to create a mood. Same people, same food!"

Vermilion came suddenly to life inside my

head. *Now!* she urged. *Do it now!*

I wanted to cry, *Let me alone!* Instead, I found myself speaking the first words that came to my tongue.

"Orva's right. Sybil asked you all here tonight because she wanted you to think about Las Vegas. She wanted you to think about Jed, and what happened to him there. I have something that may help you to remember."

Rick said, "Don't, Lindsay!"—though he couldn't know what I intended.

"I have to do this," I said miserably.

I could feel their eyes upon me as I left the table and went outside to the terrace rail. There I knelt and reached through to pull out what I'd hidden there. I picked up Jed's ivory-headed cane, carried it to the table, and set it down lengthwise like a macabre centerpiece, with the dragon's mouth open, ready to emit fire.

Someone gasped, someone cried, "No," and when I looked around the table at all those staring faces I saw that only one person was no longer looking at me. Alice was weeping softly into her hands. I had to go on—no matter how dreadful I felt.

"One of us here knows who picked up Jed's cane that night," I said. "Perhaps I can even guess who it was."

Rick broke the shocked silence that had enveloped the table. He sprang up and snatched the cane from its place, carried it outside and flung it across the terrace, where it clattered on the tiles and lay like a long black sword upon the terra-cotta. His dark fury seemed to pour out toward me as he returned to us. Yet all the while I knew that something was stirring in one of us at that table. Something horrible, something terrified and dangerous. In a moment there would be a sign.

Alice raised her tear-stained face and reached across the table to place her hand on Rick's arm. Some calming power seemed to flow from her into him, and he sat down and was still.

It was already too late. We could hear the slam of a car door and voices outside. In a moment the chimes rang. Consuela ran to the door. Whatever it was that had begun to rise in desperate hysteria ebbed away. Everyone looked tense, but everyone looked the same as always, and there could be no telling now where danger might lie.

This time it was the Coconino County sheriff who came into the house. He asked to speak to Rick, requesting that he come outside. I think he was mildly surprised to see us dining there together so soon after Sybil's death.

When they'd gone, Parker got up apologetically. "My dessert won't keep," he said, and hurried out to the kitchen.

For the first time the conversation turned general and desultory. I wanted to ask Alice why she had wept, but I didn't dare. The references to Jerome had meant something to her. I would have to find out what it was later.

I knew, however, that I had one more task to perform.

I excused myself and walked out to where Jed's cane had skittered across the tile, knowing they were all watching me. Just before I reached it I stopped. *Don't touch it,* the voice whispered. *Not again.* I stared at the cane. It *was* like a black sword pointing straight at my heart. I shook off the fantasy. I was weary of listening to imaginary voices, and I picked up the cane and carried it across the bridge to the guesthouse, where I placed it once more in the living room closet. For some reason, I wanted to keep it in my possession. Perhaps there was still something I could learn from Jed's cane, or something I could do with it. Or perhaps it was only that I wanted to defy Vermilion, who was struggling to tell me something.

Revelation had been very close, before the sheriff had timed his visit so badly.

When I returned to the table, Consuela was serving stemmed crystal glasses with Parker's lemon soufflé. It was as delicate and light as though it had never been in danger of last-minute neglect, and its sweetness melted on my tongue. Before I'd eaten more than a mouthful, the woman deputy I'd met at Tlaquepaque came in to ask if I would join them outside.

I followed her to the big garage, where the doors were open and the sheriff was kneeling to examine the wheels of Rick's pickup truck. He seemed to be scraping dirt and bits of red stone from the tires, collecting it in an envelope, while another man in plain clothes stood by. The deputy murmured to me that he was detective Atkins from Flagstaff. So the investigation was under way in earnest.

The sheriff rose and handed the detective the envelope that held bits of reddish earth and stone.

"When did you last drive your truck out in the back country, Mr. Adams?" Atkins asked.

Rick hardly needed to consider. "I haven't been out there for months. I did make a trip to Oraibi some weeks ago, and I went over some rough side roads. What's up?"

It was the sheriff who answered. "We found tire tracks out beyond Steamboat Rock that seem to match the tires on this car. And these scrapings seem to be the same composition as the earth out near where your wife's body was found. The lab will have to confirm it of course."

"I haven't been out there," Rick said grimly. "Not today or any time recently. Besides, you'll get that sort of stuff all around Sedona."

Detective Atkins was a tall man, with slightly rounded shoulders—as though he'd spent his time bending over "evidence." But he looked wiry and strong—unflappable. His voice was low-pitched and deceptively gentle. He spoke courteously now to Rick.

"Your wife's car is still in the garage. We have reason to believe that she either drove this truck out to Steamboat Rock or was driven there. Certainly she had a companion with her who drove the truck back here to your garage, without reporting her fall."

"My wife *never* drove this truck," Rick said. "I don't think she'd have gone into that rough country on her own. Especially not to a place she feared, unless there was a very strong and urgent reason."

"Why do you say urgent?"

"You've seen her shoes. If she'd had time and knew where she was going, she'd have put on something else."

"So it's possible that someone either persuaded her to go out there in a hurry, or else she was taken by force."

Rick said nothing, and the detective gestured toward the house. "Is there somewhere we can sit down and talk? There's no point in taking anyone to the office at present. I'd like to ask this lady some questions." He looked at me.

"Sure," Rick said. "My study."

We went into the house, and he led the way down the long living room. Outdoors on the terrace, the light was fading to a reddish glow. I could see that the mushroom lamps had come on. Everyone still sat at the table near the windows and we didn't disturb them.

Rick's study was a big comfortable room with a desk of polished walnut. All around was a mixed clutter of objects he had collected in his travels throughout the Southwest. The young woman deputy remained at the door, while the rest of us sat around the desk.

Detective Atkins looked at me. "Miss Phillips, will you tell us why you wanted to go ahead tonight with this dinner your sister had planned?"

I threw a quick look at Rick and knew he wouldn't help me. How could I explain? How could I say that I suspected that the same person who had murdered Jed Phillips had killed Sybil? And that I'd engineered this dinner because I'd hoped—perhaps not so futilely—that someone would give himself away. Nevertheless, there was still the key. Perhaps I could now do something with it.

"I thought we ought to talk over together what had happened," I said firmly. "Then perhaps we'd have something useful to tell the police."

"Not a bad idea," the detective said. "Will you tell me, Miss Phillips, when you last saw your sister alive?"

I explained then about the last time, and told of Sybil's upset over Jed's sculpture.

Atkins studied me thoughtfully. "Tell me how you happened to come out here for a visit after all these years?"

All right, Vermilion, where are you? I said silently. *Why aren't you telling me what to do?* But my alter ego was quiet.

"I came out," I said, "because I was troubled about my father's death and wanted to learn more about it firsthand.''

"After waiting a year?''

"Orva Montgomery sent me a note that brought me here. She felt Sybil knew something about my father's death that she wasn't telling.''

Atkins looked at the sheriff, who nodded. "I know Orva Montgomery well. A good solid woman.''

"Then we'll talk to her.''

Good solid Orva wasn't going to like that, I thought, and wondered how far she would go to protect her son, if that seemed indicated.

"There's one other thing,'' I said, and once more took the key from my handkerchief. "I found this in that—that place today. Near where I saw Sybil lying.''

Rick said, "That key belonged originally to my wife's father, though it's a key to this house. Jed always filed his keys with special notches, so he could pull them out by touch. I don't see how Sybil happened to have it—if she did have it.''

"We'll look into that,'' Atkins said, and placed the key in an envelope. "Now then, Miss Phillips, is there anything else you can tell us? Has anything come out at this dinner tonight?''

"There's nothing sensible I can tell you,'' I said, "but if you want to know what I think, it's that whoever murdered my father also caused Sybil's death.''

"Anything you can give us to back that up?''

"Only the key. That is, if the person who killed Jed took it from him in Las Vegas."

Rick and I walked with them to the door and Detective Atkins turned to me again before he left.

"I knew your father, Miss Phillips. Everyone liked him, though sometimes he worried us a little. He was given to doing the unexpected at times—and not always wisely. However, no one seems to have turned up who had a grudge against him. Or at least no serious grudge. I worked on the case at the time with the Vegas police. I still want to solve it." He told us good night and went quietly away.

I stood beside Rick and looked up at stars that were beginning to appear in the sky. How bright and close they seemed in Sedona. I longed to touch him and to be comforted, but for all that he stood so close, he was miles away.

"You've got to get out of this, Lindsay," he told me curtly. "If it's all right with the police for you to leave, I want to see you on a plane as soon as possible."

"I'm not going," I said.

"Right after the funeral, you'll go," he repeated. "You can't stay here any longer."

I spoke with stiff courtesy. "Do you mind if I remain in the guesthouse for a few more days? After that, I'll find a room somewhere. Perhaps Orva can put me up."

Rick seemed to explode. "Stay away from

Orva and from that son of hers! You can live in the guesthouse for now. But not for long.''

''Rick,'' I said, ''stop being angry with me. I want to help. And I *need* help.'' To my distress, my voice cracked as I went on. ''How I wish I could have been older when you came to New York that first time!''

For a moment, I thought he'd softened toward me. Then he stiffened again. ''I want you to stay alive—and uninvolved. You said something pretty foolish at the table tonight— that you had some idea who it was that used the cane on Jed.''

''But I *don't* know!'' I cried. ''I'm not even sure why I said that—except perhaps to stir someone into revealing something.''

''Anyway, you did say it. I'm going to send Alice over to stay with you tonight. I don't want you to be alone.''

I wasn't anxious to stay alone either, and I knew Rick couldn't come to me now. Perhaps he never would—not ever again.

I tried another question. ''Do you know what it was about the mention of Jerome that seemed to upset everyone tonight? And why did Alice cry?''

''I'm not sure, but I am very sure that Sybil was asking for trouble when she went to Jerome. She always believed that arrogance and authority would get her by. Well, it didn't.''

I hated the way he sounded. It was as though all his long-restrained anger with Sybil had surfaced out of the evening's tensions, so that he wasn't hiding it anymore. Even though she was gone, his anger was alive, and I remembered what Orva had said about Sybil's not changing just because she was dead. Unhappily, I found myself thinking of the truck in Rick's garage, with its telltale tires, and I shivered.

"Shall we go back to our guests?" Rick asked.

The only comfort I could take was that he had said "our." He was concerned about me—and I about him—yet I wanted more than that. So much more.

When we returned to the table we found everyone getting ready to leave. Parker was in the kitchen, and Orva and Clara came at once to question us. Brian had apparently gone off on his own, and Alice drew aside to another part of the room, more sensitive to Rick's tension, and mine, and willing to let us be.

"What did the police want?" Orva demanded of Rick. "Have they figured anything out?"

I couldn't bear to listen any longer, and I said, "Good night," though I doubt if anyone heard me. For once, it was a relief to hurry across the bridge. When I reached the little house it looked all too lonely and empty, and I was glad that Rick would send Alice to stay with me later.

The door, as usual, was unlocked. I'd just put my hand on the knob to open it when a shadow rose from a chair on the deck.

"It's only me again," Brian said. "Can I

come in and talk to you for a minute?"

I didn't want to talk to him. I didn't want to talk to anyone else for a long time, but I stepped aside and let him through the door.

He stood looking around the living room. "I slept in this house once. I came back with Sybil late one night after one of her speaking trips. She said not to go home and wake Orva up and that I should stay right here, since it was empty. So I did. I left early in the morning, and I don't think Rick even knew I'd stayed overnight."

What I wondered, what I questioned, must have showed in my face, for Brian shook his head wryly. "No—it wasn't anything like that. I was always useful to Sybil, though never part of her life. She was too cold to go in for any philandering."

I didn't want to talk about Sybil. "Why did you want to speak with me?"

Gently, though firmly, he put his hands on my shoulders and pressed me into a chair. Then he sat down nearby, bending earnestly toward me.

"Maybe I can help," he said.

I glanced at the door and saw that it was closed. "In what way, Brian?"

"You've had a terrible day. And the dinner tonight didn't help any, did it? There's too much emotion around—a sort of psychic emotion that affects us all, even when we're not consciously aware of it. Every possible emotion except grief, I think. I don't believe anyone, except perhaps Marilla, will grieve for Sybil. There's a way for you to ease all this, Lindsay."

"I'd certainly like to do that," I said doubtfully, "but how?"

"All you need do is remember back to when you first stepped through into the place of the Fire People. Go back to that moment when you heard me playing the drum—when you looked up at the Shining One. There's all the peace the universe holds in that face. There's some sort of wonderful promise, as well. The Ones-Who-Came-Before *knew*. Just think about it, see it again in your mind and listen to the drum. Then you'll be calm. It always works for me, Lindsay."

Here was that mysticism of Brian's emerging again, and I was already shaking my head. "No, it won't work for me. That face seemed almost too terrible to look into. Not calming at all. Perhaps because whatever it stands for knows about all eternity, and I'm only an earth person. I can't look out into the sky like that. It would terrify me."

Brian seemed sad, almost regretful, as though he really did want to offer me an escape from all that would torment me for a long time to come. "Jed found inspiration in them, a lifting of his spirit. He talked about it once to me. That's why I wanted to play the drum out there—to see if I could free *our* spirits."

"What do you think Sybil found there?"

He considered my question as though I'd

asked something profound. "Perhaps Sybil was a sacrifice," he said.

"To the gods? Oh, Brian!"

"She had to be sacrificed, didn't she? I could almost see it coming. It was inevitable." He seemed more eager than ever to convince me.

"And Jed?" I asked softly.

Suddenly somber, he stood up. "I expect it's no use talking to you, Lindsay. You have it in you to feel and understand these things, but you're not ready yet."

As he started toward the door, something caught his eye and he stopped. "What's that?" he asked, pointing.

He was indicating the glass-topped coffee table in front of the sofa, and I saw that a film of Sedona's insidious red dust had collected over its surface. I knew that it was always a continuous battle to keep up with the dust, and now I saw that there were markings on the coffee table—lettering!

I went quickly to the table and stood looking down. Barely visible, since the film was thin, a name was scrawled: VERMILION. I sat down in the nearest chair with a suddenness that jarred me.

"Vermilion?" Brian said. "Oh, I remember. She was your imaginary playmate when you were small, wasn't she?"

I couldn't look at him. I could only stare at the name written in the dust. "How did you know?" I asked.

"Sybil, of course. She said you often used your friend Vermilion against her. She said you didn't outgrow her as you got older, and that you'd begun to imagine her as almost real by the time you were in your teens."

Then she'd have told others, too.

"Sybil never understood," I said bitterly.

Brian was silent for a moment. When he spoke his tone was gentle. "I think *I* can understand, Lindsay."

"You mean you think I'm a little crazy?"

"No. I didn't believe that, even when Sybil hinted at it. I've been trying to tell you that there's a lot more out there than we humans can understand. Maybe we're nearer to it here in Sedona. There are so many—mysteries. I feel very near them sometimes when I'm hiking through the canyon—as though some sort of revelation might be close. But there's a danger too."

His rapt expression made me uneasy, but I said nothing.

"The danger lies in the fact that we *are* human. To come too close—to see through the curtain—might only mean the end of life as we know it."

I shook myself back into the real world. "You're missing the point," I said. "What I want to know is who scratched a name here in red dust? Who else did Sybil tell about Vermilion?"

"I suppose she could have told anyone.

Aren't *you* missing the point? Who else could have written it, except your—Vermilion?"

Pushing him out of my way almost violently, I ran into the kitchen to get a dampened sponge. Then I returned to kneel before the coffee table and wipe it clean of red dust. Brian didn't speak until I was through, and the table was free of any trace of lettering.

Then he said in an ordinary voice, "You shouldn't have done that."

"Do you think I'd stay here, staring at that scrawl all night? I couldn't stand any more of that!"

I was still kneeling before the table with the sponge clutched in my fingers when Brian bent over me, drawing it from my grasp. He raised me carefully to my feet and put his arms around me, resting his cheek against my hair.

"Oh, Lindsay, you have to learn to let go, to relax. Everything will be all right. I can help you, Lindsay, if you'll let me. I can help you find peace." He was smoothing my hair as tenderly as though I'd been a child, and I felt more frightened by his intense gentleness than if he'd been rough with me. Somehow I didn't dare remove myself from his embrace in any sudden way. In the most peace-loving person there could be violence—I had seen hints of it in Rick—but this man frightened me because he was just a little out of touch with reality.

Sensing my stillness in his arms, he released me and stepped back. "It's all right, Lindsay.

278

All I want is to help you. I never really wanted to help Sybil, but just to get her to promote something very important, and not only for Sedona. For everywhere today. You're Jed's daughter in a better way than she was, and that means a lot to me. When I was a kid, I worshipped him. And the feeling I had for him didn't change until the last year or so before he died. That was because *he* changed, and he began to scare me."

"What do you mean—changed?"

"I don't want to talk about that. Not now. You're tired, so I'll go. You'd better think about some of the things I've said tonight. Lindsay, if there's trouble—of any kind—you can count on me. Lock your door tonight. After this you'd better lock it whenever you leave."

Locking the door was first in my mind too, and when he'd gone I turned the key with a sharp click, then went into the living room, where I stood looking down at the coffee table, wiped clear of red dust.

Who could possibly have written that name for me to find? Who had meant me to feel the terror this act had aroused? Not for a moment would I believe that some product of my own mind, my imagination, had taken on corporeal life and traced a name in red dust. *Never!*

Somewhere inside my head that familiar laughter seemed to ripple mockingly.

I was ready for bed, wrapped in a light robe,

and sitting in the kitchen drinking hot milk when Alice tapped on the front door and called to me. I went gladly to let her in, and locked it after her. Her expression seemed solemn and concerned as she came out to the kitchen with me.

"I'm sorry if I've kept you up," she said. "I've been talking to Rick."

"It's not really late, though I feel as though it must be past midnight because so much has happened."

"I'm concerned about Rick," Alice said. "He thinks it's only a matter of time before he's picked up as the only suspect. It's too bad that Sybil must have gone off in his truck yesterday."

"Who do you think was driving it? That's the crucial point."

"I wish I knew. Lots of us around here can drive that sort of vehicle. I have one myself. But now Rick is especially worried about you. He wants me to persuade you to go back to New York as soon as possible."

New York? That faraway place—lost to me already? How strange to think that only a short while ago all my life had been tied up with New York. I'd talked to Nan today, after we'd found Sybil. Everything was going fine, and she understood that I must stay for a time. I had a feeling, talking with her, that we already belonged to different worlds, and that matters which had been important to me a little while ago and were still important to my partner no longer had much significance in my life. Everything changed in the face of—murder. In the face of love.

I repeated the words I'd said to Rick. "I'm not going to leave. Not yet."

"I know," Alice sighed. "I didn't think you would. You're Jed's daughter."

"What does that mean—being Jed's daughter?"

"So many things. I can see Silvercloud in you as well. Such stubbornness in the two of them, and such devotion to what they believed in. Though she was gentle, and sometimes he was not."

"What *did* my father believe in? I've always wondered."

"I'm not sure of that anymore. Perhaps he believed in helping—when he could. He hadn't many illusions about himself, about his own appetites—and he didn't always like the way he lived, or the fascination the next turn of the tables always had for him. The big gamble. He tried to compensate in his own way, and I think he did, some of the time."

"Not with your young friend Celia," I said bitterly.

"No, not with her."

If there had been anger in Alice Rainsong against Jed at one time, it was no longer there, though it was still strong in me.

"What can we do to help Rick?" I asked.

He was the present. I could do nothing about the past.

"Perhaps we could find out about Jerome," she said. "Perhaps we could go there."

"What do you think can be found in Jerome?"

For the first time she seemed uneasy. "Your father lived in Jerome for a while, years ago."

"Then he knew this Mrs. Jessup, whom Sybil and Brian went to see? Is that what you think?"

"Yes, he knew her, but I don't want to bother her, Lindsay. If we go to Jerome, it won't be to visit her. There may be someone else left who knew Jed, since there aren't all that many people in the town."

I still felt strongly that the mysterious Mrs. Jessup was the connecting link, but I would wait until we reached Jerome before I urged Alice again.

"Let's go tomorrow, then," I suggested. "I have a feeling there isn't too much time."

She nodded gravely. "Shall we leave for Jerome early? I'm usually up by daylight."

"Not that early. Let's say in the morning." I couldn't know then that we wouldn't get to Jerome tomorrow, no matter what we planned. "I want to tell you what happened here tonight," I went on. "Brian Montgomery was waiting for me when I came back this evening."

Alice Rainsong was a woman who could listen, who tried to understand what lay behind spoken words. She paid me quiet attention as I related the details of Brian's visit, though she offered no comment. Not until I told her of the name, "Vermilion," being written in dust on the coffee table, did she seem disturbed.

"I don't like that. It means that someone not only entered this house maliciously but chose this way of striking out at you."

I liked her calm practicality. Just having her understand helped me.

"It's a good thing I'm staying here tonight," she went on. "Two of us will discourage anyone who might try to reach you alone."

"I'm glad you came." I held out my hand and she clasped it in both of hers. Her quiet strength brought me a little of that peace that Brian had talked about so grandiloquently.

A half hour later we were in our twin beds, and after a little more desultory talk we fell asleep.

My awakening came in the small hours of the morning. It seemed to me that there had been a muffled sound from the living room, though I couldn't be sure whether it was in my dreams, or real. When I opened my eyes and stared into what should have been darkness, I saw a shimmer of light beyond the bedroom door.

It can be frightening to awaken suddenly from a deep sleep and see a light in another part of a house where there should be no light. Frightening, even when I knew that I'd simply forgotten to turn off one of the living room lamps before I went to bed. I raised myself on my elbow and looked across at Alice in the dim, reflected light. She was sound asleep. I would slip out of bed and turn off whatever lamp we'd forgotten.

The early morning hours were chilly, and I put on a robe and slippers before I went quietly out of the bedroom. Across the tiny hall a lamp was indeed burning in the empty room.

Now I was puzzled. The lamps Brian had turned on when we came in earlier were connected to the switch by the door. This was a corner lamp that I couldn't remember lighting at all. Perhaps Alice had done so. It didn't matter. As I went to turn it off I noticed that one of the sliding doors of the living room storage closet was partially open, yet I could remember clearly that I'd closed that door earlier in the evening, when I'd put Jed's cane away. Alice would never have opened that closet. Alarmed now, I pressed the lamp switch.

At once the room was dark, with only a glimmer from stars beyond the windows. As silently as possible, I edged toward the bedroom. If I called out, I might be in greater danger than if I moved quietly and swiftly. Almost at once I knocked against the coffee table with a thud, and I heard the closet door sliding further ajar.

With sudden clarity I remembered that moment on the terrace when I'd been about to pick up Jed's cane and the voice in my mind had warned me not to touch it. Now a word exploded through me as though a fuse had been lighted.

MOVE!

This time I obeyed instantly, stepping to the side, only to be blocked by a chair. I caught a glint of something flying in the starlight and heard the swish of air as the dragon's head came down. Pain cracked through me and a black curtain descended.

12

I dreamed about Vermilion. A shimmering, dancing Vermilion, with hair that seemed to stream like flames from her head. Her laughter echoed endlessly in my mind—a laughter that sounded strangely triumphant.

It seemed as though she spoke to me aloud as she'd done when I was a little girl—and only seldom after I grew up. "You need me, Lindsay. You mustn't try to deny me. I saved you, you know. If only you'd listened on the terrace! I tried to warn you about the cane."

I attempted to turn in my bed, but pain attacked, slashing and throbbing, until I lay still. Yet I could hear my own voice, faint and very far off.

"Go away! I don't want you! You frighten me!"

I could hear her whispering close to my ear. "By frightening you, I keep you alive. Because I can only be alive if *you* are alive, Lindsay. If you die, we die together. Listen to me, Lindsay! There are people around who can't be trusted."

"What people?" I demanded.

But she only fluttered and shimmered beyond the foot of my bed, and I knew she wouldn't—or couldn't—tell me.

I continued to lie still and the pain faded a little, though I knew she was still there. I could see her clearly, and I'd always loved to watch her dance—light as confetti blowing through the air, graceful, and so beautiful! Now it seemed as though my eyes were open and I could see her swirling, floating, her feet keeping time to her laughter.

She was my friend. My long-ago friend. Yet sometimes she was not my friend, and then I could sense her malice. Perhaps she wanted me alive, because as she said, I was her life. But there were times when she wanted to hurt me, and suddenly I comprehended.

"You're jealous!" I accused. "You want what I have that you can never have—life!"

Her shimmering became angry and a little wild, but her laughter had been silenced.

"I *can* send you away," I said.

I think in that moment she chose not to risk it. For an instant more the flames of her hair gleamed brightly and then faded into shadow. There was no sound or movement where she had been.

An intense awareness of my body possessed me, of the throbbing in my head. Of course I had been dreaming—only dreaming. When I opened my eyes it was to see a brightness everywhere that made me blink. The light color of walls, the white uniform of a nurse. Out of sight I could hear a man's voice speaking to someone I couldn't see. I could hear the words clearly—the sound of authority.

"Since she wasn't unconscious for long, it's probably not serious. We'll know better when we see the X-rays. The medication is making her sleepy, and she may be a little confused for a while and not remember. You can see her, if you like."

"I'm awake," I said in the same faraway tones I'd used to Vermilion.

The doctor must have gone, but the nurse smiled at me benignly and beckoned to someone who stood in the doorway. Rick came into the room and pulled a chair near the bed where I could see him without turning my head. "Don't stay too long," the nurse warned, and went away.

"It's morning," Rick said. "You're in the hospital in Cottonwood. It's a good hospital, and closer than Flagstaff." He picked up my hand and laid it against his cheek. "Don't try to talk, darling. Luckily you just missed receiving a lethal blow. The doctor says there was no laceration, though you'll have a lump on the side of your head for a while."

I reached up gingerly and felt the soreness and swelling. "What about Alice?" I whispered.

"She heard you fall and ran out of the bedroom, but she had trouble in the dark, and whoever it was got away. By the time she turned on the lights and saw what had happened, it was too late to see who was there. She called me, and we brought you here right away. The lock on the guesthouse door hadn't been touched, so whoever it was must have come in earlier and stayed out of sight in that closet."

"That's where I put the cane," I said, and closed my eyes because the light hurt me. The world—even a hospital world—was beautiful and dazzling, and right now my eyes had to get used to it.

"Who were you talking to just now?" Rick asked.

I wasn't strong enough to equivocate. "Vermilion," I said. "She comes back too often lately. She says she helped me last night. I know something told me to move just in time."

He squeezed my hand and stood up to look at someone else who had entered the room. I had no wish to move my head. Alice came around the end of the bed and spoke to me.

"I could almost sense her there last night," she told me. "Your Vermilion. There was something strong and good in the room that was trying to help you."

I managed to smile at Alice. "She's not always good. Only when it serves her to be." I looked uncomfortably at Rick. Alice Rainsong might understand, but I wasn't sure of Rick.

"You *are* your father's daughter," he said a bit ruefully. "And both you and Alice belong to Silvercloud."

Relief ran through me. Rick would never mock me as Sybil had done.

"Have you talked to the sheriff?" I asked.

"Yes. Jed's cane was dropped on the terrace before whoever struck you went down into the wash and ran away. Everyone who came to dinner last night is being questioned—whatever good that will do. So far there's not a lead. It wasn't necessarily one of us, of course. It could have been anyone at all."

"I don't think so," Alice said calmly. She sat beside my bed, straight-backed and poised. "The connecting strands with Jed and Sybil are too clear. Someone is frightened, and the frightened can be dangerous. What was Sybil after, that last day? Someone knows."

"She didn't confide in me," Rick said dryly.

I asked a question of my own. "Were there any marks on the cane?"

"I doubt it," Rick said, "but it's being checked."

"Is Marilla all right?"

"Orva is keeping her occupied. She can stay there as long as we like."

Urgency was rising again, and I knew that Vermilion's mistrust and suspicion were still alive.

"Bring Marilla home, Rick," I pleaded. "Don't leave her in that house with Orva and Brian. Don't let her become a hostage."

"What are you talking about?" He sounded

angry now, and I knew how stretched out he was.

My courage was fading with my strength. "I don't know what I mean—I don't really know! *You* told me to stay away from Orva and her son—remember?"

"This is different. She's devoted to Marilla."

"Just the same, bring her home!"

Alice put a calming hand on my arm. "Hush, Lindsay. Rick will bring Marilla home soon." She looked up at him. "What should we do now?"

"First of all, I'd better make it clear to everyone who heard her that Lindsay was talking off the top of her head at dinner last night. I mean, when she said she might know who killed Jed, and perhaps Sybil. I don't suppose I can undo the damage, but I'll try. In the meantime, Lindsay, be quiet and rest. You're safe here, and the doctor thinks you should stay overnight. If the X-rays are all right, he'll probably release you tomorrow."

Gradually my head seemed to be clearing, though I still felt far too excited.

"I can stay as long as you like, Rick," Alice put in. "Though I don't think last night will be repeated. We're on guard now."

"What about Sybil?" I asked.

Rick understood. "The police are holding her body for a few days. So the funeral must wait."

A nurse returned to motion Rick and Alice

toward the door.

"We'll see you later, Lindsay," he said. "Let me do the worrying for a while."

Alice, however, stayed where she was. "I'm not leaving the hospital yet. I'll let Lindsay rest, but I want to be here in case she needs me."

Her words reassured and comforted. I wanted to rest. The hurt, physical part of me wanted to rest, though my wakeful mind longed futilely for action. Once more there was a pill to calm me down, and I went to sleep.

Not until later that day did the police take Rick to Flagstaff for further questioning. In the meantime, all four of the "friends" who had been at the dinner last night came to see me. All were disquieting.

During the next hours I slept and wakened and ate a little. With Alice there, I began to relax—and I didn't dream about Vermilion.

The first of my visitors arrived in midafternoon. Parker brought me a thermos of what he said would be the most strengthening eggnog in the world. Since no voice warned me not to drink it, I sipped a glass right away, and could feel its power flowing through me. Perhaps the touch of brandy helped.

For once Parker seemed rather subdued, and he showed concern for me. It occurred to me that Sybil's absence made a difference to all of us. We might regret the way of her death, but things were easier without her presence.

A sad epitaph.

"Are you really all right, Lindsay?" he asked as I drank eggnog. "That was a hell of a thing to have happen. Any idea who it could have been?"

I wished that I needn't remember that it might be any of four people, with Parker one of the four.

"No," I said, "I've no idea." Even if I'd had an answer, I'd never boast about it again.

"Clara's coming to see you later—if you're still here," he went on. "She probably can't get away from the store for a while. This is a bad affair. Terrible! You get to wondering who's going to be next."

Perhaps the eggnog was helping, because I seemed to be thinking a little more clearly. There was a special question I needed to ask.

"We're all worried now," I agreed. "And we will be until this is cleared up. Did you see anything of Sybil the day she disappeared?"

He had brought another chair to the opposite side of the bed from Alice, and he sat down, considering the question. "Sybil telephoned me early in the morning. Just more details about the dinner. I'd wanted to give her a better meal than the one she planned, but she wouldn't have it. That was the last I heard from her. I never saw her again."

There was nothing I else I could ask, and he chatted pleasantly with Alice, speaking knowledgeably about her paintings in the

Tlaquepaque store. He even asked about her teaching at the university in Flagstaff, and about the satisfaction she must get from working with young people.

"You sound like someone who would have liked to teach," Alice said.

That seemed to startle him. "Afraid not. All I know is cooking, and I've never wanted to teach my tricks to anybody."

Not until just before he left did he say anything that disturbed me.

At the door he looked back as if in afterthought and said, "What's Orva's son up to anyway?"

"What do you mean?" I asked, startled.

"Clara told me he came to the store this morning. He wanted to have another look at that Fire People piece your father carved, Lindsay. Clara said he plunked down on the floor in her office and just stared at it for a while."

"Perhaps it was speaking to him," Alice said.

Parker moved his shoulders derisively. "Not in any language Clara could understand," he said, and went away.

Alice walked to the window to look down into the hospital grounds. She was the one who could accept Vermilion most easily, I thought, and I wished I could open up with her more. But she too liked to go off alone in her mind and seek for answers, and I said nothing, respecting her silence. When she turned back, however, I knew that she'd found none.

"Jed talked to me once about Sybil," she said. "He knew there was something in him that caused him to torment her at times, and I think Sybil really hated him. What bothered her most of all was his mysticism. Young Brian learned that from him. She fought the way he drew Marilla into something she couldn't understand. She disliked anything to do with the Fire People, and perhaps she feared her own fear because she couldn't accept it."

"And of course my father played on her fear?"

"That's right. I told him once that he was being cruel, and he laughed at me. The point is that everyone knew about Sybil's dread of that place. But of course this was before Jed changed."

"Brian said something like that too. How did he change? Why?"

Alice shook her head sadly. "I'm not sure, exactly. There was a time before he died when I seldom saw him, though before that he used to come often to stay at my house in Flagstaff. The last time I saw him there he seemed morose and depressed. The change came after the car accident, and I'm sure Celia's death was often in his mind and on his conscience."

"Why shouldn't it have been?" I challenged. "He *was* to blame. He always had a weakness for young, pretty women."

"I know. We all knew."

"Then why did you send her to him?"

For the first time Alice's quiet control seemed to falter. "Celia was in love with someone else. She was even talking about marriage, so I thought she'd be safe. I didn't count on that attraction he had for women—something he could never keep from exerting. I trusted him at the wrong time."

"Was he really having an affair with this girl?" I could hear the bitterness in my voice.

"How can we know? Perhaps we have to give them both the benefit of the doubt. Afterwards, he kept going back to Jerome."

"Why Jerome? And why did Sybil make Brian take her there?"

Once more, Alice seemed to remove herself from her immediate surroundings. Her eyes took on a distant look, and everything about her became very still. It was as though she turned herself inward and locked all doors and windows that might open her to the world. Almost imperceptibly, she went away to a place where I couldn't reach her, and I knew there was still something she didn't want to tell me.

"I'd rather not talk about Celia right now," she said after an interval. "There are others concerned, and I haven't made my peace yet with what happened. There was so much about Jed that I loved. I always looked to him as a father when I was growing up, yet there was that other side of him. That wilder side that led him down strange roads."

"I know. It was like that for me too."

At least, by this time, I was sure of one thing. *I* must go to Jerome. There were answers in Jerome, and it was possible that I could find them, and through them find the truth that would help Rick. The inaction of lying in a hospital bed was frustrating, yet I found myself all too ready to close my eyes and doze again. I must stop taking those pills they shoved at me.

Alice roused herself and went to draw the draperies, shutting out the light, so that I could nap again. Hospitals were far from quiet places, and someone was always popping in and out, but I was still able to fall asleep.

When I woke up, an hour had passed, and Orva was in the room, sitting where Parker had sat. She and Alice were quiet, letting me sleep, and they seemed comfortable enough in each other's company. Alice had a rare quality of meaning harm to no one, yet I couldn't forget those angry pictures I had seen in the shop gallery. Nor would I forget what she'd said about Jed, and the uneasiness about him that she too had suffered.

When I opened my eyes, Orva said, "Good, you're still alive. I was wondering if you were going to sleep all afternoon. "Look—I brought you some fruit. How're you feeling, Lindsay?"

"Better," I said. "Thank you for coming."

Alice opened the draperies and then came to raise the bed so I could sit up.

"That was pretty awful—what happened to you last night," Orva went on. "You were crazy to go ahead with that dinner. Not that I haven't done a few crazy things myself. But if you hadn't gone ahead with Sybil's plan, maybe you wouldn't have been attacked. When poison's stirring around under the surface, the way Sybil was stirring it, it's better to leave the brew alone."

I asked a direct question. "You've already told me that you saw Sybil the morning of the day she disappeared. You said she came to talk about the dinner. Was there anything else?"

For a moment I thought Orva might not answer. She sat beside my bed looking as angular and ungraceful as ever, her thin face marked with deepening lines of worry. Then she glanced briefly at Alice, and straightened her shoulders, making a decision.

"You might as well know, though I haven't said anything about this to anyone else. Sybil came to see me mainly to talk about Brian. She claimed that he was making her very uncomfortable. I think she had a feeling that he was pushing her in some way, and she didn't like it."

"I should think she'd have been the first to deal with him herself, if she didn't like something he was doing. What does Brian say about this?"

"I haven't mentioned it to him. Finding Sybil dead has shaken him badly. He hasn't talked

298

to me much lately, and I'm getting worried. Sometimes I think Jed inoculated him with some of that anthropomorphism he went in for. Stone faces that could be human—or maybe inhuman. I don't like it a bit. I never wanted him to get mixed up with Sybil. She always spelled Trouble with a capital "T". I liked Jed some of the time, but toward the end he was off in another country."

Orva stood up, elbows thrust out aggressively, as though she wanted to hear no more questions.

"I mustn't tire you, Lindsay. Just be careful. You're here because you talked too much at dinner last night. That's obvious, isn't it? I'm glad Rick's trying to counteract that, though it may already be too late. He says you were bluffing. Were you bluffing, Lindsay?"

"I'm afraid I was," I said feebly. "It wasn't very smart of me."

"Just hold to that," she said, gave us both a sober wave of her hand, and went away.

Alice took an apple from the basket Orva had left and cut a slice for me. Its juicy sweetness was refreshing. The scent of apples was more pleasant than hospital odors.

"Why did you say what you did last night?" Alice asked.

"I'm not sure." Just the same, I was sure. When an impulse as strong as that came, I obeyed it. I'd never been able to resist.

"It was Vermilion again?" Alice's tone

was matter-of-fact.

"I don't like to think that," I said. "I hate to go around hearing voices in my head. Sometimes it happens. It happens as sharply as though someone very powerful has come to life inside me and has to be obeyed."

"She isn't always right, is she?"

"I don't know. She was certainly wrong if she prompted me to say what I did."

"Perhaps you need to resist a little more. After all, you're the one in control."

She sounded as sure about that as I wanted to be.

"Just the same," I told her, "I think Vermilion kept me alive last night."

"We all have inner 'voices.' Sometimes an instinct that cautions us, even though it doesn't become as tangible as those you've experienced."

"Her name was written in dust on the coffee table," I reminded Alice.

"A *voice* didn't do that. She's part of you, Lindsay. You've just made more of a separation than most of us do."

That was true enough, but how was I to absorb Vermilion so that she'd never separate from me again?

Clara Hale spoke from the doorway. "Is it okay if I come in?" Then, without waiting for an invitation, she walked into the room and sat down by my bed. Clearly, she was in a glowering mood.

300

"How are you feeling, Lindsay?"

The question sounded grudging, and I had felt better.

"I'm all right," I said. "I mean to get up soon and walk around."

"One thing ought to be clear to you by now," Clara went on. "You'd better go back to New York as soon as you can. There's been nothing but trouble here ever since you arrived. I'm beginning to think you brought a lot of it with you."

"*Clara,*" Alice said, and I heard an edge of warning in her voice.

Clara paid no attention. Anger and indignation were driving her, and she began to spit them out at me. "They've taken Rick to Flagstaff for questioning. *His* pickup truck is the one that took Sybil out to that place. There's not much doubt about it. And someone has hinted at his problems with Sybil. His motive is getting stronger all the time. We know he didn't do it, but the police are closing in."

I shut my eyes and wished that I could close my ears as well against her words. Because all she was saying was true. I'd had nothing to do with the breakup between Rick and Sybil, though my coming appeared to have brought everything to an explosion. Sybil had been marching down an arrogant road of her own, and somehow she'd stepped into dangerous territory that had nothing to do with Rick.

"I can't go away until it's over," I said

doggedly. "Have they arrested Rick?"

"Not yet. I don't think it will be long, unless something can be done."

Anger against injustice was beginning to strengthen me. "We have to do *something* to help him. *I* need to do something—not just lie here!"

"Could be you're a likely suspect too." Clara was exploring now, maliciously.

Alice had heard enough. "Lindsay isn't feeling well, and you're not helping, Clara. I think you'd better go now."

Clara had the sense to know that Alice could be her match if she chose. "All right then. I'll get back to the store. Parker's helping out, though even with Connie there, I can never be sure he won't give away something he ought to be selling."

"Tell him I enjoyed his eggnog." I could offer that, at least.

"Hah!" Clara headed for the door, where she paused. "Good-bye, you two," she said more mildly. "I'll keep you posted on what happens."

When she'd gone, Alice closed the door. "You've had enough visitors for a while. See if you can sleep again."

Instead, I sat up on the edge of the bed and put my feet on the floor. "I've had too much sleep. Lying here doing nothing is making me feel worse than I need to. Do you think they can really arrest Rick?"

"I don't know. In the end it will come out that he's innocent, but it can be unpleasant until then."

"That's why we have to do something," I said. "Alice, will you take me to Jerome?"

"Right now I'll take you to the end of the corridor and back." She pushed my slippers near my feet and brought my robe. "We'll talk about Jerome another time."

"But you know the house Sybil went to. You could take me there."

She was already shaking her head. "I'll take you to Jerome, though I don't see what good it will do. I won't take you to that house. I know Mrs. Jessup and I'm fond of her. She's old and not well. All she asks is to be left alone. Besides, I don't see what possible answers she could give you."

"Sybil went there. Sybil got an answer—so she was killed. I think she meant to tell everything at dinner last night. And she would have, if she hadn't been stopped."

"So now you're going to ask for the same sort of trouble?"

"This *has* to end."

"Of course. But not by getting yourself hurt."

"So what do you propose?"

"I'd like to know why Brian is behaving peculiarly, and why Orva's so worried about him. This could be a first step, but it can't be hurried, either. Now I want to get something from my car. You'll be all right for a while?"

I wasn't sure I'd ever be all right again. Whether I liked lying here or not, I had to rest until my head felt better and my energy returned.

Out the window, white clouds drifted across deep turquoise. I watched them for a time, finding the slow, windless movement soothing. The land baked in the sun and I knew it would be warmer than in high Sedona. In spite of Alice's words, there was one thing more I could try. I was not, after all, ready to let Vermilion go.

When I closed my eyes, I was ready—quiet and waiting. I knew she would come. I had always depended upon her, and she had never really failed me.

Almost at once, she was there against the darkness of my eyelids, her hair aglow, her lips parted with that familiar laughter that could ring through my mind.

Help me, I said, though I knew the words had no sound. *Help me to help Rick. Help me to find the answers.*

She flipped around in one of her graceful little dances, her bright hair flying. *Think,* she commanded. *Concentrate.*

Stillness was all around me and I emptied my mind of all but Vermilion's bright figure. I could see her shimmering in every detail, even while one part of me knew that if I opened my eyes she would be gone.

Suddenly the word was there in my mind. *Eggnog.* Eggnog?

I don't know what you're talking about, I told her. *The eggnog was delicious. It made me feel better. Parker was hardly trying to poison me.*

Of course he wasn't. She sounded impatient. *You can be so slow. You really aren't intuitive at all.*

She had only taken to picking on me lately, and it worried me.

You'll have to do better than eggnog, I said. *What else?*

All right then, slowpoke! Why don't you ask Brian about his lost love?

This was certainly a fresh thought, though it didn't seem to take me anywhere. Nevertheless, I knew that she—who was a part of my own mind—had the faculty of taking bits and pieces that were already embedded in my unconscious and adding them up to something new that hadn't been grasped. This was the creative process at work. I mustn't doubt it.

Vermilion, of course, could read my thoughts, and was quickly impatient again, and resentful as well—in a new and disturbing way.

Why do you have the right to be out there? Why are you the one Rick loves? Why should I be trapped in this little corner of your mind, when I could have such a fine time if you'd let me out?

This was going too far. I opened my eyes, half-afraid that I might find her there in my hospital room. Thankfully, she was gone with

305

a flick of my eyelids, and I was left with the new thought she had put into my mind. *Brian's lost love?* I seemed to remember something someone had said . . . But this was hardly of any use, since every man probably had a "lost love." And I didn't know what Brian's had to do with anything. Nor did the word "eggnog" make any more sense. In the end, it was I who had thought these things, I reminded myself. Why?

I sat by the window, still puzzling, when the banging started on the door that Alice had closed behind her. Not a light tapping that someone might use in a hospital, but a peremptory knocking that demanded access at once.

"Come in," I called.

Brian opened the door and walked in explosively. He came straight to where I sat and bent over me angrily. Yet the moment he touched my shoulder, I knew his anger was not for me.

"I just heard," he said. "Are you all right, Lindsay? I've been away—all night. When I came home Ma told me what had happened. So I came straight over."

He'd grasped my hand with an intensity that crushed my bones, and I drew back from him. "You're hurting me, Brian."

"I would never *want* to hurt you," he said. "Never, Lindsay. You've got to believe that."

"All right, I believe it. I'm not feeling very

strong right now, and I wish you'd sit down and be quiet."

In a moment he had brought a chair from the other side of the bed and placed it near me—independent even about where he sat, his eyes hardly moving from my face.

"Are you really all right?"

"No," I said. "I feel dizzy, and I had a terrible fright. I might have been killed."

"Yes, I know. Ma said it was luck you weren't killed."

"Where did you go last night, Brian, after you left me?"

For a moment he hesitated, then gave in to my question. "I went out *there*. I put a sleeping bag in one of the jeeps and drove out to the place of the Fire People. I went through the crack in the rocks and spent the night in there. There was just enough light so I could see the faces looking up at the stars."

Though he was trying to contain his excitement, I sensed it surging up in him.

"Why, Brian? Why did you go there?"

"Because that's where the truth is. It's been marked into the rocks. A bloody happening must leave some sort of psychic stain, and that place, especially, would be sensitive. So I wanted to be close to it, to feel it run through me. I needed to live it, so I could understand— everything."

I wished Alice would return. His excitement was disturbing, whatever it was that drove him.

"What did you learn?" I asked.

"I'm not sure. I looked up at the Shining One until I couldn't stay awake any longer. When I slept, I dreamed in strange ways that I've never experienced before. I think I lived through it all. I lived through everything that happened there with Sybil. She had a reason for trying to climb that column of rock. She must have been terrified and trying to get away from whatever threatened her. But in my dream there was more. All the answers were there and perfectly clear. Terrible answers. When I woke up, it was daylight. I was cold, and all my dreams were gone. I found the answers, Lindsay —and then I lost them. So I just stayed for a while, hoping they would come back to me."

"You stayed all day?"

"Sure. I wanted answers about *me,* too. I've done some pretty strange things, and I'd like to know why. I don't always understand what drives me."

"I wonder if any of us do."

"Anyway, I'd brought something to eat and a thermos of coffee, so I could be comfortable enough. This morning I heard the police coming back, so I crawled into one of those crevices of rock and listened. They were talking about Rick. Has he been arrested?"

"Clara was here a little while ago, and she said they'd taken him to Flagstaff for questioning. He hasn't been arrested."

"I was afraid they'd do that, Lindsay. After

the sun came up this morning and I could see, I made a gift for you. Though I didn't know you'd be in a hospital when I gave it to you."

He reached into his jacket pocket and brought out a flat piece of red rock on which primitive symbols had been carved. I examined it, puzzled.

"It's the mark of your clan," he explained. "The Cloud or Water Clan that Silvercloud belonged to, as well as Rainsong."

So Brian knew about this, though he'd never mentioned it before. But then, he had been Jed's protégé long ago.

He went on. "Among the Hopi, the woman is very important, you know. She's the heart of the family, the dwelling, the field. The man builds the house and cultivates the field, but it's the woman who's the owner, and she repairs the house and keeps it clean, and when the harvest is ready, it's given into her hands. Everything belongs to her. Even when the man speaks of these things as his, everyone knows they're not. Even the family name comes down through the woman, and when a man marries he goes to live with his wife's family. The Cloud Clan symbol is those three clouds, with the concave sides down, and lines below representing falling rain. Rain is more important than anything else in the Southwest."

I turned the rock about in my hands, feeling strangely moved that Brian should have done this for me.

"I was thinking about you when I was out there." He spoke more quietly now. "About how everything has changed since you came."

I winced because these were Clara's words, though she'd intended them harshly.

He shook his head despairingly. "I didn't want to follow Sybil around anymore, no matter what she could do for the things I believe in. Without saying anything, you made me a little ashamed of the way I'd acted—playing up to her."

I felt ashamed, because I hadn't thought of him very much at all—or only in passing because he was a rather strange young man.

"Thank you for making this for me," I said.

He reached out to touch my hand lightly. "Last night I thought about you almost as much as I did about what had happened there."

Whatever Vermilion had meant by Brian's "lost love," he was apparently well over her by now, and I must put a stop to this.

"Don't think about me, Brian. Not that way."

"Oh, I know. You're already Rick's girl, aren't you?"

I said nothing, and suddenly he grinned at me. "That's right—you're part Hopi, and a Hopi never tells all."

We could smile at each other more easily, and for the first time since he'd stormed into my room, I could relax a little. I wouldn't ask him about his lost love, but I remembered the other strange thing Vermilion had put into my mind.

"Parker Hale was here a while ago," I said, "and he brought me a thermos of the most delicious eggnog."

"Ah? The famous eggnog!"

"You know about it?"

"That eggnog was the cause of a terrible fight between my mother and Sybil a couple of years ago. Or at least I suppose it was an excuse for a fight that Ma had been spoiling for. Silliest thing I ever heard. It was on Christmas when we were having open house, and Sybil said she'd bring eggnog. Only her recipe didn't suit Ma. So they practically had a shouting match over which recipe to use. It's a good thing Rick was around to settle it before they got violent. He said to put both recipes together—and that's what's been served around here ever since. It was such a success that Sybil gave it to Parker when he came to Sedona. So that's what you undoubtedly got—the Adams-Montgomery eggnog."

I tried to smile at his story, but I wasn't satisfied. What was it, really, that Vermilion had been trying to tell me? What was buried in my unconscious that I didn't know how to get at? I shifted gears and made a direct request. If I wanted to do this, I knew I must ask before Alice returned.

"Brian, can we try to help Rick? Will you drive me to Jerome tomorrow?"

He was suddenly still. "Why don't you ask

Alice to take you? Since she knows the old woman.''

"Alice doesn't want me to bother Mrs. Jessup.''

He thought about that for a moment, and then agreed reluctantly. "I suppose I can take you, if that's what you want. But it's not going to help. You couldn't possibly talk to her the way she was—if she's even alive by this time. Anyway, do you think you'll be up to it?''

"I'll be up to it. I have to be. Will you pick me up here, and then perhaps you can drive me back to Rick's afterward?''

He nodded soberly and stood up. "I suppose this all goes back to the time when Jed lived for a while in Jerome. Though I don't think we'll find out a thing. Anyway, I'll see you in the morning. Ten o'clock?''

Alice returned just as he left, and he greeted her casually and hurried away.

"Well!'' she said. "Did Brian have anything interesting to tell you?''

I held up the rock. "He brought me the symbol of the Cloud Clan.''

I didn't tell her about where we planned to go in the morning. I would have to let her know, but not until it was too late for her to stop me.

13

Two more visitors came to see me before the evening was over. The two I most wanted to see—Rick and Marilla. I was alone when they arrived, as Alice had gone out for dinner. Strain showed in Rick's face and there were new hollows in his cheeks. Marilla seemed more subdued than I'd ever seen her.

At least her antagonism toward me had apparently faded, and perhaps I had Orva to thank for that. With a shyness that seemed foreign to her, Marilla held out a small package. When I'd unwrapped it I found the little unicorn smiling at me.

"The other time I just said you could have it, because I didn't want it," Marilla said. "But now it really is for you. Orva showed me how to paint it and put on the pink glaze before we fired it. Unicorns are for love and luck—and to keep you safe."

"I'll keep it always," I told her.

"You'll come back to the house, won't you?" she went on anxiously.

I looked up at Rick, questioning, and he sat down beside my bed. "Alice is going to stay for a while, and we'd like you there too. Marilla will feel more comfortable. Are you all right, Lindsay?"

"I'm fine. I'll be out of here tomorrow, and I'd like to come back to your house. This time I'll be more careful. How did it go in Flagstaff?"

"Not badly. They're inclined to believe me, I think, though anything might change that. I'll have to go back tomorrow. The trouble is, they've nothing else to go on but my truck, which it appears really was out there."

"Will there be a grand jury hearing?"

"Only if they're ready to indict. The medical examiner's report and that of the police have gone to the county attorney, and they want to talk to me again. Then perhaps there'll be a preliminary hearing before a local magistrate. I don't really know what will happen. I can account for some of my time, but there are blank spots."

"Couldn't this have happened while you were driving me to Flagstaff?"

"They think it happened later than that." He glanced at Marilla and stood up. "We'd better go along now. Marilla will spend another night with Orva, and then I'll bring her home. Shall I pick you up in the morning before I go to Flagstaff?"

I shook my head. "Alice is here, and

I have a lift.''

I couldn't risk being stopped by anyone who might think I shouldn't go to Jerome. Not even Rick.

When they'd gone, I lay back against my pillow, feeling limp again, and depressed. Getting to Jerome had begun to seem the one thing I might be able to take action about. If I could find the same answer that Sybil had found, and if I could handle it more wisely, perhaps I really could be of some use to Rick.

When Alice returned, I told her first about my visitors and then brought up the subject of Jerome.

"Brian is driving me there in the morning. I realize that you don't want me to talk to Mrs. Jessup, but I must go, Alice. This is what *my* instinct says I must do."

"Vermilion again?"

"No! This is only my decision. She's been quiet for a while."

"Perhaps because you're doing what she wants you to do?"

I didn't want to even think about that.

The room had grown dusky, with only light from the hospital corridor shining in, and the echo of trays being collected sounding far away. My muscles tensed as if for resistance as I lay there, waiting for Alice's opposition. This time it didn't come.

"Since you're so determined about this," she said, "I'll go with you and Brian. Perhaps you'll need me there."

"Thank you. I think I can sleep now."

All night long my dreams were quiet ones, and Vermilion was quiet too. Alice's offer to come with me had finally enabled me to relax, and perhaps her intention might really have worked out, if it hadn't been for Brian.

He came for me promptly at ten. I was wheeled to the downstairs door, where his car waited. While Alice went to the desk to take care of checking me out, Brian started the motor and drove away.

I protested quickly, indignantly. "You can't do this! I told Alice that she could come with us. Brian, you've got to go back!"

"If you really want to go, we'll be better off without Alice," he said.

"No—I won't treat her that way!"

"Oh, stop it," he said impatiently. "You don't really need a built-in nurse! Just keep still and enjoy the drive."

He had changed again—not at all the sympathetic man he'd seemed last night. I was furious with him, but at least I felt better physically this morning than I had yesterday. Though there were still soreness and a lump on the side of my head, the dizziness and over-excitement seemed to have passed, and my energy had returned. In fact, I felt as though I were bursting for action. To do *something* was to allay last night's depression. So I would go with Brian without further protest, and I would explain to Alice later.

Luckily, Jerome was no great distance from Cottonwood, where the hospital was, and after Clarkdale in the Verde Valley, we began the steep rise of two thousand feet—"over the mountain," as I'd heard the phrase used. Cleopatra Hill, a great spreading mound on the side of Mingus Mountain, rose behind the town, and it seemed amazing that tiers of houses could cling to the steep sides. A great barren scar that was the old mine pit was visible, long since abandoned.

"Fifteen thousand people used to live up there," Brian said. "Now it's mostly a ghost town. Oddly enough, it was named for a New Yorker—Eugene Jerome. He more or less started it all, and you may remember that he had a famous cousin named Jenny. Underneath the town there's a hundred miles of shafts and tunnels, mostly filled with water. There used to be cave-ins and buildings could slide down the mountain. Houses were pretty solidly packed up there at one time, but now you can see the gaps where buildings are gone, or empty and wrecked."

The road began its steep turns and traffic that funneled into the narrow way moved slowly. We were nearing the end of our trip.

"Do you know anything about Mrs. Jessup?" I asked Brian.

"Only that she's an old-time resident who has always refused to be moved out of her rickety house. I gather she has no relatives left. A few neighbors look out for her, and she's kept her independence until this illness. Of course we can't be sure she's still alive by this time. Or that she hasn't been moved to a hospital."

"Didn't Sybil say anything that would give you a clue when you brought her here?"

"I think she was looking for clues herself. She wouldn't let me come in with her, and she didn't tell me anything. Though she seemed pretty pleased when she came out."

We made a last steep turn, and I saw that people who lived here must get around mostly on foot, by trails and steps. Cars were kept in garages dug into the mountainside, since there was no parking space. Brian knew his way, however, and found a spot where he could leave his car temporarily.

"Now we walk," he said.

He led the way up wooden steps to a higher level, and once when I stopped to catch my breath I looked back over the great panorama of the valley. Far out there were the red rocks of Oak Creek Canyon. I felt a slight lift of my spirits, thinking of Sedona—and Rick.

Up we went again, climbing to a small brown house that perched on the edge of nothing. More steps brought us to the front door. When Brian knocked, a woman came to look out at us doubtfully.

Brian turned on his easy charm and smiled at her disarmingly. "We were going through," he said, "and we wondered how Mrs. Jessup is. The last time we called she was pretty sick."

The woman accepted his words without question. "She's some better. She's a good fighter, so she's still hanging on."

"That's fine," Brian said. "Her friend, Alice Spencer, asked us to stop and see her."

How glibly he managed, I thought, glimpsing an aspect of Brian Montgomery that I hadn't seen before. He wasn't all mystical naturalist by any means, and apparently he could be pragmatic enough when he chose.

The woman recognized Alice's name. "You want to come in? Just so you don't stay too long. Though prob'ly she won't talk to you anyway."

The main room of the house had been turned into a downstairs bedroom for Mrs. Jessup. All the windows were carefully closed, though they looked out upon magnificent views. The room had the musty, mediciny smell of a sickroom and the bed was set against the far wall in the dimmest part of the room. It took a moment for my sun-filled eyes to make out the figure of the old woman who sat propped against pillows, her gaze fixed on emptiness.

Our escort spoke to her cheerfully. "You got company, Emma. Some folks are here who know Alice Spencer. You remember Alice?"

Dim eyes seemed to return from a distance and with an effort focused upon us as we advanced into the room. Wrinkled lips almost smiled. She made no attempt to speak.

I glanced helplessly at Brian. It seemed unkind to intrude upon the frailty of the woman in the bed.

"Look," Brian said under his breath, "*you* wanted to come. Now let's see you do your thing."

I went close to the bed and spoke clearly to its occupant. "Alice Spencer is my sister," I said.

Some sort of spark came to life in the old eyes, and this time she made an effort. "Alice's a good woman. Always tried to help."

At least she could talk, and I sought for another means of getting her to open up. "Mrs. Jessup, I have another sister—another half sister who came to see you not long ago—Sybil Adams. Do you remember her?"

She closed her eyes, pressed her lips together, and said nothing. I couldn't tell whether she had even heard what I'd asked.

Brian moved closer to the bed. "I brought Mrs. Adams here that day, though I didn't come in with her. We'd like very much to know what she said to you, and what you told her. It will help us in something we need to do. Please try to remember."

The old woman moaned faintly and turned her head from side to side. "It's so hard to remember. I can remember when I was a little girl, but sometimes I can't remember yesterday. What was her name again—the lady who

320

came to see me?"

"Sybil Adams," I repeated. I could see that the name meant nothing to her.

Perhaps there was another approach, I thought, remembering that Jed had lived in Jerome at one time. I bent toward her again.

"I believe my father lived here years ago. Perhaps you knew him? His name was Jed Phillips."

This time there was a reaction, sudden and startling. Mrs. Jessup pushed herself up in bed and glared at me with a fury that seemed to shake her thin body.

"That awful man! Wicked, wicked, wicked! I won't talk to anyone connected with that man. Go away!"

"Well, that settles it," Brian said. "We'd better go."

I had to make one last try. "Sybil Adams was his daughter too. Didn't she tell you that? Why did you talk to her?"

But her outburst of anger had shaken her badly, and she lay back upon her pillows with her eyes closed, rejecting us, refusing to accept our presence in her room.

The woman who had let us in beckoned from the doorway. "I guess you'd better go. She won't talk to you now. You shouldn't have mentioned that name to her."

We followed her from the room, and I made one last try. "Can you tell us why she reacted that way?"

She answered evasively, uncomfortably. "I only came to Jerome last year to stay with my daughter. She works at the museum here, and her husband has a job in Cottonwood."

I had a feeling that she could tell me if she wished but would say nothing more. Her manner had cooled and she too wanted us to leave.

We went out on the porch, thanked her, and started down the steep flight of steps that appeared ready to slide down the hill. At their foot, Alice Spencer waited for us. She looked calm and unruffled, except for a light of anger in her usually serene dark eyes. Again I recognized depths of emotion she seldom revealed.

"You didn't need to kidnap Lindsay," she told Brian.

He smiled at her as we went down the steps. "Oh, yes, I did. I don't think you'd have let her see Mrs. Jessup. You knew why she'd react the way she did. Certainly you'd have kept me out. But I wanted to see for myself."

"You're right," Alice said. Her look seemed to soften a little. "You, especially, I'd have tried to keep away from her."

"Maybe you'd better tell us why," I said.

"There's no need to be secretive any longer," Alice admitted. "I'll tell you what I can, though it won't do you much good. Let's stop for coffee and we'll talk."

The steep descent led us quickly to the main

street, and in a few moments we were seated at a table in a small café. I couldn't wait to ask the question that had been haunting me ever since I'd seen what Jerome was like.

"Why did my father come here to stay?"

"Because Arizona fascinated him," Alice said. "He loved the Southwest, and since he never put down real roots anywhere, he could stay where he liked. He enjoyed places where he could get back into history and feel as though he were part of it. Jerome is where all the copper ore came from in the old days. He used to talk about writing a book about Arizona someday, but only when he got too old to get around and explore it. He'd have felt at home in the last century."

"Wasn't there some sort of scheme he was trying to cook up for Jerome?" Brian asked. "Something that was supposed to revive it and make everybody rich?"

"There were always schemes," Alice agreed dryly.

"Then he must have known Mrs. Jessup when he lived here," I said.

"She was his landlady for a while. She isn't really as old as she seems. It's just that she's given up wanting to live, and that can age anyone fast."

"What did Jed do to make her so angry with him?"

Alice sipped black coffee, watching Brian. "So she told you how she feels?"

"She called him an 'awful man,' " I said, "but she didn't say why."

"She was never able to make allowances or forgive him. She blamed Jed for the accident to her granddaughter, and that was that."

"Her granddaughter?" I cried. "Celia was Mrs. Jessup's granddaughter?"

Alice was looking at Brian. He'd made a small sound of pain, and I saw the tightening of his mouth as he stared at her.

She nodded. "Yes—that's it, Brian. I didn't want you to go there. It would only have hurt you all the more if you knew."

"I *didn't* know. If I had, I'd never have taken Lindsay to that house. Though I'd have gone alone, perhaps. Celia never told me she came from Jerome. I thought she had no family left at all. You were the one who took care of everything when she died."

"I knew her grandmother was ill, and that she had no one else. Afterward, I went to tell Mrs. Jessup what had happened. There were family connections Celia didn't want anyone to know about, and though she was fond of her grandmother, she'd have kept you away from her. I told her often that she wasn't responsible for the past, but she could never get away from it."

"Just explain!" I pleaded.

Again she looked at Brian and he nodded. "Go ahead—tell her."

"Celia and Brian met at the university in

324

Flagstaff. That's right, isn't it?"

He nodded. "I wanted to marry her, but she wasn't ready then. Maybe I was too patient. I waited too long."

Alice went on. "I don't think there was anything more you could have done. She wanted to live in San Francisco, and I knew Jed had friends there who could help her. After all, he'd known her when she was a child, and he'd roomed at her grandmother's. He was almost like family—the way he was for me—though he hadn't seen her for some time."

"Some family!" Brian said bitterly. "He didn't have any intention of remaining a benevolent uncle."

There was a submerged rage in his voice that I'd never heard before, and I could understand why all too well. Jed's age had never mattered to women. His good looks and his charm could be overwhelming, as even I knew. Perhaps Brian's "nonviolence" that Marilla had mentioned was only an abstract concept. I was beginning to feel very uneasy indeed.

Alice spoke to him gently. "You can't go on letting what's happened destroy you. You have to live with what's real. *You* matter now."

I felt saddened and sorry, both because of the old woman and because of Brian's pain and loss. I also felt a little haunted, since Vermilion's words about his "lost love" were sharp in my mind. Not that I might not have made some unrecognized connection and come

325

up with this consciously in time.

Alice glanced toward the door and her face brightened. "Good! I knew he'd find us if he could."

I looked around to see Rick coming through the door and my spirits lifted as they always did at the sight of him. He came to our table at once.

"I got your message at the hospital," he told Alice. "When I found I was free this morning, I went directly there. Thanks for letting me know. I tried the Jessup house first, then thought you might have stopped here. Lindsay, you shouldn't be running around like this."

He sat down next to me and Brian looked at him without welcome. "You've just missed confession time," Brian told him. "We're baring our souls. But of course you knew about Celia and me."

"I knew." Rick spoke quietly. "And I saw Jed when he came back to Sedona after what happened. He never stopped blaming himself. I think he'd have given his own life, if he could have saved Celia's."

"Her suitcase was in his car," Brian said tightly. "They were off for a weekend together. A lot of good it did for him to be sorry afterwards. Sure, he was sorry enough—so what?"

Alice put a calming hand on his arm. "Sometimes I think the old idea of not speaking badly of the dead is a good one. It's easier for the living if we can give them the benefit of our doubts. For all we really know, he might have been taking her to a train."

Brian snorted derisively. "You're right about one thing. She would never tell me much about her family. She couldn't remember her father, and said he had died when she was small. She loved and hated her mother, but she would never open up and talk about her. She said it hurt too much, and perhaps she would tell me someday. So *you* tell me now, Alice. There'll never be a better time."

"There's no reason not to—*now*," Alice agreed. "Celia's mother was in prison. She was accused of killing a man when Celia was small. Someone who had used her badly. She claimed she was innocent, but the State took a dim view, and she was tried and sentenced to life imprisonment. She died in prison—of pneumonia. Celia said her mother didn't want to live. She visited her two or three times and always came back broken up. Brooks was a name Celia chose, of course. She didn't want any connection with her real name and her mother's past. I was her friend and adviser, so she talked to me. But she was afraid to have anyone else know."

"She might have trusted me a little," Brian said. When he rose from the table abruptly and walked out of the café, his expression frightened me. I had the feeling that he had been pushed to some extreme.

"I'm sorry," Alice said. "It was time for him to hear these things, no matter how much they hurt. Shall we go back to Sedona now? I have my car, Rick, if you want to take Lindsay. There are some things I need to do in Sedona."

It seemed to me that she and Rick exchanged a look that carried some meaning I didn't understand. I would be only too glad to go back with Rick. I touched the lump on my head lightly, and found it hadn't gone down much as yet. I still felt a little groggy at times.

We parted with Alice. When we were in the car driving toward home, we had little to say to each other. He mentioned that he was to see the police in Flagstaff again this afternoon, and after that he was silent. Too much still lay between us, holding us apart. Once I tried to put my uneasiness about Brian into words.

"He's been holding all this back about Celia, but it's been churning inside him ever since her death. He must have hated Jed more than almost anyone else. Do you suppose —"

Rick cut in. "It's too easy to speculate. If he'd killed Jed, wouldn't that have vented a lot of his rage?"

I didn't know. I didn't know anything.

When the red rocks were near, Rick turned off down a road I didn't recognize.

"There's a place I want to show you," he said. "A quiet place I think you'll like. Maybe we both need it now."

14

As we drove across a flat area of valley, Rick pointed. "Look up there."

Above us a narrow structure of white stone grew out of a red mountain, a great white cross supporting the roof and sides. Behind it, red cliffs towered hundreds of feet, and at its feet golden aspens rustled.

"The Chapel of the Holy Cross," Rick said. "We're going up there."

It was awesome to see the great slabs of aggregate stone that sloped narrowly downward from the top of the cross, to be rooted in rock. A cross that celebrated a younger faith than the giants behind it had known. The chapel stood like an exclamation mark, a challenge flung down against the forces of evil.

"It was built as a memorial," Rick said, "and it's there on the mountain for anyone who has need."

The road curled up from the valley, cutting through rock, circling as it rose. High up, we found a place where we could leave the car and walk the rest of the way. The approach was from the rear and over a curving, steel-supported ramp of concrete. Red rocks encroached all around, enfolding what men had built, so that only the chapel stood free, dominated by its white cross.

At the top, the pavement widened into a spread of gravel, with rails and low stone benching. But it was still the chapel that held my full attention. At the rear it came down from the ninety-foot cross and widened into a curving wall of glass panes that reflected red mountains of rock. The flat roof slanted upward away from us, and it too narrowed at the top of that challenging cross which faced out across the country, to be seen for miles around.

"Let's sit down for a moment," Rick said.

There was no one about. We sat on an outside bench, close, not touching. I felt a new awareness of everything around me. I was especially conscious of the cliffs that stood like great red statues, frowning and stark. Aware, too, of the glowing panes of the chapel, and above all, aware of the man beside me, warm and alive in a world where there was so much death. This was a moment to cherish, no matter what happened.

"This afternoon when I go to Flagstaff," Rick said quietly, "I'm going to give them the motive they're searching for. It's better to offer the truth than to have them digging to find something they think I'm hiding. They know by now that Sybil and I were breaking up. So I mean to tell them we'd eventually have been divorced."

I waited tensely and he went on.

"I'll also tell them that when this is over and a decent time has passed, I'll ask you to marry me."

I slipped my hand through the crook of his arm and held on tightly for a moment. But for Rick's sake, I couldn't approve what he meant to do.

"You mustn't go through with this," I said, "It could count against you too strongly."

"Perhaps. I have to persuade the police to look into other possibilities. They need to look for someone who has something to hide—and I'm not hiding anything."

Before I could speak again, he stood up and drew me with him. "Let's go inside," he said, and we walked together through the door of the chapel.

Stone walls slanted inward and upward toward a rear version of the great outside cross. It stood against panes of blue glass that reflected the sky. Under our feet the carpet was a soft desert brown, and benches had been set on either side of the central aisle. The altar, set a few steps up from the aisle, was small and covered with white linen.

It was a place for prayer or meditation, a place where one might ask silently for help—

from whatever outer or inner source there might be. The quiet seemed intense and peaceful, and it held off the clamor of the world, offering that gift that was peculiar to man alone—hope. I closed my eyes and asked for help against those forces the cross had challenged. I asked forgiveness for Sybil, for Jed, for me. I asked for Rick's safety. And I gave thanks for life itself.

In a little while we rose and went again into sunshine. After this small space of time set apart, I could feel renewed, strengthened. Whatever was to come, I could face it with more courage now.

"We'll stop at Orva's and pick up Marilla," Rick said when we were in the car again and heading toward town. "She'll stay out of school for a few days. The funeral will be quiet, private, of course."

When we reached Orva's, we found her in a state of nerves, and the moment we stepped into the house we heard the drum. It came from the outdoor patio at the back. Brian was using a heavy beat followed by two light quick ones, over and over. It was a quickened version of the beat I'd repeated for myself—a beat that still stirred the pulses and demanded action, that built toward some explosive climax.

Orva shook her head despairingly. "He came bursting in a little while ago and went straight out there. Come and look."

She led the way to a glass door at the rear, and we stood staring at the strange tableau out on the patio. Brian knelt with his back toward us, the drum before him, the beater in his right hand. He was totally unaware of us, oblivious to anything but the drum.

"I don't know what he's trying to do," Orva whispered.

Marilla came running from her room, wearing a paint-smeared smock that was too big for her, a crimson smudge on her chin. The puzzle of what drove Brian was nothing we could solve, and when we turned to greet Marilla, she once more clung to her father. Rick said it was past lunchtime, and if she wanted to hurry and clean up he would take us into Sedona for a quick lunch. He hadn't much time left before he must start for Flagstaff.

Marilla hurried, and when Rick had thanked Orva we left her to her concern for Brian and drove downtown.

The restaurant was Mexican in atmosphere, name, and menu, with whitewashed walls, a dark, beamed ceiling, and tiled floor. We talked about anything and nothing as we ate, skirting dangerous territory as if by mutual consent.

Now and then Marilla's eyes widened, as though she still held horror away. She knew, as we knew, that nothing was finished, and that we didn't know what might step out of the shadows around us.

When we'd eaten, Rick drove us to the house. Consuela came to the door at once and motioned anxiously with her head. When I looked toward the terrace, I saw that Parker Hale was out there, pacing the tiles.

"Have you any homework to catch up on?" Rick asked his daughter.

She sensed that she was being sent away, but she went quietly, and I knew she was afraid.

Parker heard us coming and whirled around at the far end of the terrace. "God! Where have you been, Rick? I've been calling all over for you, and no one knew where you'd gone. You might have left word at a time like this."

"You apparently didn't try the sheriff's office," Rick said. "I told them where I'd be. We went to Jerome."

"Jerome!" The word rang with disbelief. "Why *Jerome?*"

"It doesn't matter," Rick said. "You wanted to find me, and now I'm here. What's wrong?"

"It's Clara," he told Rick. "You'd better come and talk to her right away. The police have been out to see her, and she's scared she'll say the wrong thing. Can you come over to the shop right now?"

Rick glanced at his watch. "I've still got twenty minutes before I go to the sheriff's office. So let's go."

"I'm coming with you," I said.

"All right." He asked Consuela to keep an eye on Marilla and I went out with him. Parker had left his car down the road. When we started up he followed us.

At Tlaquepaque we all went into the shop

together. Clara, looking thoroughly distraught, was waiting on a customer. The neat braid she usually wore down her back or around her head had given way to a mass of thick hair caught up carelessly with a barrette. When she saw us, she nodded toward her office and we went straight back. As soon as she could leave the shop to her assistant, she joined us.

"Do sit down, Parker, you make me nervous," she snapped at her husband, and he dropped into a chair, where he fidgeted with his sweater. Clara sat behind her desk, while Rick and I took the small sofa. I'd never seen Clara so close to losing control.

"You shouldn't have gone off to find Rick," she told Parker. "You just pop off on impulse sometimes. I needed you here, because the police came back. I'd held off telling them anything, but this time they got it out of me."

"Take it easy," Rick said. "Got what out of you?"

She made an effort to speak more quietly. "There's something I hadn't told anybody till now, because I didn't want to hurt anyone. That last morning, when Sybil disappeared, she came here after she'd seen Orva. She came to make trouble, and she tried to stir things up. I didn't say anything about this at first because I thought it was better if the police didn't know she'd come here, and that I might have been the last person to see her alive—except one, of course. But someone saw her come in here and

335

told a deputy. So I had to admit that she'd been here. At first I didn't tell them the whole story."

It was Parker's turn to snap. "Get to the point, Clara. Tell us what happened."

She raised her hands helplessly, then let them drop back in her lap. "Sybil sat right here in this room and gave me the details of what happened that night in Vegas—the important thing she'd never told the police. She was angry with her father, and they'd had a quarrel earlier in the evening. She wanted to have something out with him. So when it was late enough and no one would see her, she started down the hall to talk to him.

"That's when she saw someone hurrying away from his room toward the elevators. His door was ajar, and she walked in to find him lying there dead. Because of the quarrel they'd had, and the long antagonism between them, she went back to her room and told the police nothing when everyone was questioned the next day. Lately, however, she'd begun to worry. She felt there was a threat against her life, and she wanted someone to know what had really happened in Vegas. Though she still wasn't ready to go the police. It's too bad she didn't—she might be alive now."

Clara's voice broke and she began to cry in great convulsive sobs. Parker put an arm about her, attempting clumsily to soothe and comfort, no longer impatient with her. She pushed him away.

I heard my own voice cut through the sound of weeping. "Who was it that Sybil saw in the corridor, Clara?"

She took a great gulping breath and stared at me with swimming eyes. For a moment I thought she wouldn't answer, and then she seemed to come to a decision. "It was Rick who was running away from Jed's room."

The silence that fell upon us seemed terrifying, as though we all held our breaths, waiting for something awful to happen.

After a moment, Rick spoke quietly. "Sybil was lying, of course. I never went near Jed's room that night. Sybil and I had separate rooms, so I didn't know she was out of hers. I didn't leave mine at all."

"I knew it couldn't have been you who killed Jed—or Sybil!" Clara wailed. "That's what I had to tell the police. I tried to hold back at first, but they got it out of me. So they're looking for you now."

"Then I'll go to them," Rick said quietly. "I'm due there anyway, and I've nothing to hide. Don't worry, Clara, I'm not blaming you. It's just that Sybil always was a liar. It's a wonder she didn't come up with this a long time ago, in order to get me in trouble."

"She told me she'd kept still because she was afraid. Nevertheless, she always liked to turn the screws and use her power. I suppose this would give her a power over—whoever it was."

"You're right—it would have been like her," I broke in bitterly. "This means that she saw the real murderer that night, and this is why she died. Whoever killed my father found out what she knew."

Rick got up. "I'm late. I'll get over to the sheriff's office right away."

He touched a finger to my cheek. "Don't worry, Lindsay. We'll come out of this. I may not be home tonight to keep a lookout, as I'd meant to. I've had a workman over to put on stouter locks, and Alice will be with you. Take care of Marilla, won't you?"

"I will," I promised. "Of course I will."

"I'd like you to do something else now. Go upstairs to the workroom we've been planning, Lindsay. Go up there and try not to worry."

When he'd gone, Clara made an effort to collect herself. "Rick's right—you'd better keep busy, Lindsay. We all need to find something to do. Parker, you said you had a special dinner on for tonight, so hadn't you better get started?"

He gave her a long look, as though she'd become a stranger to him. Then he nodded to me and went away.

Perhaps Rick could forgive Clara for talking. I couldn't. "I'm going to be very busy," I said, "and I think you'd better help. There's only one job I'm interested in right now. That's trying to find out who killed my father and my sister—and tried to kill me."

I didn't wait for her answer but went outside and up the stairs to the second level. Through show windows I could see that several pieces for furniture had been brought into the shop, and that Alice was inside. So this was why Rick had wanted me to come up here. This was what Alice had wanted to do in Sedona. I could only feel apathetic as I tapped on the glass.

She came quickly to open the door. "Rick thought it would be a good idea for us to start on some of the things we'd intended." Then she saw my face. "What's happened now, Lindsay?"

There was no one I'd rather talk to. We had come that far in this short time. I dropped into one of the chairs and told her what had happened, while she listened gravely, offering no false words of consolation. Instead, she made an effort to interest me in what she'd been doing in this room.

So I made an effort too. I tried to remember who I was—who I used to be—even though New York was a thousand light-years away. It seemed strange to realize how fully Arizona had moved in to possess me. My ties were here now, not only because I loved Rick and wanted to be part of his life, but because of a heritage that must still be explored and realized.

Trying to orient myself, I checked through the items Alice had been able to find. There were pattern tissue, lightweight unbleached muslin, packets of pins, shears with a bent handle, smaller scissors for trimming. She'd brought me somebody's yardstick, though its edge was no longer smooth and might snag on cloth. There was even a tomato-shaped pincushion that made me smile.

"This is fine," I said, "but since I haven't a dressmaker's form to work on, how about using you, Alice?"

She blinked, suddenly self-conscious. "I don't know. Will I do?"

Old habit was instilled in me, I found. My mind clicked into the familiar groove, and I knew that I was still the Lindsay Phillips whose name had become well known on a dress label.

"Stand up and turn around," I directed.

She obeyed gracefully enough. At the moment she was wearing brown slacks and a beige blouse, and I studied her. Alice Rainsong was fairly tall and rather squarely built. Good shoulders that would allow a dress to drape well, hips that would need to be watched, the long legs of a model. For now, I would pin muslin over her clothes and make allowances.

"You'll do," I said, and smiled at her. "Schiaparelli used to say that a woman must train the body to fit the dress. That's good advice, but hardly anyone minds it. I always like to think of a particular woman in a special background, and then I design for *her*. Now I have you, and I have this beautiful blue cloth, so I want to put you together. In New York I do the sketches and the beginnings myself. Then I turn the detail work over to others. Here I'll need to get back to basics—I'm the whole show again—and what a good thing that is for me now!"

"For me too, if you can give me something to do," Alice said. "I'm pretty good at sewing."

"That will be useful when we have a machine. First I'd like to do some draping." It helped me to talk as I worked. Talking could fill spaces into which frightened thoughts were too eager to pour.

"Explain as you go along, so I'll begin to understand," Alice said, and I knew we had the same need to fill those empty spaces.

"Some designers start right in with the cloth," I told her, "but I like to make a muslin toile first on the form. That's you, right now. Later I'll cut a pattern from this shape when it suits me. I wish we had a long mirror, so you could see what I'm trying. I'll get one as soon as possible because it helps me to see all around a model." As soon as possible? I wondered when that would be. At least we were managing to hold off the waves of anxiety that threatened to engulf us.

As I worked, Alice talked about some of the symbols I could think about using in my designs. Kachina dolls and masks would offer great ideas. And there were so many symbols —the whirlwind that was so familiar in this country, the rain, the lightning.

"You haven't seen a storm over the rocks yet, Lindsay. It's breathtaking. And there's always the sun, of course—the life-giver—and clouds that sometimes bring rain we always need. Then there are the birds and animals, the eagles and antelopes and snakes. Of course the dancing gods, and the endless geometric patterns that can be very precise. If you want to be authentic, you mustn't invent there."

"You're my guide now," I said, and stopped in my pinning to look up at her from where I knelt. "And so much more—so quickly."

She smiled. I knew that she'd begun to feel what I was feeling, and that was something to marvel over.

What a strange afternoon we spent together. While I draped, pinned, scissored, and talked about dress designing, Alice stood patiently, moving only as I indicated, and we both managed to hold time at bay. Strangely enough, in the midst of threatened disaster, I found that I could still kindle a feeling for what I was doing.

"The Indian designs can be done in appliqué for this dress," I said. "Eventually, I hope I can meet and talk with your family of weavers."

"*Your* cousins, and an aunt," Alice told me.

I was kneeling, as I cut and pinned the length, and I looked up at her. "Then I'm all the more eager to know them. It's still not real to me, I'm afraid—this blood relationship. With you, yes. I already feel that we are sisters. But not all the rest."

342

"Perhaps it never will be. Because you belong wholly to the Anglo world. I'm mixed up in both, and that's a lot harder."

I went on pinning, using the little tomato cushion. The first lesson every dressmaker learned was never to put pins in her mouth. Not only because of the risk, but also because lipstick smears were easily transferred to materials.

When a telephone rang in the room, I started and dropped my shears. I hadn't known a telephone had been put in. Now I saw it sitting on the floor in a corner, and its ringing seemed a dangerous threat.

"They connected it just a little while ago," Alice said. "You'd better answer."

I picked it up doubtfully, to hear Rick's voice at the other end.

"Lindsay? I'm glad you're there. Is Alice with you? . . . Good, I'll talk with her in a minute. I'm going to Flagstaff now, and I expect I'll be gone overnight—if not longer. Don't worry. They haven't anything real to use against me. The sooner they find that out, the better. They want me now for more questioning. Take care of Marilla, will you? I have an uneasy feeling about her, and this is going to frighten her a lot."

"I'll go straight out to the house," I assured him.

"Fine. Now put Alice on."

They talked a while and Alice made notes. Apparently Rick was asking her to call a lawyer

343

they both knew, to get him up here soon. When she hung up, I removed the muslin toile carefully and folded it away.

"This can wait," I said. "Let's go back to Rick's."

We locked up and went downstairs and out to Alice's car. When we reached the house, Marilla came running to greet us, asking for her father. Alice and I explained as well as we could. Not that he might be accused of anything, but that there was police business that might keep him in Flagstaff for a few days. She understood that an investigation of her mother's death was under way, and I was sure she sensed more than we were telling her.

"Let's go over to the guesthouse now," I said. "It will be a lot cozier there."

"Like a castle on top of a rock." Marilla's imagination was already at work.

"That's right," Alice agreed. "We'll tell Consuela to go home, and I'll raid the house refrigerator and make dinner for us over there."

With plans for the night shaping up, we felt a little better, safer. We filled a basket with groceries, then went across the bridge.

All I wanted was to be shut away in safety for the night—though even the guesthouse hadn't been safe night-before-last. Another part of me fretted impatiently because I was only marking time, whatever I did. I wasn't in the least sure that Rick's confidence in the future was justified. He had needed to reassure me, just as I must reassure Marilla. If only there was something I could *do*.

Shiny new deadbolts were in evidence on the doors—Rick had thought of that—and Alice had the keys. Nevertheless, I walked in cautiously. By mutual agreement we looked in all the closets and the bathroom before we relaxed.

Alice was, as always, perceptive, and she'd been watching me. "Marilla is going to help me get dinner, Lindsay. So for tonight you do as you like. I have a feeling you want to be by yourself for a while. So why not run along and do whatever you wish."

There *was* something. It had been at the back of my mind ever since my last effort in that direction, though I hadn't given it my full attention. Now the urge was there, and I still wasn't strong enough to resist it. Perhaps *she* was the only one who could help me now.

I thanked Alice a little absently and went into the bedroom. There I pulled open the draperies and stood before the glass panels looking out at the now familiar view. It was late afternoon. The sky had grayed so that the sun was setting behind clouds and the usual flaming sunset red of the rocks had been subdued. I hadn't noticed until now that the sky had a stormy look. Rain would be welcome if it came. Clouds often piled themselves high in the afternoon, only to soar away to drop their moisture elsewhere.

After a moment of watching, I turned my back

on the view and sat down in an armchair, closing my eyes. Softly I spoke to her in my mind.

Come. I need you now. Tell me what to do.

There was only a deep silence inside my head, and no figure with swirling red-orange hair danced into view.

"Vermilion, do come!" This time I spoke her name aloud. I even tried to flatter her a little, because sometimes she responded to flattery. "You're wiser than I am—help me to help Rick. Please come."

A small voice spoke in my mind. *Why should I?*

I still couldn't see her. It was almost as though I'd forgotten how she looked, though she'd been vivid enough at the hospital.

"You want me to stay alive, don't you?" I said. "So help me now to know what to do."

Why should I? the faint voice repeated. *Why should I help you to go away from me?*

So that was it! She was jealous of Rick. I tried to empty my mind, merely waiting for her to fill it. When nothing happened, I permitted myself a question not addressed to her. Were Vermilion's powers growing weaker, vanishing?

She caught that thought at once, and in a burst of angry energy she was there, flowing through my consciousness, burning as brightly as a flame. Not for a long while had she given me such an angry performance, and I made no effort to resist. I let her take possession and command my thoughts fully, though even as I let myself

346

go, a part of me wanted to check her. If I allowed her in to this extent, might it not give her a life that could overpower my own? Was there an edge that led to madness?

Almost in the same breath, however, I knew she wasn't trying to take me over completely. At least not yet. She had come because I called her, and she still knew that she depended on me for her existence, that if I refused her she would be lost. So, having vented her annoyance in the burst of energy that had swept through me, she did what I asked—she spoke to me. And it was almost as though I heard her voice there in the room with me:

Think about those who loved Celia. Maybe there's an answer there.

Having offered what could only be further suspicion of Brian—and no use to me at all—she was gone in a flash. I felt an annoyance that was entirely my own—because she'd given me nothing that I didn't already have. Brian had loved Celia. Who else? Alice, of course, though she wasn't the one I searched for. Otherwise, there was only old Mrs. Jessup in Jerome, who had dearly loved her granddaughter. It was possible there was still some sort of answer there, but it was out of reach.

So must I really focus on Brian? He was a strange, haunted young man, who appeared to be reaching out at times toward another dimension. Reaching out rather dangerously, perhaps, as he asked the very questions that I was asking.

I opened my eyes, feeling weary, and wondered if this time I had simply been dozing. I hoped that was the case, because I must stop this nonsense about Vermilion and her powers. It had been foolish to think some answer might come to me from that direction. I could excuse myself only for the reason that I needed to try everything.

In any case, she was gone now—far away into her own mysterious silence—and I knew that if I was to be of any use to Rick, I must act on my own. Yet the thought was not entirely a strengthening one.

15

The three of us dined that night at the small round table at one end of the living area nearest the kitchen. The wind had begun to rise outside and towering thunderheads rode a darkening sky.

"It's really going to storm," Marilla said. "I love it up here when it storms. It's exciting. Look at those clouds, Lindsay. You can see the unicorns are out riding them tonight, and the dragons and griffins and firebirds!"

Her last word caught my imagination. I remembered the ballet with its stormy Stravinsky music. That's what Vermilion was! If Alice was a quiet Rainsong, Vermilion was a Firebird.

I watched the sky and saw that the clouds beyond our window had indeed taken on wildly imaginative forms that kept changing even as we watched them roll above the rocks, sometimes touching down and hiding them from view.

"Perhaps the kachinas are out there tonight," Alice said softly. "The spirits of our ancestors riding the wind. Listen—do you hear the drums?''

My scalp prickled, but it was only distant thunder that I heard, and moments later the sky brightened for an instant with lightning, then turned dark again. The storm was still far away.

Inside, the house was cozy, sheltered, safe. By candlelight we ate Alice's savory meal with good appetite. There was a lightly browned omelet and a salad into which Marilla had mixed everything she could collect, including bits of Swiss cheese and crunchy pecans. Alice had even made hot muffins that we piled with butter and marmalade. She'd found a bottle of white wine, and milk for Marilla.

Later, when we'd finished, I washed dishes while Marilla wiped, and Alice stood at a window watching the storm blow closer. If I had felt sure of Rick's future, I could have been quietly happy that night.

Contrast between the wild sky and this peaceful interior brought a heightened sense of safety. Perhaps a false sense? Even the candles Alice had lighted added to the sense of stillness and peace as their flames burned high and straight, untouched by the outer turmoil that rumbled around the house. Yet always the thought of Rick's danger was there—a danger that could threaten all of us—until we knew the one name that could free us from danger. Or open us to attack?

I shook off the edging of terror that wanted

to intrude. We could only live in this moment, and for *now* we were secure.

I was almost right.

When the storm broke, it was more spectacular than any I'd ever seen. Alice pulled the living room draperies wide, and we stood together at the great window. I had seen storms in New York. I had seen lightning play around granite and concrete towers and listened to booming thunder in city canyons, but here it was far more terrible. The lightning was very close. When it darted its arrows at red peaks and thunder crashed, all the rock echoes took up the sound and clattered it back and forth above the red stone mountains that cut into an attacking sky.

The rain came, and it was like none I'd ever seen. Sheets of water slanted across the deck outside our window as though a solid wall had struck the house. Though we could feel the shock of wind and water, the house was solidly based in rock, and it barely trembled.

After a time, even such a spectacle grew to be more than one could bear to watch. We turned back to the room, switching on lamps we'd left dark so we could see outdoors.

"Let's read aloud," Marilla begged us. "It's a wonderful night for reading. Alice, you begin, and we'll take turns. I have a book."

Alice was willing. Marilla got out the Lewis Carroll she'd brought with her. It seemed a proper night to follow the adventures of another

Alice, and our Alice Rainsong read about her beautifully. Together we went down the rabbit hole and into a Wonderland no more strange than I had found in coming to Sedona.

Nervous energy still surged in me, however. I couldn't sit still. While I listened, I moved from window to window, following the course of the storm as it swirled around the house, lighted by splitting skies.

When I came to the window that looked out across a deep arm of the wash, I found myself studying the main house intently—as though I expected something to move over there. Alice had left lamps burning and draperies open, so I could see dimly into the living room, its glass panes awash with rain. The great room was empty. I could imagine that high row of wooden heads from Oraibi all staring hard at nothing, heads my great-grandfather had carved!

A gust of wind knocked over a chair on the terrace. In the light from the mushroom standards I followed its tumbling course as it crashed into an anchored table and stopped. At that moment something else moved out there— something human. The rain had lessened and I could see the terrace clearly—wet and glistening with water that flowed across it but no longer blurred by solid sheets of rain. Thunder had rumbled away into the distance and no lightning flashed nearby. But this was what something in me had feared all along—human movement on the terrace.

A figure stepped out from the shelter of the overhang onto the tiles. A man stood looking off toward the peaks of rock, and even as my attention fixed upon him in a sudden wave of fear, I saw who it was. Brian Montgomery faced into the blowing wind, hands in jacket pockets, his bare head tipped back so he could gaze at the sky. As I watched, he flung both arms upward in a gesture that seemed to evoke the powers of unknown gods. He braced against the wind, with legs apart, arms reaching for the heavens, and I turned from the window, meaning to call out to Alice.

Before I could move, *she* was there—Vermilion.

All of her this time, shining and shimmering in my mind in bright flaming light—stronger than I'd ever seen her before. And her voice seemed stronger than I'd ever heard it. A firebird indeed!

"Go to him," she said. "Go out there to him. *Now!*"

I could neither resist nor disobey. Near the door a raincoat hung on a rack. I pulled it on, turned the key in the new lock, and stepped out into the wind.

It struck me like the flat of a giant hand, and I staggered as I caught at the bridge railing. Planks under my feet shuddered. I waded in water that flowed over my shoe tops. Yet the rain had stopped and was hardly more than a misting now, so that the water left behind was flowing away. I went over the bridge, clinging to the rail, hurrying lest the wooden planks be swept from under me. Far below, I could hear the voice of the water, where Oak Creek had grown to a river, pouring down the hill past town, heading toward the valley at Poco Diablo. All the black, glistening surfaces of rock were chutes for the water, hurling it through every gully in Oak Creek Canyon. At least the rising flood was far below our rocky crags.

I was safely across, and Brian still stood as I'd seen him, his wet face lifted toward the sky. The wind released me, gentled its pressure a little, so that I could move out toward him. Once I glanced toward the house, looking into the lighted living room, but nothing stirred inside.

Vermilion was still pushing me. In my mind— or outside it?—she laughed, knowing her own power now, growing stronger than ever. I had let her in deliberately, and this time I didn't know how to stop her.

Brian paid no attention as I came to stand beside him. His face was rapt, his eyes wide and staring. I spoke to him softly.

"Brian, what do you see out there?"

If my presence startled him, he didn't show it. He simply took me for granted, as he might have taken any wild thing that appeared suddenly beside him in the night.

"All the answers are out there—in the sky and in the rocks," he said.

"Why did you come here?"

He seemed to return from some faraway place. "I was looking for Rick. But the house is empty. Do you know where he is?"

I tried to speak in an ordinary voice, though my teeth had begun to chatter with the cold. "He's gone to Flagstaff. Alice and Marilla and I are staying in the guesthouse. Come in with us and get dry."

He pulled away roughly, and I think he would have gone off and left me there alone if Vermilion hadn't prompted me again. I spoke the words she put into my mouth.

"Brian, come inside and tell us about Celia."

Her name cut through to wherever he had gone, and he really looked at me for the first time. The deepened lines of his face relaxed a little, and his more familiar jaunty air returned with a hint of bravado.

"Okay," he said. "I'm wet through and frozen, so I'll accept."

This time I clung to him as we crossed the bridge, and the wind let us pass without trying to fling us down the cliff. Only when we were close to the guesthouse did I see that Alice and Marilla stood together in the doorway, watching us. The moment we reached them, Alice took charge.

"Give me your wet jacket, Brian. Come here by the fire. Marilla, will you put a kettle on, so we can fix hot coffee?"

Brian gave himself meekly into her hands.

He wasn't trying to be jaunty and confident now but seemed only a wet young man who wanted to get warm again. He sat cross-legged on the hearth, with a blanket around his shoulders, and reached out his hands to the fire. I ran to get a bath towel so he could rub his head and face dry and brush off some of the wetness. I wasn't as soaked as he was, except for my feet, and I kicked off my shoes and put on slippers.

When instant coffee had been made, Brian sat before the fire, warming his hands around a mug, drinking the brew black and strong. If only Rick could have been here, I thought. Rick would know how to handle Brian.

The voice in my head said, *You can handle him. He likes you. Ask him about Celia.*

Now that he'd relaxed a little, his expression had grown dreamy as he stared into the flames. In some strange way, it was as though he heard Vermilion before I could speak. He glanced at Alice, who had drawn an easy chair close to the fire, while Marilla and I sat on the other side on the sofa.

"You remember—I drove Celia out to San Francisco before Jed came into the picture," he said to Alice. "I was there in the city when she died in Jed's car."

"Can you tell us about it?"

"We had our best time together when we made that trip. Celia was more alive and vital than anyone I've ever known. It was as though she had to gulp down every kind of experience —as though she knew she hadn't much time. Those first weeks in San Francisco were great. Except for one thing that made me uncomfortable. There was someone else out there—a friend she didn't want to tell me about. And I started to worry."

Brian was silent again, staring as though the figure of Celia were there before him, moving through the flames. After a moment, in which the wind seemed to lessen its attack, he went on without prompting.

"I don't know whether this friend was a man or a woman. She said it was someone who could tell her more about her mother. She'd always been terribly alone, with no one to talk to about the past. I knew she had a grandmother somewhere, but I never even knew her name or that she lived in Jerome." He broke off, considering. "I wonder how Sybil knew about Mrs. Jessup? Anyway, it made me uneasy that Celia kept putting off telling me about this friend. She said she'd tell me later, when she was sure about something.

"Then Jed appeared. Celia said he was going to open doors for her, introduce her to people who might help her. She had some idea of going on the stage, though I tried to discourage that. She wasn't physically strong enough for that sort of life, for all her vitality. Yet I couldn't stop her from seeing Jed and trying to go ahead with her plans."

"I wish—" Alice began and then broke off, perhaps hearing the futility in her own words.

Brian went on, his voice hardening. "Then the day came when she went away in Jed's car. We'd planned to have dinner together, but she didn't meet me. I didn't know what had happened until Jed got word to me from his bed in the hospital, and I went straightaway to see him."

Strain had deepened the lines in Brian's face, so that he no longer seemed so engagingly young. No one spoke, and he went on as though he were talking only to himself.

"I stood by his bed, and I *wanted* to kill him. Even though I knew it had been an accident, he was the instrument, and I wanted to pay him back for what he'd done. He was badly broken up—especially his leg. That black cane with the ivory head was leaning against the wall in a corner, and I thought how easy it would be to pick it up and kill him right where he lay. He was too weak to talk to me for long, and the nurse had told me I couldn't have more than five minutes with him. But five minutes are a lot more than it takes to end a life.

"I suppose it was the look in his eyes that stopped me. They were the only part of him that moved. There were staring at me with such awful pain and pleading. He knew what was in my mind, and he wasn't asking for his life—he was asking me to *end* it. That's why I couldn't do it. When I walked out of his room without

358

touching the cane, I told myself that later on would do as well. When he'd had time to pay for causing Celia's death. If he could ever pay enough."

As Brian's voice died away, I put my face against my raised knees and tried vainly to shut out the vivid pictures he'd painted in my mind. Beside me, Marilla's hand found its way to my arm and pressed hard, as if in reassurance. Then she stood up, indignant, facing Brian where he sat before the fire.

"Grandpa Jed wasn't bad, like you say!" she cried. "He was better to me than anybody else, ever—except maybe my father. He never *meant* to hurt anyone."

We stared at her—a small, angry defender, confronting Brian.

"Besides," she spoke more quietly now, "I don't think you ever went to the hospital to see Grandpa Jed. I don't think you ever stood by his bed and thought about killing him. You made it all up!"

Brian sat staring at her as though her words had stunned him into silence. Then, slowly, he seemed to relax, as he gave her his open, appealing smile.

"How did you know, Marilla?" he asked.

"I know because lots of times you've told me about not wanting to kill anything. Not ever. And because of the cane. Grandpa Jed never had that cane until after he came out of the hospital with a limp. That's when he needed it to help him walk. That's when he bought it in a San Francisco store and took it everywhere with him after that. He told me so. But he didn't have it *before*."

Brian's laughter came easily, and without embarrassment. "How right you are! You're smarter than any of us, Marilla."

"No, I'm not," she said earnestly. "It's just that Lindsay and Alice are thinking about other things."

She returned to the sofa and sat beside me again.

"So now what?" I said. "Why did you give us that rigmarole, Brian?"

He swiveled around with his back to the fire, regarding me gloomily.

"I'll tell you," he said, "and this is the truth. That whole scene was something I thought about over and over again. It was what I *wanted* to do. Wished I'd done. I'm sorry, Marilla. I do believe in the things I've told you—they weren't lies. But, I guess after Celia died, Jed wasn't the only one to change. And maybe it helped me to play that game in my mind and keep on adding details long after Jed was out of the hospital and I'd come home. That's how the cane got in—because it seemed such a good idea to have it there, in case I wanted to use it."

"You never did use it," Alice said. "Isn't that right, Brian?"

"I don't *think* I could ever have used it,"

360

he said. "I know that sort of imagining can be dangerous—if it takes over. One of the queer things about that time was the way Celia's mysterious friend never turned up. Not when you came, Alice, and took care of everything. Not even to see Jed at the hospital. Whoever it was just disappeared."

"If there ever was anyone," Alice mused. "Sometimes I think Celia lived in a dream world of her own."

The sudden ringing of the phone brought me to my feet with just one thought in mind—Rick!

It was only Orva's voice, asking for her son. "He said he might go over there. I rang the house, but got no answer, so I tried you. Is Brian there?"

"Just a minute," I said, and held out the phone. "It's your mother, Brian."

He shook his head. "I don't want to talk to her."

"Can I take a message for him?" I asked.

"He is there, isn't he? Well, tell him I want him to come home right away. We have trouble on our hands. Clara's here and she's scared. Parker got drunk tonight—for the first time since she's known him—and he knocked her across the room. She came straight here, and she's afraid he may follow her. So I want Brian home."

"Hold on," I said, and transmitted all this to her son.

He got up from the hearth wearily. "Okay. Tell her I'll be there right away."

Alice brought his wet jacket. He threw it about his shoulders as he went out. She locked the door behind him, and we listened until we heard his car start up and move down the hill.

"I'll fix some cocoa," Alice said as she came back to us, "then perhaps we can turn in early."

A good idea. I was beginning to feel shaky again, and remembered that I'd spent yesterday in a hospital. Marilla hurried to fetch milk from the refrigerator, and I set out cups. Movement helped—once more doing *something*. We didn't talk about Parker and Clara or even about Brian, or any of the things that troubled us. We needed a respite—needed to do small ordinary things. The lump on my head felt hard to the touch, and very tender, and I was tired and ready to lie down.

When Marilla fell asleep over her cup, Alice took her off to bed. I was ready to follow but the night's surprises weren't over yet. We had just carried our cups into the living room, when someone knocked on the door. Alice opened it a crack, and when I heard Parker's voice, I tensed again.

"Please let me come in," he said. "I thought you might be here, Miss Spencer. I need to talk with you."

I held my breath while she hesitated.

"I'm not drunk," he told her. "I expect

you've heard what happened. I've been out walking around for a while, and it's cold enough to clear my head."

When she unfastened the chain and let him in, he headed straight for the fire, giving me a look of no great pleasure as he went past.

For a few moments we waited for him to explain. When he didn't speak, I said, "Would you like to talk to Alice alone, Parker?"

He didn't look at me, directing his words to Alice. "Though I don't know you very well, Miss Spencer, I've heard a lot of good things about you from other people. I need someone with real sense to talk to." He glanced at me without much hope. "You'd better hear this too, Lindsay—because of Rick."

"We'll listen," Alice said. "Orva phoned a little while ago and said you'd hurt Clara. Is that what you want to talk about?"

Long and lanky, he dropped into a chair, his knees jackknifing. "I never meant to hurt her. She's only a little thing. I just couldn't take it anymore—about her and Rick."

"That was over years ago," Alice told him.

"No! It's not over. I can tell from the way she looks at him and listens to him. And then after—after what happened to Sybil, I think she began to want him back. I tell you, I know what's happening, though I don't know what to do about it. So tonight, when the storm started to get to me, I got as drunk as I could—and I told her off. She went a little crazy. She came at me with her fists, pounding me. *Me!* And I got mad and hit her. I didn't hit her as hard as I could have, but I slapped her and she fell. Then she got up and ran out of the house. After a while, I just went out and walked in the rain. All my life I've messed things up, and now I've done it again."

I could only wonder what Clara had seen in him in the first place—why she had married him. Perhaps because he was vulnerable, and she had thought she could help. And because she was vulnerable too?

"I think you have things wrong, Parker." Once more Alice spoke with her own quiet authority. "You came into Clara's life when she needed someone badly. Rick's only her partner now, and her friend. That's *all*. Clara loves you, and you shouldn't doubt that. Besides, Rick is in love with my sister, Lindsay. You've mixed things up in your own mind, Parker."

He stared at her for a moment. "What do you think I should do?"

"Let me call Clara at Orva's. Let me tell her that you're perfectly sober, and then you can let her know how sorry you are."

He seemed to recoil from her words. "I can't do that! It's too soon. You don't know Clara. She never forgets and she never forgives."

"I think she will this time," Alice said. "She'll want to forgive *you.*"

Parker pulled himself up, looking only a little less distraught than when he'd come in.

."Thanks, Miss Spencer. I needed to talk to somebody. Go ahead and tell Clara for me—I won't try to talk to her now."

He still looked so miserable that I suggested coffee, and asked him to sit by the fire for a while, but he only shook his head and got up. When Alice let him out, I went to a window and watched him cross the bridge. On the lighted terrace he stopped for a moment, staring at the main house as though he expected someone to come out of it. Sybil, perhaps? Then he walked around toward the driveway and disappeared. The wet terrace with its overturned chair had a lonely look, as though no one would ever sit out there again.

When I came in to get ready for bed, Marilla opened her eyes. "Will my father come home tomorrow, Lindsay?"

"I hope he will. We can't tell for sure. What we can count on—the big thing that will get him out of this—is that he hasn't done anything, Marilla. And we all know that."

"Then who—?"

I touched a forefinger lightly to her lips. "Let's wait on that. It will come."

"Maybe you should ask Vermilion."

"I won't do that," I told her. "Vermilion was only a game that your grandfather helped me to make up when I was a little girl. She isn't someone real outside myself. She's only a make-believe part of me, and I know that very well. So she hasn't anything to tell me that I don't already know." My words were blocks of defense against something that might begin to terrify me.

"Why are you afraid, Lindsay? You are afraid of Vermilion, aren't you?"

I bent to kiss her cheek. "You know what I think? Sometimes I think you're a witch's child. Do you ride out on a broomstick at night? Or on a unicorn?"

At least that made her laugh, and she rolled over sleepily.

I didn't ask Vermilion. I only asked myself. Which one of them?

Somewhere I seemed to hear her laughing, though I hadn't summoned her. *I know,* she whispered. *I could tell you. But you'll have to ask.*

Once more I reminded myself that what Vermilion knew, *I* knew, and a reassuring memory returned to me. Even in that matter of Brian's "lost love," *I* had known. It was Sybil herself who had said when I'd first arrived that she was glad Brian was over "that girl." I'd never picked up on the thought again. It must have been lying fallow in my mind—for Vermilion to produce.

I lay awake for a long while, but I still didn't ask Vermilion.

16

The next day seemed endlessly long. Alice persuaded Marilla to go to school, and she drove her there. I wanted to stay by the phone, waiting for word from Flagstaff.

None came, and in midafternoon Alice urged me to leave the house and do anything at all that would be a change. She would stay by the telephone, so if Rick called someone would be here.

"Perhaps I'll go to Tlaquepaque and talk with Clara," I said. "I have a strange feeling right now. As though that drum is beating again in my head. I can almost hear it building toward something frightful."

"Vermilion?" Alice asked.

"No! This is *my* feeling. How can I make it stop?"

"Maybe you can't. Not deliberately. We can only go on with whatever we need to do."

"What I must do is get the truth out of Clara. She hasn't told it all yet."

"Be careful," Alice said, and then smiled

ruefully. "The two most futile words in the language!"

There was no way to be careful when I had no way even to guess the direction of the threat that might come.

"I'll use Sybil's car," I said, and went to get the keys to the red Spitfire from Consuela.

A little while later I was walking through the central plaza in bright afternoon sunlight. All traces of last night's storm had vanished. Only the flowers showed evidence of having been beaten by heavy rain.

It wouldn't have surprised me if Clara had not come in that day, but when I went into the shop I saw her at the back, working at her desk, with Connie taking care of customers.

Once more, Clara was her neat, well-ordered self, with her long braid down her back. That one eye was circled by a stain the color of an eggplant was something she chose to ignore, greeting me guardedly.

"Have you seen Parker since last night?" I asked.

She shook her head. "I haven't been home, and he hasn't come here."

"He really was upset. I think he hates what he did."

"Of course he does," Clara said calmly. "He's like Jed—he's sorry afterward. It will do him good to suffer a little. He'll come—I'm all he's got."

The bruise about her eye was hers, and so

were the decisions she must make.

When the telephone on her desk rang, it was Alice asking for me.

"Good news, Lindsay. Rick just phoned and he's coming home. He left his car at the sheriff's office when he went to Flagstaff with the detective. So I'm going there to pick him up. Orva will bring Marilla home from school, and Consuela's here. You'll come back soon?"

Was the drum tempo picking up an even more threatening rhythm? Why should I think that anyway? Why did I feel it so strongly?

I told Alice that I'd be home shortly and said I was glad she would go after Rick. Then I sat down and looked at Clara.

"We need to talk. I mean about what you say Sybil told you. There's more, isn't there?"

She shifted papers absently on her desk, avoiding my eyes. "I don't want to go through all that again. I shouldn't have told the police what I did. Rick will never forgive me, and I'll never forgive myself."

"You must know Sybil was lying, and that Rick was telling the truth?"

Though she looked miserable, she was growing angry with me. "Stop it, Lindsay! Let it alone. The police can't prove anything and Rick will be all right. I just needed more time to figure things out."

"I want to see him cleared—soon. And you can do that."

"I want to see him cleared too. But there's

369

nothing I mean to do about it now.''

It was hopeless to try to cut through her defenses, and I had a growing feeling that I should get back to Rick's, that perhaps I should never have left the house to come here.

"Just think about it," I said to Clara, and went out to Sybil's car.

When I reached the house, Marilla wasn't there. Consuela said she hadn't come home from school yet. There was nothing to feel uneasy about, but I phoned Orva at once. When I got no answer I began to worry, though silence probably meant that she had gone to pick Marilla up.

Because I couldn't sit and wait, I drove the short distance to Orva's house. There was no answer when I rang the bell, and neither she nor Brian appeared to be home.

Just as I returned to the car, she drove up. She had taken Marilla home from school and then gone into town on an errand. She didn't know where Brian was. I didn't stay to talk. The drum was suddenly, ominously silent—as though whatever was to happen had happened. And now Vermilion was beginning to chatter. I shut her out and drove quickly back to Rick's. There I searched the main house and then the guesthouse, calling Marilla's name, while Consuela trailed after me, alarmed by my behavior.

I found nothing until I went into the bedroom, where Marilla had slept last night. There it waited for me—a folded sheet of paper on my pillow, with my name scrawled upon it, as though written in haste.

I snatched it up and, as I read the note inside, my first feeling of relief faded. There were only a few words.

Dear Lindsay:
I have to go out to see the Fire People. If I go there I can help my dad. I'll get a ride to the turnoff and hike in.

Love,
Marilla

Vermilion was almost screeching in my ear. *Go after her! Don't let her be there alone. Go —go!*

I didn't need her to prompt me.

While I changed my shoes, I questioned Consuela. She hadn't known that Marilla had come home from school, hadn't seen her come or go. Which was perfectly possible if she'd come around by the outdoor path to the guesthouse.

I explained carefully to Consuela where I was going, so that she could tell Rick the minute he got home. Then I picked up the keys for his truck, got in and backed it out. Not for a very long time had I been in this sort of vehicle. After a little fumbling I familiarized myself with the gear shift and drove down the hill and out along the highway toward the dirt road. Now I must find the right way in.

I missed it the first time and had to turn back, but eventually I was bouncing along the rough road in low gear, watching for Marilla around every turn. I saw no jeeps out this late in the day, and the loneliness of the country touched me as it hadn't when I'd come here with the others.

At least the road seemed familiar now. When I reached the great beached whale of a rock I got out and left the truck. I could see the trail that led toward high red cliffs, and I began to run, trying not to trip on the rocky ground. I didn't know what I was going to find but only that fear drove me on.

Once through the stand of dead pines, I could see the rock barrier that hid the Fire People, and that thin, high crack in the rocks through which I must go. Once more I scrambled up through loose scree and stopped just below the opening. This time I shouted Marilla's name as loudly as I could—and this time I had an answer.

Her voice came back to me from inside, rising in a scream that repeated its terror in echoes. "Lindsay, go back! Don't come here! Go back! Lindsay—!" She choked off her shouting and was silent.

The silence frightened me even more. I stepped into the slanting gap in the rocks, once more pushing instinctively at the walls on either side, as though my feeble strength could hold back their terrible weight!

There seemed to be more loose sand on the floor of the crack as I went through, probably washed there by last night's ferocious storm.

Marilla didn't cry out again, but the moment I stepped out of the far opening, I saw her, and a wave of relief filled me. She sat alone in the middle of that oval pocket in the rocks, the great figures of the Fire People rising behind her. Her arms were clasped about her small body and her shoulders were huddled protectively.

"Are you hurt?" I called, starting toward her.

She raised her head and stared at me with a strange helplessness, as though my coming had caused her to give up entirely.

For the first time, I noticed that the afternoon was growing dusky and that the sky glowed with a red that was deeper than that of the rocks. The Fire People stood with their bright faces turned toward the sunset. The light wouldn't last much longer, and I'd never find my way in the dark. I ran to where Marilla sat and took her hand. There was no time for explanations either way.

"Come quickly. We must hurry and get out before it's dark. On the way you can tell me why you came here."

My words seemed to give her sudden new hope, and she reached for my hand and pulled herself up. "Yes, we must hurry!" She was whispering now. "Maybe we can get out!"

I didn't know what was wrong, but I heard her terror and knew it was real. As we turned together and started toward the crack in the rock, a thundering boom came out of the sky, and the ground beneath us trembled. All around us the rocks reverberated with the sound, as though they might crash in upon us. This time there was no glimpse of a plane overhead, but I knew that one had flown across.

In an instant the ground was still. I pulled Marilla by the hand. Now she resisted me. She stood rooted beside me as though she had lost the will to move.

"It's too late," she said hopelessly, and her eyes were fixed upon a wall of rock opposite the Fire People.

I looked up to see that a figure had emerged from what must have been a cave or crevice high in the rocks, and a man stood looking down at us. It was Parker Hale, dressed in Levi's, plaid shirt, and scuffed shoes. No sight could have seemed more incongruous at that moment, and I stared up at him, not believing.

"He brought me here," Marilla whispered. "He made me write that note for you. He said you'd be sure to come after me. I'm sorry, Lindsay—I couldn't help it." She was crying, and I held her close against me.

Out in the clearing behind Parker something began to whirl and dance, and I knew that

Vermilion had broken free at last. My eyes were open and I could see her. She had broken through all the barriers I'd raised, and she was *there!* I could even hear her voice.

Run! Get away from him! He's the one! Take Marilla and get away!

With a strange irrelevance I saw that her hair was almost the color of certain rocks that my father had once promised to show me in Arizona.

Only an instant had passed. There was still a chance for escape. Parker was high up on the rocky cliff, where he must have hidden when he heard me coming in. If we could get out ahead of him and run for the truck . . . Perhaps we could still move faster than he could . . .

But even as we moved toward the passage-way, a new whispery sound seemed to fill the tiny valley, growing in volume until it became a strange moaning, as though the great cliff cried out in pain.

"Look!" Marilla cried.

I stopped beside her and saw that a new crack had opened in rock already eroded further by last night's cloudburst—waiting only for the slightest jar of the earth to tear it loose. As I stared in horror, rock broke away to fall in upon itself with a tremendous roar, sealing off what had once been the way out. A precarious balance that had prevailed for who knew how long, had ended as rock split away, closing off the entrance forever.

There was no longer anywhere to run. Above us, Parker dug his heels into loose shale and rode it down in a small landslide of earth and stones, reaching our level all too quickly.

Marilla whispered to me frantically. "He thinks you *know.*"

And now I did know. Not the reasons, not the whys, but only that this harmless-seeming man had killed Jed, and then Sybil. And had already tried to kill me.

"There's another way out." Marilla's whisper was urgent. "It's harder, but it's behind us, up the rock."

"Then we'll reach it," I said under my breath. "Show me."

Once more, hope had revived, and she clasped my hand tightly. "It's up there on the cliff behind the Fire People."

Slowly we stepped backward, not daring to run and spur Parker into movement. He saw and shook his head as he came toward us.

"There's nowhere for you to go, Lindsay. I never wanted to hurt you in the beginning. I tried to scare you off by throwing a rock at you on the terrace that night. Just as I threw an egg at Sybil at her meeting, and left that note on her windshield. You should have run when I cut up that blue cloth and left it for you to find. But you kept right on threatening me! Neither you nor Sybil had any respect for what I could do."

Step by step backward . . . we mustn't stumble.

He kept on, almost apologetic now, as though he must make me understand the reason for my own death. Only now there was Marilla—and we *had* to escape.

"In the beginning it was only Sybil I hated. Next to Jed. When I married Clara I didn't know how closely she was connected to one of Jed's daughters. Not that it would have made any difference. I had no idea then that Sybil had seen me that night leaving Jed's room. She didn't know who I was. But when I moved to Sedona she recognized me and sprang the whole thing, turning the screws. Power over others—that's the only thing that made her count with herself. It wasn't you I was after, Lindsay—not in the beginning."

I could tell that he'd been drinking again, though not enough to make him helpless—only enough to give him a dangerous courage. Yet, in some strange way, he really was sorry. That was the awful thing—that evil men never knew they were evil. Or evil women—like Sybil.

He'd slowed his approach and we ventured another two steps backward.

"When I tell you to," I said softly to Marilla, "you must run and get out."

"I won't leave you," she whispered.

"You *must!* I can't move as fast as you can, and you know the way. Get out and bring someone to help."

Help would never come in time for me, but Marilla might escape. She pressed my fingers, and I knew she would obey.

Parker rambled on, releasing his own rage—and a strange sort of grief—in words. "I had a close call that time when you almost caught me in the shop. I'd come for Jed's sculpture, and I just got out in time. I took it straight to Rick's and left it for Sybil to find. Then I managed to get home just after Rick called Clara and told her the shop had been broken into. So I went into town with her. But that's when she began to wonder about me, and I knew it was nearly over."

He broke off, and I sensed the source of his grief—he had already lost Clara. He was staring at me with a queer defiance.

"Where's your Vermilion now, Lindsay? Marilla said you were going to ask her. Remember when I wrote her name in the dust for you? I'd been waiting for you, though you never guessed that I was hiding in that closet. With Jed's cane right there with me!"

In her own indirect way, perhaps Vermilion had tried to warn me about him when she'd said "eggnog" at the hospital. Because it was *Parker* who had brought that thermos to me—and one suspicious part of me that was Vermilion had picked up on something. Only she was outside of me now.

I could have told him she was there behind him, shimmering and dancing, shining in the sunset light, with her hair on fire . . . a crazy figure of mist that I'd projected from my own

378

mind. I didn't need her any more. In this terrible moment of danger I was whole within myself and I could let her go. Whatever had to be faced, I would depend only on me. With a strange clarity, I realized with a new intensity that she really had been the hating, jealous part of me, useful whenever I was threatened. Now I'd learned something about loving, and I could let her go. Love for Rick, for Marilla, for Alice. Even a strange forgiveness that might allow me to love my father again. Even forgiveness for myself?

Once more we retreated, though slowly, trying not to startle Parker.

Marilla whispered. "My mother knew about the other way out. She was trying to get away from him that day. It's just behind us now—the cliff."

I spoke to Parker as calmly as though nothing desperate was happening. "I don't understand what you had against my father. What possible reason—?"

"That's what your sister Sybil wanted to know. I was a fool to let it slip that I'd lived in Jerome a long time ago. That's why she went there. She'd known about Mrs. Jessup through Jed, so she went to her—and hit pay dirt. That's why she asked the question of old Mrs. Jessup that you and Brian never thought to ask."

"Did you know Jed in Jerome?"

"I never knew him. I left before he came. I

never saw him before the time I went to his room in Vegas. You're right, of course, if you've guessed. *I* cooked the food for that dinner Jed gave. Not much of a dinner, but I had to do what I was told in those days. I never meant to kill him. I only wanted to talk to him, tell him what I thought of him. Maybe see him suffer a little. And then he laughed at me."

Marilla clutched at me from behind, and I whispered to her, "Go! Go *now!*"

For just a second her hand tightened on my jacket. Then she fled toward the base of the rock columns and I could hear her scrambling up.

"Hey!" Parker shouted. "Don't go up there—you'll fall!"

He was starting after her, and I blocked his way. "You don't want Marilla. Let her go."

"She's not going anywhere. You saw what happened to the passage. I've been all the way around this place, and there was only one way out. We're all here together, and everything's going to be settled. Oh, I won't hurt the little girl—she doesn't matter now."

"Rick's coming," I said. "He knows where we are."

"And *he* can't get in!"

I dared not think about that, and I asked the question that would give me all the answers. "What did Sybil want to find out from Mrs. Jessup?"

Parker smiled at me almost pleasantly and

came a step closer. "She asked Mrs. Jessup if she knew me."

I wondered if I could turn and try to climb up behind the Fire People. I couldn't hear Marilla now, so she must have reached the ledge. I took another step backward, and felt the ground beginning to slope upward.

"Tell me the rest, Parker," I said. I was close now, but I dared not turn to look up. Already the space around me was bathed in a twilight glow from which the pink was fading.

Parker seemed almost pleased to tell me. "The old woman must have exploded when Sybil mentioned my name. She knew me all right. She never approved when I married her daughter. She thought I was nothing but a drunk. And she thought I'd ruined her daughter's life and got her sent to prison—for something I did. Though nobody was ever sure. Sometimes I'm not even sure myself. They were all against me. I loved my little daughter when she was a baby. Celia was all I had for a while. But they kept me away from her. When she grew older, they told her I was dead. I couldn't blame her for disowning me and taking another name. Then I found her in San Francisco and we started to be friends. Until Jed came along and turned her head around. She was going off with him that day in his car. Only she never got to wherever they were going."

He broke off, choking on his own anger and remembered grief. All of it was perfectly and dreadfully clear now. Sad and tragic and terrible.

He looked almost eager for me to understand. "You can see how it was, Lindsay. I never meant any of this, but I've never had any luck. Clara was my one chance. And now I've lost her too. She knows. She even tried to give me some time by lying about Rick. But she's through with me now. So what happens doesn't matter. If you hadn't come here everything would have been fine—beautiful. In spite of Sybil. I could have shut her up and gone on. But you came, and you're Jed's daughter. He's tried to get back at me through you. You opened everything up. You destroyed—and you have to be stopped."

I dared not wait a moment longer. I whirled to run for the base of the cliff and began scrambling up the slanting mound of scree at its foot. I clung desperately with my fingers, my toes, while sandy rubble slid beneath me. When I looked up I could see the narrow ledge that sliced through the rock behind the Fire People. Marilla was there, holding out her hand.

"Come up, Lindsay! Hurry, hurry!"

Parker did not move. When I glanced down, I saw that he stood at the foot of the slope watching me in grim amusement.

"It's no use, Lindsay," he told me. "Sybil tried that too. I made it look as though her head struck one of those rocks as she fell, though I had this wrench in my jacket. Like I do now. Too bad I had to drop some stuff that time when I pulled the wrench out—that key of Jed's that I took from him in Vegas, so it would look like robbery. You never guessed, did you? I was too smart for all of you."

Another few inches and I was up. Marilla helped pull me onto the ledge and we stood looking down at Parker.

"We can get out this way," Marilla pointed back.

If I followed her, Parker would come after us. This was a better place to make a stand. "You go," I told her. "Do as I tell you. Get away!"

She didn't want to leave me, but again she obeyed and I heard her running along the ledge behind the Fire People. I looked around for any sort of weapon that would help me. There was nothing. Not a stick or a big-enough stone. And he was coming up now. I braced myself against the walls of rock with both hands. At least I had the advantage of gravity, and he had only emptiness behind him. He would need hands and feet to climb onto this ledge. And I would fight to stop him.

Suddenly I heard sounds at the far end of the slit that offered a way to freedom, and I was afraid that Marilla had turned back. But she was talking excitedly now—talking to someone else. I turned to warn her and saw that Rick was there beside her, coming toward me. In spite of the shock of enormous relief, I knew it wasn't over.

Rick drew me gently out of the way and stood looking down. "It's no use, Parker. You're through now."

Parker paid no attention. The very fact that there was nothing left for him to go back to must have kept him coming. As he neared the top, he reached out to grasp Rick's leg, and Rick braced himself against the walls as I had done. What happened next seemed almost like slow motion. Rick shoved him away with his foot and Parker never tried to save himself. He let go of Rick and went backward into the air without a cry. The interval before he struck the ground seemed very long, and then the crash reverberated repeatedly. Parker lay still.

"Stay with Marilla," Rick said, and climbed down. He knelt beside the man who lay at the foot of the cliff, and after a moment he looked up at us. "It's over—he's gone."

Rick climbed back to our ledge and for a moment he stood with an arm about each of us, holding us tightly. It was getting darker fast, and we had to get away. The rescue team must wait until daylight to bring out Parker's body.

As I squeezed through the narrow space behind the darkened head of the Shining One, I reached up gratefully to touch the rock— because all the gods were one. I never looked back into the clearing where I'd left Vermilion.

Much of what happened that night is a blur to

me now. The sheriff came to Rick's house, and so did Clara, weeping a little, and yet controlled. Marilla went to sleep in her own bed. Alice stayed with her.

When all the words had been spoken, and everyone had gone, Rick and I stood at the rail of the terrace, listening to the enormous silence. And to the buzz of night insects that was somehow a part of the silence. Out among the rocks a coyote wailed its lonely, almost human cry. A strange sense of belonging came over me. A part of my blood was speaking to the land, responding with a recognition that lay somewhere deep inside me. Someday soon I would go to Oraibi.

Once, a long time afterward, I dreamed that I heard Vermilion crying. But when I woke up I knew it was only a dream.

The publishers hope that this Large
Print Book has brought you pleasurable
reading. Each title is designed to make
the text as easy to see as possible.
G. K. Hall Large Print Books are
available from your library and
your local bookstore. Or you can
receive information on upcoming
and current Large Print Books by
mail and order directly from the
publisher. Just send your name
and address to:

G. K. Hall & Co.
70 Lincoln Street
Boston, Mass. 02111

A note on the text
Large print edition designed by
Cindy Schrom.
Composed in 16 pt English Times
on a Compugraphic Compuwriter II
by Adhanet Elias